"THEY SAY ~~POISON~~ WAS THE MURDER WEAPON," SHE SAID, BLOWING SMOKE INTO MY FACE.

"Listen," I said. "No one's going to say 'It's a wrap,' Camelia. Not on this. This one's for real." I wanted her to stop this acting. I wanted her to come clean.

"You won't abandon me, will you?" It was more of an observation than a question. "I didn't kill him, you know."

"The money."

She sighed and stubbed out the Camel. "Let's work with this script idea," she said. "We now work it so that I took the money, but for a good cause. No one believes this except the lone private eye. And why he persists in believing this, no one can understand."

"What was the good cause?"

She shook her head. "Go with this version. Can you do that?"

"Do I have a choice?"

"No." She tried to wink at me but got it wrong. We would have to do another take.

———————— ★ ————————

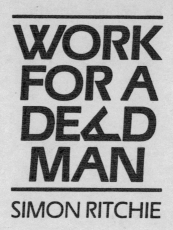

WORK FOR A DEAD MAN

SIMON RITCHIE

W♦RLDWIDE®

TORONTO · NEW YORK · LONDON · PARIS
AMSTERDAM · STOCKHOLM · HAMBURG
ATHENS · MILAN · TOKYO · SYDNEY

For my father, John Henry

WORK FOR A DEAD MAN

A Worldwide Mystery/January 1991

This edition is reprinted by arrangement with Charles Scribner's Sons; an imprint of Macmillan Publishing Company.

ISBN 0-373-26064-4

Printed in U.S.A.

I should like to express my thanks
for kind assistance received from
W. Leigh Thompson, Clarence A. Hirsch,
Jerry M. Mann, and Anita N. Martin of Eli Lilly and
Company; and thanks as well for help from
Dominic Clarke, Martin Hawkes, and Mark Alfano.

ONE

"YOU DIDN'T HAVE to hurry. He's not getting any deader." Sergeant Hornbeck gave me a loose grin and jerked his head at the body that was sprawled between the table and the over-turned chair.

"Move," I told him, and I pushed past his bulk to get to my dead client.

Bench came up behind me. "Don't touch, Jantarro," he barked. I ignored him and squatted down next to it. "Your message was on his machine," he said.

There wasn't a smell, and I was grateful for that. Sometimes there is. Sometimes if a man dies a certain way, the smell is unholy. But always there is something around a corpse that reaches me, that has me fighting against fear and anger.

Because this had been a client, I made myself be near it. I saw my scuffed running shoe two inches from its face. I heard Hornbeck's stertorous breathing and I thought the stray thought that he should quit smoking. My shirt felt clammy against my skin. My palm was sweating, and I had a mad urge to wipe it dry on the dead thing's clothing.

"Well?" Bench again. Impatient as always. He had had me paged at the baseball game forty minutes ago. The announcer told all forty thousand of us that Manny Lee was pinch running for Fernandez, and then he told all forty thousand of us that I should come to the customer information booth. When I left, we were winning. Toronto six, New York two.

I rocked back on my heels and managed to stand up. I turned to face him and nodded once. "Alan Laki," I said. I looked at Hornbeck and then away. "It was Alan Laki."

Bench grunted. He'd known. Now he knew for sure.

ALAN LAKI was fair-haired and thirty-five years old. His face was pale, long. Sensitive, I suppose you could say. He wore a thin white linen shirt fresh from the cleaners, and a pair of baggy black linen pants with half a dozen pleats at the waist and no crease down the front. His fingers, too, were long—delicate—and he used them to sketch what he was telling me, as though he were signing while he talked.

"I'm quite embarrassed about this, really," he told me. He threw one long leg over the other, decided that wasn't comfortable, and took it off. "It isn't what you think it is. I know you don't do..." He found it necessary to breathe, and a hand finished the sentence for him, before he had the chance to say "divorce work."

"No one does anymore," I said quietly. We were in my living room, because I don't have an office. Most private investigators have offices, but I just never seemed to get around to renting one even though I've been in the business for seven, nearly eight years now—ever since the insurance company decided they didn't want me working for them any longer. Cases keep showing up, I keep taking them, and an office keeps getting pushed into the future like a whole lot of other things. Maybe in a few years' time, when I'm fifty, I'll deal with it and everything else. Maybe.

But not now. Now I had a client who was embarrassed. Who didn't want me to do divorce work.

The August sun was streaming through the narrow slits in the blinds, overpowering the air-conditioning and hitting everything with thin gold stripes. The room was tiger skin. "There's no need for divorce work now," I said. "Not with the new laws. Not really."

"Yes, yes," Laki said. He was impatient with his own hesitation, not with me.

"So why do you want me to follow your wife?" I was trying to help him out with a simple, direct question. He made movies—films, I guess people would say—for a living, and things probably got cut together in funny ways inside his head sometimes. Even so, a big director and producer like Laki, a man with half a dozen commercially successful features to his credit, should have been able to tell a story.

"Yes," he said again, but affirmatively now. He came forward in the big easy chair, elbows on knees, hands flickering in front of his face. "I want to protect her," he said. "And I want you to believe me that I love her. Very deeply. This is not to be some . . . some cynical . . ."

"Rip-off?" I suggested. I'm not touchy. What I do for a living is considered to be more disreputable even than making movies. The fact is, though, that I do it well.

"Okay, rip-off," he said, looking at me to see how I'd take it.

"You know my reputation or you wouldn't be here."

A silence emerged, and I considered the golden stripes on the wall behind him and how they seemed to ripple a bit in the heat like the skin of the beast itself. I heard him sigh.

"Look, Jantarro, she's in trouble. I know it." It all came tumbling out now, so fast that I forgot to watch his hands. "And what kills me is I haven't the faintest idea what the problem is. She won't talk to me about it. She just says I'm making it up, or I'm crazy. But I can see it in her face, the way her eyes are screwed tight. I can feel it when we . . . when we're together. And she's spending money. A whole lot more than she usually does. I'm ashamed to say I got her bank manager to tell me about her account. I don't think I can show my face in there again. He thinks I'm scum. I'm ashamed to be here, doing this, if you want the truth. It isn't the money. Shit, I wouldn't care if she spent me down to the lint in my pocket. It's just . . . it's just . . ."

"That she's in trouble."

"And I don't know what else to do."

"YOU WERE working for him." Bench, God's gift to the Homicide Squad, went over to the window and poked aside one of the slats of the venetian blinds with a stubby finger and peered out into King Street traffic.

"How did he die?" I couldn't take my eyes off Laki's body, even though it hurt to look at him.

Bench sighed and turned away from the outside, considering the dust on his fingertip. "When did you last speak to him?"

"What was it?" I asked him. "Poison? It looks like poison." Laki's hand was clawed, the one that wasn't trapped underneath him; and his face was badly contorted, his neck corded. His knees were drawn up unnaturally high, as if at the moment of dying he'd tried to fit back into the womb.

"Today?"

"Have you told his wife?"

Bench snapped his fingers. "This isn't going to work, Jantarro. Not this way." I looked at him, seeing him for the first time since I'd entered the room. It was a face I knew very well, as well as one knows the face of a friend. The boxer-dog face with the funny little mustache to cover up the fine harelip scar. The eyes that gave the impression of protruding aggressively even though they didn't. The bristle of graying hair like hackles permanently raised.

Only it wasn't a friend's face. Not anymore. Not for perhaps five or six years now. When the insurance company figured I was the one who was skimming off a good portion of their profits, it was Bench, working Fraud then, who made the case against me and got me locked up. It didn't matter that he was only doing his job; it didn't matter that his enthusiasm was natural in an ambitious man; it didn't matter that when I was released, vindicated, that he said he was pleased. What mattered was that he had thought I was capable of it and had gone ahead and got just enough evidence against me to make it seem likely. Friends don't do that. Not my friends.

"Well," said Bench tightly, "when did you talk to him last?"

"I spoke to him yesterday," I said. "On the phone. About three in the afternoon. He seemed jumpy. But then he always seemed a bit jumpy to me."

"What were you doing for him?"

It was my turn to go to the window. The traffic was thickening, packed streetcars clanging, squealing, groaning on their way through the sea of automobiles like giant groupers through schools of shiny herring. Some of it would be the crowd from the stadium going home. I wondered if we had won and tried to see if the kids with baseball caps were happy or not.

"It was poison," said Bench. He is not stupid. He understood it would go faster as tit for tat. "The ME hasn't given us anything more than an opinion. He's guessing strychnine. There's a bottle in his other hand. Underneath him. We took a look."

"So you're done with it. Why's it still here?"

"ME's been and gone. We're still waiting for Photography and a couple of the forensic people."

"Suicide?"

"What were you doing for him?" Bench insisted.

He was right. It was his turn. So I told him.

IN THE THREE MONTHS before her husband came to see me, Camelia Laki had spent $235,000 and change. You have to respect that kind of spending power. And if it's your money, you have to worry about what it's buying. And Laki did.

Drugs come to mind.

I know people who can do a lot of coke. Mostly, I used to know them, because you can't keep up a really good intake rate for too long without needing a rest cure of some kind or other. But at nearly eight hundred bucks a day, every day, for that length of time, you'd have nothing but snot where your septum used to be, or tracks on your arms that they could switch Diesel locomotives on.

I didn't think Camelia had either. "It's plastic," I told her on the afternoon we met. "On the outside, that is. A kind of polyvinyl." Her eyes were lovely. Clear, but not overbright; steady, but not fixed; wide, and not at all objectionably so.

"I think it's fascinating. It really does look real!" She had her arm stretched out next to mine, comparing. It was beauty and the beast. My left arm is a prosthesis, cunningly made to resemble the real thing, but in fact a tube of wires and levers and motors and myoelectric switches that more properly belongs in a factory than on anyone's shoulder. The good arm of flesh had been left behind in the prison hospital after it had attracted the attention of a couple of sadistic guards and an incompetent prison surgeon. But some things you never leave completely behind, and now I could feel the ghost hairs on the phantom limb tingling, rising with some excitement. I couldn't blame them, for Camelia's arm, bare to the shoulder of her sleeveless T-shirt, was lovely. Delicate. Pale, smooth, and very womanly. If she shot up, she didn't use that arm. Ever.

Now she laid her fingertips on my plastic skin—for her, I had taken off my jacket and rolled up my sleeve—and said, "It's a wonder."

"I'll pass along the praise to the folks who made it."

"And what can you do with it?" Her grin was just right. She was flirting and letting me know that she was only flirting.

"All sorts of disgustingly normal things," I said. And I grinned, too. I hoped it was just right.

We were drawing a small crowd from her cocktail party guests who'd wandered through the French doors onto the black marble patio. I could have felt like a court dwarf, the ones that the rich nobility kept around for fun and general amusement. You see them in Velázquez's sublime painting of the little Spanish princesses. But I'm nicely over six feet tall. And although I don't usually demonstrate my prosthetic left arm in Tupperware party fashion, Camelia had me doing tricks and feeling not an ounce of discomfort.

Then some guy in electronics and a red blazer came up and importuned me to show him the insides. Camelia winked at me and somehow had me twenty yards away in no time at all. She was holding my good hand, swinging our arms as we walked; and I thought it was one of the finest days I could remember in a long time. We stopped, apart from the crowd, and I looked over at her, our gazes meeting with an unexpected honesty. She blushed and dropped my hand as if it were hot. It was.

"These are my flowers," she said, fingering a bright green bush with nothing blooming on it. "Sort of." She looked at me. I looked back stupidly. "Camellias," she said. She found a dead blossom hiding in the deep shade and picked it to sniff at. There was nothing at all wrong with the septum inside that nose. I was willing to swear.

"Of course," I said, feeling slow.

She laughed. "Come back in the spring and they'll knock your eyes out. They're really something." She turned back to the plant. "*Camellia japonica* 'Magnoliiflora.'"

I frowned.

She laughed again.

Her husband, my client, came over to stand between us. "Don't get excited," he said. "It's the only Latin she knows."

"It's also the only name of a flower I know," she said. Perhaps I imagined it, because I'm no expert in matters connubial, but it seemed to me that he tried to slide an arm around her waist and that she glided out of reach. He contented himself with reaching over to touch the nakedness of her shoulder.

In the following week there were three other parties like that one that I didn't attend. Laki said he would have fixed it for me. I'd been that jack of all services, a "consultant," at his party, and I could pose as one again. But there wasn't any point. She wasn't spending his money to make snow fall on her friends. It wasn't drugs she was buying.

"THAT WAS a couple of weeks ago," I told Bench. It felt like yesterday and like all of a year past. Death makes time too liquid to hold easily in the mind.

"They party a lot," said Bench. It sounded half-envious, the way a criticism usually will.

"And write it off against income, and enjoy it, and still have millions left over."

"Not any longer." We both looked down at Laki's shell. I could hear the sound of men and equipment coming up the hall to the room.

"Does she know yet?"

Bench shook his head. "No," he said. He straightened the blue knit tie he always wears and adjusted the jacket of his perennial gray suit, as though he were preparing even now to go calling.

I almost wanted to say "Let me tell her." And I shivered. Perhaps I meant "Let me see her again. Let me be close to her."

"So it wasn't drugs she spent the money on. What was it?" Bench's voice was tired.

A young guy in jeans and a black T-shirt came in carrying a fat aluminum briefcase. He set it down on the floor near the door and snapped the catches. Two more people strolled in with baggage of their own, and the three of them started a private conversation, as if the dead man weren't there.

"I DON'T KNOW what it is. Not yet."

Alan Laki interlaced his long fingers and, stretching, cracked all his knuckles at once. He got out of his chair and began to pace. "Okay," he said, nodding as he paced. "Okay, that's okay." Today he was in blue espadrilles, white pants, and an outsize blue short-sleeved shirt. Sunglasses hung from a cord around his neck. "It's only been a week."

"Have you got any further ideas?" I'm never too proud to ask the client for help.

"Nothing. Nothing." He whirled at the end of the room and stopped. "She's been"—he batted at the words with those butterfly hands of his—"more *there* this week. More with me. Maybe it's over."

"Do you want me to stop?"

He started up pacing again. He shook his head. "No. It isn't over. I can feel it. And besides, I want to know what it was even if she never spends another red cent."

"I want to put a tap on your phone," I told him.

"Listen to what we say?"

I nodded. "What she says."

His mouth turned down at the corners. "That's pretty...creepy."

"Mr. Laki, I've followed her, I've watched her, I've even talked to her pretending to be a friend of sorts. I don't think eavesdropping is going to push us over any moral boundary we haven't already crossed."

He was standing above me, shifting his feet, moving his arms, his head and neck, his hands. The smile on his face was grim. "I guess you're right. Okay."

"Sit down," I said, and I pointed at the chair he had left. "I want to talk to you about blackmail."

BENCH NODDED. "That's what I would have figured," he said.

"I've got the telephone tapes," I told him. "A week's worth. At home."

"They give you anything?"

I shook my head. "She's got a nice voice. She talks girlie talk when one of the girls calls. She talks firm to her husband's business partners. She talks sexy to the plumber and the grocery man. She's got a charity—cerebral palsy—kids. She talked a lot about that."

"Bring them in," he told me. "The tapes."

"Now?"

"Hornbeck will drive you home. You can give them to him."

"I want a copy of the reports." I waved my only hand at the boys scampering around the remains.

"You're finished," he said, without looking at me. "You're off the case. Your client is dead. He's my client now."

"I don't know if I can put my hands on those tapes right away." I can work for a dead man, too, I thought. And contesting with Bench was almost a reflex.

"Last known person to talk to him. We'll need to hang on to you for a couple of days at least."

"I didn't talk to him. I just left him a message."

"MR. LAKI, this is Jantarro. I've just listened to the tapes. I'm going to the ball game this afternoon, and I can come there, to the King Street office, after it's over, say around five. Don't get your hopes up. I still don't know what's happening."

"SHIT," said Bench.

"Yeah," I agreed. I was looking at Laki, wondering if he'd thought his life had been a good one, wondering if it *had* been a good one.

"Get the tapes, Jantarro."

There didn't seem to be much point in fighting it. There was nothing in them, and I was prepared to give him nothing. "Okay," I said, and I wondered as I left if there was such a thing as a good life anyway.

TWO

LAKI HAD LIED to me. I was fairly certain of that because all clients lie. Everybody lies, but clients lie especially. This is because: clients are in trouble; trouble means blame; and things have to be found that will shift the blame elsewhere. QED.

I get paid to find those levers that will do the shifting. Which can be a problem, given that I have this strange belief that there is a truth beyond blame, and that, moreover, I'm capable of recognizing it.

I blame my father for this obsession of mine with the truth, himself a contradictory man the truth of whom I still have not been able to determine. A man who, on the one hand, was a successful academic economist, a sober Protestant toiler at the "dismal science," and who, on the other hand, was a revolutionary manqué, having fought in Spain for the losing side with a splendid passion. A man who graced me with the elaborate name of J. K. G. Jantarro, but who always called me simply "John." Who taught me that everyone lies, and who showed me good truths behind those lies. I blame him, but, since his death, I blame him less and less each year. *Nil nisi bonum.*

And that would be another problem with the late Alan Laki. Not only would I have to sort out his truths from his lies, but I'd also have to watch for people beginning to paper over any cracks in his life through which I might have glimpsed the truth.

All of this mental meandering happened over a cooling cup of coffee. It was morning, the day after Laki's body had been found, a time for fresh starts and the breakfast of hope. But the image of the dead man's contorted body, that horrible cast of his attempt to clench life at the last, had stayed with me through the night and it hovered oppressively over me as I thought about what to do.

Even my hallowed piano music failed to lift my spirits. My machine was offering me early Rachmaninoff, from when he was twenty—a piano duet played by John Ogdon and his wife,

Brenda Lucas. We were in the second movement, a scherzo with faintly jazzy moments; and although I could hear the fun Rachmaninoff was having, all I could think of was how in later life he abandoned fun and became what someone once described as a "mauve depressive." All I could hear was four hands tinkling.

Perhaps if I'd worked harder, Laki would still be alive. That notion was the obvious source of my pale blue funk. And I told myself that perhaps if I worked hard now, I could find out why he died.

The money was the obvious place to start. Laki had said that his wife had spent huge sums over the last three months. It would make sense to find out if that was the truth.

I got up from the table, left the toast crumbs where they were, and walked out on Rachmaninoff, Ogdon, and Lucas. The ghost of Laki came with me into the sunshine.

WILLIAM BRODERICK was a busy man. The receptionist told me that, and so did his appointments secretary. His private secretary didn't actually use those words, but the theme was the same. Everyone in the hushed, bustling office was therefore surprised when, less than a minute after I sent in my card, Broderick came out to greet me. He led me into the sanctum sanctorum, ordered coffee, and did something to his telephone that would stop it from ringing.

"It's been what? Two years?" he said. His smile was genuine, even if his teeth were perfectly capped; and his eyes showed that perfect mix of amusement, watchfulness, and interest that I remembered. His desk was clear, and the filtered light from the window behind him made it shine richly. It was appropriate: he had touched it, and he was Midas.

"At least two years," I agreed.

"You prospering?"

"In my own way."

"You know, Jantarro, I think of you quite a lot—every time my kids visit, in fact." I had helped put the blocks to an extortion attempt that had threatened his children. And he was one of the people who had given me financial advice from time to time. When I came out of jail minus an arm, I sued everyone and everything; and for my seven and three-quarters pounds of flesh the law gave me a very large sum of money, which, although it couldn't scratch my right elbow or caress a woman's cheek, fixed things so I didn't have to work again unless I wanted to. Broderick and others had helped to turn that original sum into something that made life without left-handed complements a comfortable proposition.

The coffee arrived in a Meissen jug on a beautiful Chinese tray. The secretary poured. I murmured that, yes, I did take cream and sugar. And then we were alone again.

"How are the kids?" The coffee tasted the way that all coffee ought to taste but rarely does.

He wrinkled the expensive tan on his forehead. "Mark is stalled in high school and Linda is too concerned about her weight. All right, I guess. Normal." He looked up at me and grinned sheepishly. "For rich kids."

It was his money. He had come from his father's struggling hardware store in tiny Markdale all the way to this aerie above Bay Street where, it seemed, he bought and sold money—as if such a thing were possible. But he could still remember how it was to be an ordinary person.

His cup steamed untouched on the burnished wood. I held mine on my lap, braced against my plastic hand.

"I need a favor," I told him.

"Anything," he said.

"It's about Alan Laki."

His eyes flicked to the right as he searched in his memory for the name. They widened and came back to me. "The man who died yesterday. The producer."

"That's right."

"That sounds like a mess."

"I think it is."

"But I don't—didn't—know the man."

"I need to find out about his money. Particularly, I need to find out how much his wife spent over the last six months."

"Ah," he said. Money was what he did know. "The accounts will be frozen."

"Will that make a difference?"

He shrugged. "It might. Although, of course, if she has separate accounts, and she probably does, they will still be active. But the police will be in there, presumably, looking through them. That could make things difficult." He made a small noise and a dismissive motion with his hand. "I'm thinking out loud. My worry, not yours. Of course, I'll find out what I can."

"I'd appreciate it." I put the coffee cup carefully on the desk. "What kind of movement are we talking about? Do you have any idea?"

"A quarter of a million? Something on that order. Or so I've been told."

He nodded. It probably seemed a small amount to him. Then he shot his very white cuffs and I knew it was time to go. He came with me through the outside office all the way to the front door. "I'll call you," he said quietly. And he gave my fake arm a squeeze.

"SWEETIE! You get to be more of a hunk every day. Come and sit where I can touch you, and tell me all about your most intimate sexual practices." Elaine Younger of the *Star* made sure it was my good arm that she squeezed. She squeezed it and then wouldn't let it go, but kept massaging it as though it were meat that needed tenderizing.

"If I told you about my sex life, Elaine, you'd be asleep in under a minute."

"In bed, maybe," she said, "but I wouldn't close my eyes for a second even if you asked me to. I like to watch." She was in that no-man's-land between fifty and the grave, where some women wind up in spite of their brains and beauty and clear mating calls. In Elaine's case, I didn't think I knew a man who was secure enough to answer those calls.

"I need a favor," I told her, and I watched her round blue eyes dance with pleasure. Laki had said he was deeply in love with his wife, but maybe he had lied. That was what I had come to find out.

"Oh, I'm so glad," she said. She was sitting next to me on the small couch in her office, and she wriggled until we were touching from knee to shoulder. "Because then you'll owe me and I like being on top." She batted eyelids painted a blue more vivid than her eyes, and then she laughed at herself, at life, and at the excitement of it all.

I laughed with her and felt the specter of Alan Laki with-draw a little. "Gossip," I said.

"Is that a command, honey? Because if it turns you on, you got it."

"It's the favor I need. Gossip about Alan Laki."

She whistled through painted lips. "Hot stuff. The late, great Alan Laki." She had leaned away a bit and was considering me with the professional gaze of a newspaperwoman. The society features were hers and had been for over twenty years.

"We could ... compare notes," I said tentatively.

She laughed again. "We could compare whatsits, you big beauty. But it'll have to be something that I don't already have. Something the world doesn't already have, and that won't be easy. Laki was a larger-than-life man, a character out of one of his flicks. Poor boy becomes rich man. Struggling artistic talent finds recognition amid the schlock troops of cine-land. Hollywood North's own Coppola, Levine, Parker—you name it—only better. Dreamer directs, director produces, producer succeeds. He shoots, he scores."

"Not that," I said. "Everybody knows that."

"Size ten shoes. A weakness for Belgian chocolates. Never slept more than four hours a night."

"Come on, Elaine."

"You come first," she said. "I like it that way. Besides, with me it's only tit for tattle." She ran her hands alongside her breasts in a parody of Mae West. "Tattle, honey child."

"What do you have?" I asked, beginning the bargaining process.

"What do I have? What don't I have! But, uh-uh, honey. You just start talking. I'll tell you when to do something else with your mouth." She ran a hand through my hair as she spoke. Then she got up from the couch, found a cigarette holder, and fitted a Kent into it. She handed me the gold lighter from her desk and leaned down. I lit her cigarette. She blew a plume and, watching it find its way into the air-conditioning duct, said, "Well, Jantarro? Don't be shy."

"Deep background?" I suggested.

She coughed on her smoke and laughed uproariously. "You've been watching too much TV. 'Deep background,' my ass." She sat on the front of her desk and regarded me steadily for a moment. "Tell you what, though. I won't use it unless I can find another source for it besides you. How's that?"

I took the plunge. "The morning papers only said that he was dead and that the police were looking into suicide among other possibilities. In fact, he died from ingesting poison—it might have been strychnine. I don't know that for sure yet."

"So he did pull the plug."

I shook my head. "I was expecting to meet him yesterday afternoon. We'd tentatively arranged it the day before. He was very interested in what I might have had to tell him. So I've got my doubts about suicide."

"He hired you."

"We had arranged to meet."

"Okay, okay. But he hired you."

"I left a message on his machine about noon, telling him that I'd be there around five. The message was still waiting when the cops found his body."

"So he was dead before noon."

"Or the killer—if there was a killer—didn't bother to check the machine."

She flicked ash onto the floor impatiently. "Or did check it and wound it back again."

I shook my head. "He had a phone hooked into a new phone mail system. Linked his editing office with his business ones, I guess. Anyway, you have to save a message or wipe it, once you listen to it. And it wasn't saved or wiped."

She frowned, ejected the butt of the Kent from her holder, and hissed softly through her teeth for a bit. "What did he hire you for?"

I shook my head. "Enough is enough."

"First crack when you solve it?"

"There may not be anything to solve."

"Don't kid a kidder, Jantarro. You got a nose almost as good as mine. And a damn sight prettier." She fitted another cigarette into the holder but just toyed with the thing in her hand. "You haven't given me a hell of a lot, you know."

"As much as I can."

She slid off the desk and delicately scratched the silk that covered her rump. Then she looked at me consideringly. "You've got some standards. I like that." The look softened.

"I want you to know that I don't kiss and tell, either. Despite..." She waved the cigarette and holder like a wand at the rest of the newspaper people outside the glass wall. And then she looked away. "I'm telling you this, Jantarro, in case you ever decide that you'd like to see what an older woman has to offer. No, no. Don't say a word. Now, what can I offer you about the unfortunate Mr. Laki? That he probably really was a genius, despite all the money he made? That he once had a mad fling with a pair of twins—underage—in Grenada? That he was sterile? Not actually sterile, but a sperm count lower than the IQ of an actor. That the sort of thing you want?"

"More general," I said. "Like, how much is he supposed to have been worth?"

"Oh, millions. Literally. Eight, nine, ten, personally. They just bought a huge place in Forest Hill. Two houses, actually, and they pulled one down to get more land. That alone must have cost three mil. His own company, Lakipix, financed most of his last two pictures—broke even on *Yours Truly* and cashed in big on *Griffin*. Although I thought *Yours* was the better film. Don't you ever read the papers?"

"His film production company," I said, "was it his alone, or did other people have shares in it?" I wanted to pad things out a little before I asked about Camelia, his wife.

"Seventy-five Laki and twenty-five Arnold Guberian. Sweet Arnold used to hold fifty-five, but Laki bought control about a year ago or so."

"*Sweet* Arnold?"

"Because he's anything but, silly."

"Why did he sell?"

Elaine shrugged and saw that her cigarette was unlit. She lifted papers on her desk, looking for her lighter. "Don't know. Word had it Laki caught him with his wife—" She stopped abruptly. "You're holding my lighter." And, of course, I was. I spun the wheel and lit her cigarette.

"He caught him with his wife?" I asked.

She breathed the smoke in deeply. "Can't vouch for it. Doesn't even seem likely," she said. "I mean, I know I'm not too particular where men are concerned, but at my most rabid I couldn't even *imagine* making the beast with two backs if he was one of them. He is a most *unpleasant* man. Still, there must have been something to make Guberian let go. Maybe he gambled it away. He does like to gamble, you know. If you happen to find out what it was, you will let me know, won't you?''

"Did she fool around generally?"

"His wife?"

"Yes."

"Now she *is* a sweet thing. You know, you meet so many people, and of all the people you meet there are maybe three or four in a year that you'd like to get to know. Really know. She's one of those."

"You got to know her?" I asked.

"Not really. I go to parties, Jantarro, but don't forget, I'm just a working girl. Not in the Lakis' league."

"And that made a difference."

Elaine shook her head. "Not to her. To me. I'm funny about stuff like that."

"And did she fool around?"

"Well, of course. Don't be such a horse's ass, Jantarro. Honestly, sometimes you make me wonder. Everybody fools around."

"And how did he feel about that?"

"How should I know? I mean, if he loved her, he wouldn't have made a fuss about it. And he didn't. Make any fuss, that is. Oh, don't look at me that way. Guberian would be one thing. The man's business partner, a regular creep and all. But the little bit of fluff here and there—that's an entirely different matter. So far as I'm concerned, the Lakis were very much in love."

"AND DO YOU?"

"Do I what?" Glenda and I were battling produce in the kitchen, trying to turn it into food. It's something that neither of us does very well.

"Love me, dummy."

"Yes," I said. She had brought the walnut oil and the bottle of vinegar with the withered-looking stick inside, so making the salad dressing was her responsibility. I was lost in the intricacies of a head of lettuce, debating about whether to cut it sideways or from top to bottom.

"Yes? That's it? Just yes?"

I gave the lettuce its tenth reprieve and lifted the carving knife. Was it just yes? Wasn't that enough? Glenda Redway and I were more than just good friends and less than married. A talented, respected lawyer, she was an independent and busy person; and with her law partner, Ann Beckman, she was on the point of being very successful. Despite matters like talent and respect, and without any partner at all, I was usually busy and always independent. We saw each other when we could. We were at the stage of asking whether there was more to it. To us. To love. Actually, I thought, we were past that, stalled at the stage of being frightened by the answers. I transferred my stern look from the lettuce to her. "Are you badgering the witness, counsel?"

"They don't really say that in court, you know. Only on television. They say things like, 'My friend has got her answer, and she should be happy with it.'"

"Glenda, which way should I cut it?"

"Doesn't it come with instructions?"

"We could go out."

"I've put the steaks on the barbecue already."

"We could take them off. I'm not supposed to barbecue on the balcony anyway."

"We'll get to bed faster if we eat here."

"I don't think I can cut it."

"What?"

"Glenda, I'm standing here with a knife poised over a head of lettuce, paralyzed because I can't make up my mind where to stick it in. This is not good."

"Is something wrong?"

I put the knife down and went to get myself another Scotch. "No," I called from the bar. "Not wrong, exactly. In fact, it's something right. I'm involved in this case."

"Okay," she said. "I know what. We'll break off little pieces and dip them in the sauce."

"I think it's because I don't have a client." I topped up my glass and went to put some Earl "Fatha" Hines on the stereo.

"In which case we might as well just tear it to shreds and dump the sauce all over it."

"And because my client is dead."

"What are you saying?" she called from the kitchen.

"I'm working for a dead man," I called back. Hines plunged into a rollicking piece as if he didn't care.

THREE

"SWEET ARNIE? Sure. I know the gentleman."

"What's his vice?"

"Hey, Jantarro. This is Lady Luck we're talking about here. Kiss-Me-Kismet herself. So do me the favor and lay off the dirty talk." Paul MacMurtry chuckled, and the pumping of his huge chest pulled at his shirt between the buttons, so that the fabric parted and closed. Ovals of white flesh winked at me from under his Countess Mara tie. He was slumped back in his specially built chair—the only place I've ever seen him—sweating under all his bulk in spite of the very cold air dropping from the ducts above us.

"What should I call it?" I asked him. I was sipping a Singapore sling at eleven in the morning, because Paulie Mac was drinking Singapore slings and he insisted I join him.

He worked the chair closer to the desk with a mincing motion of his heels and began picking up objects from its battered surface—a huge red die, a black book, a pocket calculator—picking them up, handling them, and putting them down again. "Pleasures," he said, wholly absorbed in this meaningless reordering. "We think of them as pleasures. A man has pleasures, not vices." A tarnished brass statuette of a bowler was in his hands, and he turned it upside down and examined its underside with great care, as though some secret of life might be written on its base.

"So what's his pleasure, then?"

"That's better. Don't that sound better? *Pleasure.*" He said the word caressingly to a small Toby mug, taking the thing delicately in his fat fingers and addressing the wizened china face.

Paulie Mac, fat, smart, and quirky, was the bookie's bookie. If you wanted to place a serious bet on the outcome of any sporting event, he was your man—or, more likely, the man your bookie dealt with. He had risen fast over the last five years, peacefully taking over small operations, quietly consolidating them, until suddenly he emerged as a major threat to the established big-time operators. Then, before they could act, he brought a lot of muscle to bear in a short, very nasty campaign that saw him installed, Farouk-like, as the undisputed king of book.

I had met him when the Jockey Club had hired me to find out who was trying to tinker with the computers they use to calculate the odds at the track. It seemed someone had been taking bytes out of their profits. It wasn't Paulie Mac, as it turned out, but one of his rivals, soon to be blown away by Paulie's sudden rush to prominence. Paulie was heavily into other nefarious things, but because my client hadn't told me to be interested in those, I wasn't. And Paulie Mac, although he had understood that I wasn't doing him favors, had been wise enough to treat me as if I'd helped him. We'd talked; he'd given me "advice"; I'd taken the good and left the rest. And so we had the kind of wary mutual respect that cops and robbers sometimes get for each other.

One of his quirks, I knew, was his love of small objects, things he could put on his desk and fondle. I had come bearing an egg-sized geode—an unprepossessing stone cut in half to reveal a miniature cave of crystal wonders. It lay untouched in the middle of the desk. He was working his way over toward it like a skittish animal.

"He in trouble?" he asked of Guberian.

"Not that I know of. In fact, I don't know anything about him at all."

"Thought he might be, what with Laki gone now." He tilted his great head and winked at me with one dark eye. It was his way of asking for something in exchange without actually lowering himself to use words.

"Yeah," I said. I had to pay everybody, it seemed, and with Paulie Mac I only had the currency of information. "I'm working on the case."

His fat white hand crawled toward the geode, a troglodyte crab seeking its home. "Who for?" he said, and his hand halted an inch short of its target.

"For nobody."

This time his whole head rose and he blinked at me. His red pouty lips came together in a skeptical moue.

"I take bets, Jantarro," he said in a cold voice. "I don't take risks. And I certainly don't take no shit. You know that. With me it's got to be all up front. I shouldn't have to tell you this."

He didn't frighten me. His manner was threatening out of habit, but unless you were into gambling, he wouldn't even consider touching you. He was a specialist. Of course, if his mother crossed him, he'd have her squashed like road kill. Ruthlessness was part of getting to the top of his specialty and staying there. "Relax," I told him. "I don't have a client. I *did* have a client—Alan Laki. Now I'm out one client."

"Ah," he said. And then absently, "Drink your drink." He drummed on the desktop. "That could make a person mad," he said after a pause.

"Losing a client?"

He nodded a fraction of an inch.

"And Guberian's a good client?" I asked him.

He had the geode in his palm now, drawn near his face, and he was poking into the glittering penetralia with his little finger. He sighed. "Good enough. But I'm not going to hang onto him if he's . . . wanted elsewhere. Lots of fat fish around. This thing is incredible, Jantarro. What the hell is it?"

I told him what it was called. He asked me to spell it. I spelled it. "I'm trying to get a handle on Guberian," I said.

"How do they make them?"

"They don't. They find them and then just cut them in half. I don't know if he's connected with this at all. It's just that I like to check everything out."

"Incredible. But how does all that stuff get inside?"

"Paulie, I haven't the faintest idea. I'm sorry."

"Well, he bets the seasonal sports. Baseball now, and the Canada Cup. NFL, NBA, PGA—the whole alphabet. You know."

"Does he win?"

He closed his hand over the geode. "I need another," he said, pointing with his free hand at the tall empty glass on his desk. His still had its little orange parasol hanging on the edge. I had removed mine, tried to collapse it, and then put the mess of paper and sticks on the arm of my chair. "You don't like it?'' he asked. "Too sweet? The sugar's good for you. Gives you energy."

"Sure," I said, "but I'm fine." He shrugged. And a weedy kid came in, unbeckoned, to take Paulie's glass.

"Thing is," he said when the kid had left, "you and me, it's kind of the same. Pleasures''—he thumped his chest lightly with the geode first—"and pains''—he punched the fist toward me. "Both real private-like."

"I understand," I said. It was enough for me to know that if Paulie saw him as a customer, Guberian was a heavy bettor.

"I mean, how would I feel, I come to you because... because..." He fished around for a reason why he might need my services. "Because my wife run off and left me." He chuckled at the very idea, and again I thought his shirt buttons would pop. "And you go around telling people, 'Hey, Paulie Mac's lost his wife!' I mean, I wouldn't feel too good about that."

"When I've got a living client, I don't talk."

"Exactly," he said with a satisfied nod and a smug expression on his fat face. "And how would one of my clients feel if I was to tell you that his biggest pleasure in life was to dump zillions of bucks into somebody else's pocket betting on teams like Cleveland? Hey? Philanthropy's supposed to be done in secret. That's in the Bible." He chuckled again at this witticism.

So Guberian was a loser, and a compulsive one by the sound of it. Out of a sense of gratitude I tipped the rest of the Singapore sling down my throat, smacked my lips, and hoisted the empty glass in Paulie Mac's direction. He beamed.

I got to my feet. "Thanks," I said.

"For nothing."

I nodded. "For nothing."

"Take the Jays," he said.

"If Fernandez's knee holds up."

"Even," he said.

I stopped at the door. "I owe you," I told him.

"No you don't." He was holding up the little geode and peering deep inside it.

I WAS PUTTING OFF the one thing that had to be done, and that was going to see Camelia Laki. There was no way this business was going to be resolved if I kept skirting the person that Laki had come to see me about in the first place. But I told myself that the widow should be left in peace for a few days at least, that she would probably refuse to see me, and that I didn't have a good idea of how I would play it with her anyway. I did at least suspect that I was avoiding her because if I ever got to know her I might never be able to get her out of my mind. And I didn't have any use for that kind of trouble in my life right now.

So I spent the afternoon working on getting the forensic reports that Bench had said I couldn't have. This kind of trouble I'm perfectly comfortable with.

You don't need a pass to get into the cafeteria of the Forensic Sciences Building—at least you don't always need to show one. I ate lunch there, a depressing affair consisting of a patty of gray meat, an ice-scream scoop of mashed potatoes, carrots boiled yellow, and a miniature haystack of coleslaw. They poured a pale gravy over everything, coleslaw included, before I could stop them.

I positioned myself so I could see the door, figuring that sooner or later one of the pathologists or technicians I knew would come in. I pushed the food around on my plate while I waited. I was looking for Henry Wilms, their top man, a good-natured guy who'd been helpful to me in the past. But no one I knew was willing to risk his health until around three-thirty when George Chin came in, got a tray, and slammed a coffee and two sticky buns on it.

I caught his eye and motioned for him to join me. He pointed at something over my head and set off in the other direction. I looked up to see a NO SMOKING sign. So I dumped my tray on the conveyor belt and went to sit at his table.

He lit a cigarette and inhaled down to his toes. "Don't tell me you want an autopsy, Jantarro, 'cause I'm plumb tuckered out. You'll have to wait till tomorrow." Smoke went everywhere as he talked. He narrowed his eyes against it, which made his round face look even rounder.

"A little pathologist's humor?"

"You mean you're not dead? You mean I get to talk to a living, breathing human being?"

"Been working you a bit hard, have they?"

"You don't know the half of it."

"True enough. But, hell, George, you're a civil servant. How bad can it be?"

He French-inhaled the last of his cigarette and butted it out with some force in the dented aluminum ashtray. "Shit, Jantarro, you can joke about it. When the hell did you ever bust your ass? But me, I'm one of four people right now standing between civilization and a tidal wave of cadavers. And as fast as I flay them, they bring in more." He sucked back half of the coffee in the crockery mug and puckered his mouth with the bitterness. He placed his fingertips on one of the sticky buns.

"Sounds really great."

Chin was munching on a chunk of sweet pastry. "Don't get me wrong," he said. He swallowed. "I'm ambitious. I want to be..." He took another greedy bite and pointed at the ceiling over his head. He said something I couldn't make out through the mastication.

"Huh?"

"Another five years," he said. There was gummy dough stuck to his teeth and he worked his tongue around in his mouth. "That's all it'll take, and I'll be head honcho."

"You want another coffee?" I asked him.

He shook his head. "Got gastritis already. That stuff's a killer." The next bun made the trip to his mouth. "Figure, what with me being a Chink and all, that ought to be about right. Five years. Time for minority leaders everywhere. Only a shame I'm not a woman."

"Listen, George, did you work on the Laki case?"

He pushed a lock of straight black hair out of his eyes and chewed solemnly, regarding me with an all too readable expression. "Yes," he said, and he resumed chewing.

"Feel like talking about it?"

"Not supposed to."

"Yeah, well."

"What did you ever do for me?"

"What did you ever want me to do?"

"That's a point." Chin examined his empty plate, then he dabbed at the crumbs with a fingertip. He tossed his head to move the stray lock of hair again. "You and Wilms are friends, right?"

"Not exactly friends."

"But you see him."

"From time to time, yes."

"See, a lot of it's got to do with timing. I figure Wilms to go five more years. But if, maybe, he should go early—or stay on longer . . ."

"You would want to know."

He nodded. "It's kind of a long shot, right? I mean, I've got my local sources. But, hell, it couldn't hurt to have a little help from the outside. Maybe Hank will talk to someone outside before he'd talk to anyone in here. What do you say?"

"Sure. Unless he swears me to secrecy."

"Explicitly."

I nodded. This was just fantasy that Chin was spinning to feed his dream. If it made him feel important to have outside sources, it was no skin off my nose. "Explicitly," I conceded.

"Laki ingested a large quantity of strychnine phosphate. Arrhythmia and diaphragmatic spasms began almost immediately, along with subsequent severe contraction of all muscle tissue. Death ensured between six and seven minutes later, given his body weight and his age."

"Ouch," I said.

He grunted. "Brutal."

"Any indications that it wasn't suicide?"

Chin laughed. "I'm a doctor, Jantarro. Bodies don't usually tell you which nervous system caused the swallowing. But there weren't any evident signs of his hands or arms having been confined, I can tell you that. No cuts or contusions around the mouth. But there was a freshly chipped tooth, as there might have been if someone had force fed him. There was also some bruising on the torso. Premortem. But he'd have been thrashing around like a pike on a dock, so I don't think that or the tooth makes it conclusive one way or the other."

"What would that shit taste like?"

"Really bitter. Worse than this coffee. Like the inside of a peach pit, maybe. But you could disguise it—tea, maybe, or beer, or a supersweet concoction."

"What else did you find in the stomach?"

Chin nodded with approval. "You're not so stupid as they say. I didn't think you were." He picked up his coffee mug, looked into it, and put it down again. "Well, for one thing, a whole lot of orange syrup."

"Like cough medicine?"

"Exactly."

"So the bitterness would have been disguised."

"Pretty much."

"And?"

"And iron phosphate in some quantity and traces of quinine phosphate." I frowned at him. He grinned. "Yeah. That was a hard one. But the great Chin pulled it out of his ass. Your dead man ingested a considerable quantity of a tonic known as the old IQ-and-S elixir—iron, quinine, and strychnine. Haven't marketed it since nineteen seventy-three, not that I know of. Not since strychnine went on the special list. Bad stuff." He wagged a warning finger. "Out of the pharmacopoeia. Officially, that is. Course, whoever doctored this guy—and I'm not saying he didn't do it himself—upped the dosage of strychnine by, oh, about a thousand percent."

I thought for a minute. Chin considered his empty plate, now picked clean of crumbs. "Anything else?" I asked.

"Yeah." He belched behind his hand. "If he was planning to kill himself, he sure did it right. He was freshly shaven, showered, and covered with cologne. And ninety minutes before he died, he'd eaten a meal of eggs Benedict, mixed green salad, and sparkling wine. We're not allowed to call it champagne, you know."

"You're still smiling."

"Am I? Never could hide a damn thing. Well, he'd recently had sexual congress. With a woman. We're not allowed to call it fucking. After the shower."

"A man in the full of life," I said.

"Or saying good-bye the right way."

We were silent for a moment, contemplating the way that up and down can be made to seem the same. Then I stirred myself. "Thanks, Chin."

"Don't forget," he said.

I stood up. "I won't." I started to walk away, and then I thought of a question I'd forgotten to ask. I waited for Chin to get rid of his tray and come over to the door. "This old whatever elixir..."

"IQ-and-S," he said.

"What is it? I mean, how do you get it and what do you get it for?"

"Well, like I said, you don't get it now—I think. But when you did, you got it from your friendly local pharmacist," he said. "On doctor's orders only. A pick-me-up. A Dr. Feelgood special." He grinned. "They used to cut dope with strychnine, you know. Maybe they still do. It gave you a good body stone. But you're probably too old to remember."

FOUR

IT WAS SHORTLY AFTER eight in the evening. I pushed the lit button next to the big white paneled door and heard the chimes echo in the hall. Behind me my cab accelerated away, dragging the noise of its leaky muffler out of the fancy neighborhood. And then there was silence.

Crickets started up in the evergreens beside the steps.

My mouth went dry, and I thought of the times in my youth when I had stood, suddenly parched, at the door of some girl's house. But this was a widow's house, I reminded myself. And a dead man's house.

I was wondering whether to ring again when the door opened. "Mrs. Laki," I said, and we looked at each other.

SHE SAT SIDEWAYS on the down-filled couch and tucked her bare feet up behind her. She wore faded jeans and a man's white oxford cloth shirt. I noticed that the collar buttons were undone. Her face was made-up, but her eyes were hollows and emitted no light.

Her brother stood behind her, his hand on the back of the couch. It seemed to me he was careful not to touch her, as though to have done so would have started something. Perhaps I had interrupted an argument, I thought. He was a tall, skinny man of about twenty-five, with a thin, beaked nose, skin still cratered from acne on his cheeks, and a luxurious head of black hair that he combed back from his forehead. Camelia had mentioned his name in that soft voice of hers, but I had already forgotten it.

His whole attitude made it abundantly clear that, so far as he was concerned, I wasn't welcome; and although I couldn't find much to like in him either at first sight, I respected him for his protectiveness. But whether or not he wanted me there, it was she who had asked me in, asked me to sit.

She had made him get me a drink, because the houseboy had been sent away.

And now she turned her hidden eyes my way.

"The funeral is the day after tomorrow," she said. And then she frowned in a little puzzlement.

"Mrs. Laki, my name is Jantarro. I did some work for your husband."

"If they release the body. They said they might, didn't they, Randy?"

Her brother patted the back of the couch. "It's all right, Cammy," he said, "I'll look after it." He glared at me, as if I might challenge this wardship.

"Do you think they'll release the body?" she asked. The question was directed at neither of us, and Randy flicked his eyes to one side, as if he thought he might cry.

"I doubt it," I said deliberately. And slowly something registered on her face. Inchoate grief, inchoate anger. "They will need to clear up certain matters first," I added, "such as whether it was suicide or murder. And if it was murder... Well, then there will be a whole lot more matters to clear up."

"Murder?" she said, as if the word were a new one to her. "I can't think...you don't think..." Her eyes emerged from their dark homes and began to roll this way and that, looking for a place for her to faint perhaps.

"It is a possibility," I said. It seemed to me she ought to have considered it, if only fleetingly.

"No," she said loudly, and she steadied herself with her hands, pressing them deep into the softness of the cushions. "No," more reasonable now. "That is not—" And then abruptly she broke into tears. She bent her head, groaned, and all the noise of grieving came tumbling out of her.

Randy looked like a boy trapped between fight and flight. So I dropped my eyes to the Scotch he had poured me and considered the murky swirls that crept between the ice cubes. And I wondered how it was that I could be unmoved by her anguish. What was the stoniness inside me that let me calmly think of all the questions that I had? I didn't like what I discovered in among the ice. I wanted to see her smiling at me again. Not weeping for a dead man whom I hardly knew.

And I wanted to know who had killed him.

SHE FINISHED CRYING at about the same time that the last of my drink was gone. Randy supplied her with tissues and murmured consolations; he had wisely decided I didn't exist.

"Who are you?" she asked when she lifted her head.

"My name is Jantarro," I repeated. "I did some work for your husband just before his death."

She bit her lip against more tears, and, unable to risk opening her mouth to speak, she waved a tightly wadded fistful of tissues in front of her. So what? the gesture said.

"He thought that you were in some kind of trouble, and he wanted me to find out what it was."

She looked rapidly between me and the tissues. "I don't understand," she said. I could tell that she did, and that she was temporizing.

Randy was paying attention, I noticed. "It's just as I said," I told her. "He believed that you were in trouble. He was to meet me on the afternoon he died to discuss it once more."

Her eyes went to where Randy's hand rested near her shoulder. "I see," she said. And then in a bright, brittle tone, "Obviously, it wasn't me who was in trouble, was it?" She started sobbing again.

"That thought did occur to me," I told her. "But it also occurred to me that if he was the one who was really in trouble, it wouldn't have helped him to disguise that fact. Particularly to pretend that it was you. Would it?"

She shook her head and spread her hands in dumb helplessness. The sound from a distant television set filtered down from a room above us. Maybe the houseboy was watching it. Or maybe it was playing to an empty house.

"I wanted to tell you," I said, "that your husband was my client. That I'm going to investigate his death. And that you are involved—at least initially."

"I know you," she said suddenly.

"Yes," I said, "we've met. At a party you gave."

"You're the man with the...the prosthetic arm." Randy looked. She didn't.

"That's right."

She peered down at the wadded tissues in her hands, and she began to disentangle them and fold them neatly. "You were spying on me." She spoke without lifting her gaze.

"I was," I admitted.

"And what did you ... spy with your little eye?"

I REMEMBERED LAKI—when we'd arranged that I would come to the party—telling me what I'd see. It was the filmmaker, I supposed, the visual man who wanted to be able to make others see. Through his eyes.

"She's a very beautiful woman." He had stopped his agitated moving and had stared at me to see if I would believe him.

"I'm sure," I had said.

"No, no. I'm speaking objectively. I'm a man who's worked with all the beautiful women in the world. And Camelia's extraordinary. On camera and off. A round face, but not at all doll-like. Sensuous features, lush mouth, wide nostrils—but not coarse or cheap. Eyes that breathe light in and out, so that they shine on film."

"She acts?"

"She used to. I'd like her to act again. God, what am I saying? She's got to act again! She's what acting is all about. What makes film worthwhile. She's got to. She will. But..." He had shrugged and had begun to pace about once more. "She doesn't want to. And I have to respect that. You've never seen her?"

"In the movies, you mean?"

He had nodded. "Camelia Noone. That was her stage name."

"I don't remember her. I don't go to the movies much."

Laki had spun on his heel and goggled at that. He had burst out laughing. "I suppose there are such people. I never meet them. People who don't go to the movies."

"Why doesn't she want to act anymore?"

He had struck out at the question with those restless hands of his. "It really is a shitty business," he had said. And then his eyes had lit up. "But she is quite beautiful. Inside and out. A wonderful ... *soul*."

I HAD FOUND myself agreeing with him when I met her at the party, but I couldn't tell her that this was what I had seen then. What I was seeing even now. So I said, "Nothing that shouldn't have been there. Nothing out of the ordinary." I waited for her head to come up and for our eyes to meet. "Nothing that would have explained your husband's real concern."

"Randy," she said, "be a dear and fetch me a glass of wine. And I think that . . . this gentleman—"

"Jantarro."

"—Mr. Jantarro could use another . . . Scotch, was it?"

I nodded. She laid the refolded tissues on the arm of the couch, pressed them flat, and adjusted her position among the cushions. There would be no more tears, her actions said, no more of the luxury of grief. Randy hesitated, and then, with bad grace, went toward the front of the house to do as she had asked.

"Mr. Jantarro," she said as a door opened and closed somewhere behind us. Her voice was low and unhurried. "I am grateful that you were thoughtful enough to come to me with this. And for your discretion. I don't know whether or not Alan told you this, but he and I discussed his . . . opinion . . . that I was in some sort of difficulty. I was unable to persuade him that I was not. It became an *idée fixe* with him, and we lived around it as best it could. I had thought he had finally given it up, but now I see that he shared this notion of his with someone else. I suppose that's why he was more relaxed the last week or so." She lifted her eyes to the hall beyond my shoulder, to see if Randy was on his way back.

"Frankly," she continued, "I had hoped it was a psychiatrist he was seeing"—she spared me a look and a wan smile— "instead of a detective. But I must tell you that there was nothing in this idea of his. Nothing at all." We heard the door close in the hall and footsteps approaching. "It would only . . . further upset Randy to learn that there was dissension between Alan and me. So I'd appreciate it if you could—"

"You mentioned psychiatry. Do you think it was suicide?" I asked her.

She gave me a warning look. "I'm afraid so," she told me, adding quickly in a firmer voice, "Thank you, Randy. That's really sweet of you, darling. I was just telling Mr. Jantarro that I'm afraid Alan's new film, *The Bengal Lancer*, won't be completed now." She sat up straighter, took the wine from Randy, and said to me, "We haven't seen any rushes. He wouldn't show them to anyone. But I know that he had twenty pages or more left to shoot. I doubt that there's anything that can be done with the scenes he had already shot.''

"I could finish it, Cammy. You know I could." It was the first time I'd paid real attention to Randy since the few words we'd exchanged on my arrival. His voice was startlingly deep, a bass as beautiful as the rest of him was plain.

She patted his hand, and he withdrew it from this attention. "I know you could," she said. "Randy is a director himself, you know," she said to me. "Quite a good one. A really good director," she amended, "for someone so young."

"Youth has got nothing to do with it," Randy protested in a rumble.

"Have you anything showing now?" I asked him. I would need to talk to him, and when I got around to it, it would help to have a basis.

He glowered. "They only show feature-length crap," he said.

"And your films are not . . . feature-length?"

"What is feature-length anyway?" he asked rhetorically, readying himself for a defense he must have delivered a number of times before, if only to his mirror. "An invention of the moneymen in Hollywood. A package to sell the masses on, like popcorn and candy. Life doesn't move in ninety-minute blocks, does it? It's more fluid and more abrupt. Art, Mr. Jananna, has to reflect and to respect the fact that life is fickle."

Camelia Laki stood up. "It's Mr. Jantarro, dear. And I'm sure he doesn't want to hear a tirade on the evils of modern filmmaking." Neither did she want an exposition on the fickleness of life, I thought.

I put down my Scotch and got to my feet.

"I'll show you to the door," she said. Nodding at Randy, I let myself be steered toward the front of the house. There was a great deal more I needed to know from her, but it would have to wait for another time.

THE DOORBELL RANG.

Camelia and I looked at each other briefly. It was a curious instant of near domesticity: we seemed to be asking each other if we were expecting company, if we were up to having guests in, if we shouldn't instead just turn out the lights on whomever it was and go to bed. I saw her lean toward me, her lips slightly parted, and I would have taken her in my arms and kissed her right then and there. But someone began knocking on the door. She went to the peep hole and looked out. Then she stepped back and opened the door a few inches.

"Camelia Noone Laki?" a voice from the other side inquired.

"Yes," she said. I could see her spine straighten. Her right hand made a fist.

"I am Detective Sergeant Pelletier," said the voice. "I have a warrant for your arrest." She drifted back, admitting two men and a woman in uniform—and Bench.

THEY DID IT up right. All the warnings, all the information she would need in order to know the exact nature of her predicament. And they put cuffs on her, as they do on everyone arrested for murder.

One of the uniforms kept Randy at bay in the mouth of the hall. His booming protests seemed to be hollow noises that came from a long way off. And Bench stood directly in front of me, silent and unmovable.

Once, when everyone began to shift around, her eyes met mine, but I couldn't read what was in them. She stood mute throughout everything, until, when they were ready to take her away, she asked if she could change her clothes. Bench nodded. And the woman cop led her to the stairs and up to the bedroom. Pelletier followed them, two paces behind.

"Talk," said Bench.

"I have the right to remain silent," I told him.

"Cut it," he said.

"I came to tell her that I was going to investigate Laki's death."

"Well, we've just put you out of work."

"Maybe."

"Tell me what she said."

I shrugged. I was having a difficult time getting my mental balance. Murder had been a real possibility, and for all I knew she was the best suspect going. But I didn't want her to be, which was a stupid thing to let dictate my actions.

I wondered what my client would have said.

"She's a beautiful soul, Jantarro." That's what he would have said. "She's in trouble, and I want you to help her." That's what he would have said.

I smiled at Bench. Once you take instructions from your client, a lot of the confusion gets cleared up. "She didn't say anything you'd be interested in," I told him.

"Donovan," he said to the uniform down the hall. The cop turned his head but stayed between Randy and the rest of us. "Mr. Jantarro is coming downtown with us. You take him in the Yellow." Bench switched his look to me. "He's going to help us," he said.

FIVE

"Milk? Sugar?"

"Both."

"These Styrofoam cups," said the young cop who was minding me, "they say that bits come off when you drink and get stuck inside your guts. Gives you cancer."

I sipped the lukewarm swill and shifted my weight in the uncomfortable gray steel-and-plastic chair. The cop shop—Forty-eight Division, because the arrest had been made there—was a warren of little offices done over in gray and shit brown. And this cubicle was as messy as the rest, with nowhere clear to put the cup down.

"Makes holes in the ozone layer, too," the kid said. I let his motor mouth run on; at 2:00 A.M. I was too tired even to complain. "It's the chlorine something or other they make them with. Gets into the air and eats up the ozone."

I would give it another half hour, I decided. I needed to know what they had on Camelia, and if Bench wouldn't tell me directly, the thrust of his questions might give me some idea. But I also needed my sleep, so in half an hour I would phone Glenda, who would either make the fuss herself that would get me out of here or call her law partner to do it. Provided, of course, that they'd let me have my phone call.

I yawned, stretched, and for what must have been the twentieth time read the sampler that hung over the desk in front of me. It said: "Stress: A condition caused by the brain overriding the body's urge to take the asshole by the neck and squeeze him until his eyeballs pop out." The cop who owned the desk had taped one of his kid's pictures next to this piece of riotous humor. It was a rendition of chaos in crayon, signed, through the help of a teacher, "Love, Jinny."

Bench came in just as I was flexing my legs in preparation for an attempt to walk out of the place.

"Sorry," he said. "These things take time. Lawyers and all." He gave my uniformed baby-sitter the eye, and the kid fled. Bench sank into a chair and rubbed at his eyes.

"You think she did it, huh?" I asked him.

He uncovered his eyes and looked at me. "Yeah, I think she did it."

"Want to tell me why?"

"No, I don't want to tell you why." He resumed the rubbing of his face. "But I will," he said. "Because I want you to tell me what she said this evening, and I'm too fucking tired to go ten rounds with you."

I had already thought things through and had decided that if I gave him a verbatim report of who said what, leaving out the significant pauses, the facial expressions, the nuances in the tones, I wouldn't be doing Camelia much harm. So I played back the evening's conversation for him while he grunted and massaged various sluggish parts of his anatomy.

"I may want that in the form of a sighed statement later on." He looked the question at me.

I shrugged. "Okay, I guess," I told him. "So why Camelia Laki?"

He sighed. "We found her prints at the King Street office." He held up a hand to forestall me. "Fresh ones. We can tell that now, you know. Laser surface...something. I don't know. These were still glistening fresh. And we got a witness saw her going in and out of the place just after noon. And—" He stopped, considered, and began again. "Anyway, that makes her the one."

They must have found out where and when he'd eaten brunch and with Chin's evidence put the time of death at about noon. "So you figure she said, 'Here, dear, drink this,' and he did."

"Something like that."

"And motive?"

"Millions of them. All dollar bills. Hell, Jantarro, you were the one who told us she was running through dough like a junkie. He just cut off her supply. Or he found out what she was buying with all that cash and it blew the lid off the thing."

I took a sip of my cool coffee. "How about," I said, "how about they had a fight and he killed himself after it?"

"I don't like suicide. Not anymore. No note. And—" Again he stopped, waved his hand, and said, "There are other things, too." I thought of the chipped tooth and the bruising. I didn't like suicide either; but I liked the thought of Camelia as a murderer just as little.

"But you've got nothing that rules it out," I said.

"You mean, do I have a witness who saw her put the shit in the bottle and make him drink it? No, I don't. But murderers of this kind tend to be a little circumspect, Jantarro. Which is why we tend to have to use circumstantial evidence. You've heard of that. Circumstantial evidence."

I shook myself awake and stood up. I had a cramp in my leg and my stump was itching furiously. I needed a scalding shower, and even more I needed bed. "Has she confessed?" I asked him.

"Not yet," he said. "The lawyer got there too fast."

"Have you found out where she got the poison?"

He shook his head. "Not yet."

"Have you even connected her with the stuff?"

This time he just shook his head.

"Even circumstantially?" I asked.

"Get out of here," he said, too weary to make it a command. "Go on, get out of here."

THE PHONE RANG at nine the next morning, waking me up.

"You didn't call," Glenda said. It wasn't exactly an accusatory tone in her voice, but it was something that might rapidly have moved in that direction.

"Didn't call what?"

"Me, Cagey, me." When she calls me Cagey—from my middle initials, K.G.—I know that it isn't serious. "John" is when it's serious.

"Oh," I said.

"Yeah, oh."

"I was busy."

"Of course."

"At the cop shop."

"Oh," she said, switching tones.

"Yeah, oh."

"Are you all right? You must be if they let you go."

"I'm fine. Just tired. That's all. How about tonight?"

"I can't, Cage. I'm tied up."

"Oh," I said.

"Oh, come on. There's nothing 'oh' about it. It's business. A client who . . . Why am I explaining?"

"On Saturday night? A client? Saturday? Night?"

"Some people work, Jantarro."

I laughed. "Tomorrow night, then?"

"You're on. And Cage?"

"Yeah?"

"I love you."

"Me too," I said. And we hung up.

I sank back into the pillows, rolled my head to see out of the windows, and found that everything outside had a bright, hard edge to it. I wasn't sure I could cope with things so vigorously, aggressively present. So I closed my eyes again, but the image of Camelia Laki rose up behind my lids, making me restless.

I looked at the phone and thought of Glenda, wondering whether she was picking up the vibrations that the Laki woman was causing in me.

And what exactly were the vibrations, I asked myself?

But now I was awake, and half an hour later I was showered, fifteen minutes after that coffeed, and in another fifteen minutes dressed and on the street.

Arnold Guberian was listed in the phone book under Guberian Enterprises, at 113 Bloor Street West. One-Thirteen, as the building is called, is a twenty-story, postmodernist thing that rises within bright red anodized aluminum cladding to a yellow peak that looks just like the roof of a two-room cottage in the Cotswolds. The doorway to the street is made to resemble a giant eye, and as you pass through the 'pupil' you feel the whole thing might nictate you into pieces without warning.

The man at the information desk wore a perfectly ordinary, almost premodern rent-a-cop security-company uniform. Since it was Saturday, he made me sign in. And since it was Saturday, I wasn't at all certain that Sweet Arnold would be on the premises.

I asked the guard which floor and which office I should go to. Guberian Enterprises, he informed me, *was* the thirteenth floor. A gambling man, I thought as the elevator carried me up.

Thirteen in One-Thirteen. Maybe Sweet Arnold had a sense of humor, along with his reputedly rotten disposition.

My modest gamble paid off. The crazy film-world people were there and working on Saturday, and from the way that the employees were scooting back and forth through the reception area with earnest expressions pasted on their faces, it was a good bet that the boss was in residence.

There are a number of ways to get in to see a rich and important person. Most of them involve lying in one form or another, and because I wanted to be able to see Guberian more than once, I had rejected all the real lies in favor of a version of the truth. So when the receptionist prepared himself to give me a hard time, I gave him an envelope from the inside pocket of my nine-hundred-dollar suit.

"Mr. Guberian wants this right away," I told him, and I wandered off to find a *Forbes* to read among the ferns and palms of the reception area. I was offered coffee and I declined. I was kept under observation and I pretended not to notice. And I was peeped at by two secretaries and still I remained unflustered. Eventually, I was ushered into Guberian's presence.

And I was not impressed. Neither Elaine Younger nor Paulie Mac had seen fit to tell me that Sweet Arnie was all of five feet one. He was balding, he wore heavy black-framed glasses, and he fit inside his dark blue suit with a perfection that my tailor would hear about. "Sit down, Mr. Jantarro," he said. His voice was a high tenor that did nothing to add to his height. I sat. He remained standing on the other side of his desk. He brushed a hand across my expensive notepaper with the deckle edge. "How is she bearing up?"

In my note I had simply told him that Camelia Laki was in jail and that I had come from there. "As well as possible under the circumstances," I said. "As you might imagine."

"The late Alan Laki was my friend," he said, and through his thick lenses he fixed me with a pair of magnified black eyes. "And not, I'm afraid, his wife. Consequently, I don't possess information about her that would permit me to imagine how she might act." He spoke without any accent at all, but with the stilted exactness of a foreigner who had determined to learn proper English and had done so with a vengeance.

I cocked my head at him. "That's not what I hear. I hear that you and she were lovers." Elaine's suggestion seemed ridiculous; perhaps it had been her idea of a joke.

"Mr. Jantarro! Do not be indelicate." His tone was sharp, but I could tell he was pleased by this report. His little chest swelled and he fingered his tie for a brief instant before checking the gesture.

"I apologize," I said. "But I was under the impression that I was coming to a close friend of hers."

"Alas, in that you were misinformed. However, that does not mean that I am unwilling to do what I can to assist her." He brought his fingertips together and taped them lightly. "After all, I owe a great deal to her late husband."

"What she needs right now is an idea of who might have killed him."

"But . . . Ah, I see. You believe her to be innocent."

"And you don't?"

"I had given the matter of her guilt or innocence no thought at all until I got your . . . note."

"So what did you imagine had happened to Alan?"

"You seem inordinately fond of imagination, Mr. Jantarro."

"I have to be. I'm a private investigator. Until I get facts, that's all I have to go on."

"As you say." He walked in choppy steps to the righthand edge of his desk and then back again to the left. He stopped and placed his hands once more on my note. "You are employed by her?" I gave him my bland look. "Yes," he said, "of course. A breach of . . . professional ethics." He let me see the trace of a crooked smile.

"I would like to be able to tell Mrs. Laki that you're willing to help."

"But you shall, my dear man. You shall indeed." His voice rose and then fell dramatically. "However, I cannot oblige her at this very present moment. You must understand: your visit comes as something of a surprise, and I am a believer in well-ordered days."

"I'll bet," I said.

"What?" He goggled at me, or maybe he just stared at me through those Coke-bottle bottoms of his.

"When will you be able to help?"

"So direct. So blunt and forceful." Now his crooked smile revealed small, pointed teeth. It was established: we did not like each other. "This evening. Will that be in time?"

"Where?"

"You are welcome to come to my house. At seven. My secretary will give you my address as she shows you out. Good day, Mr. Jantarro." And he left the room and me.

AND THAT LEFT ME with the rest of the day to turn to some advantage. There were two or three things I knew I needed to find out, things that the cops were better equipped to pursue; but it would be bad policy, I decided, to hope that Bench would share any more information with me—at least until I had something else to trade. I needed to know when Laki ate his last meal, in order to know the time he died. As well, I was curious about who had shared his last brunch with him, and whether the same person had shared his last bed. And I needed to know for whom the iron, quinine, and strychnine elixir had been prescribed.

To learn these things would require footwork, the patient slogging up and down streets that demands a personality different from mine. Or a personality like mine that is slipping into the thrall of a woman nearly named after a flower.

I chose the hunt for the restaurant, because, although there are perhaps a thousand more restaurants than drugstores in town, I could feel lunchtime approaching, and because I had another idea for the drugs that would save me all that exertion.

There were two ways I could go: either I could start canvassing the eateries near Laki's King Street office, or I could begin with the chichi places that might attract a big-name director.

Then I had a thought. I rang Elaine Younger at her office. She, too, was in on Saturday. It seemed the whole world was working overtime, including me. "Brunch," I said.

"Name the place."

"That's the problem."

"I'll name the place, then."

"Where would you go on a Wednesday morning—early, maybe—for brunch?"

"It's Saturday, Jantarro."

"I know."

After a pause she said, "I see. The Laki thing again."

"*Still* the Laki thing."

"Wednesday what time?"

"Ten, eleven."

"That narrows it down considerably." There was crackling and faint conversation on the line as she thought. "Well, I'd say the Grill Room, Astarte, or Fenton's. If I had to, Sutton Place, maybe."

"For eggs Benedict."

"Ugh. I wouldn't."

"Pretend."

"Well, anyone will make you eggs Benedict if you force them."

"What about the King Eddie?" I asked. The King Edward Hotel was one of my favorites, and it had a fancy, upscale dining room or two. It was also on King Street.

"Yes. I suppose so. Certainly, it's chic enough."

"I'll meet you at the King Eddie"—I checked my watch—"at one."

"Splendid," she said. "I'll book the whole afternoon off."

I had time to take a cab up to the Sutton Place Hotel to check it out. And if I had to, I could hit the other places for dinner and nightcaps. An investigator's life needn't always be hard.

SIX

THE SUTTON PLACE dining room was a dark-wood-and-thick-carpet place. The lighting was too low and the classical Muzak too high. And in the center of the room, under a baby spot, the largest arrangement of fruit I had ever seen rose precariously above the white-linen-covered tables.

I stopped at an oak lectern that held the reservations book like a gospel, and while I waited, I leafed through it back as far as last Monday without finding Laki's name. But that didn't mean he hadn't been here. Then I counted Red River grapefruit until they disappeared among the dozens of bright-eyed Sunkist oranges and the shambling shapes of the Ugli fruit. I was steeling myself to tackle the bananas when the manager of the room appeared.

"I'm acting for the late Alan Laki," I told him. It wasn't wholly a lie.

"You don't want a table?"

"Not today."

"I'm sorry but I'm quite busy at the moment."

I looked around. Over half of the tables were empty. And then our eyes met. If anyone lies with more panache than a private investigator, it must be a maître d'hôtel.

Experience told me that there was only one thing to do in such situations. And I did it: I reached into my pocket, withdrew my money clip, and attracted his attention with a fifty-dollar bill.

"A terrible loss," he said promptly.

"What?"

"Mr. Laki, sir."

"Indeed. He dined here?"

"Not often enough."

"But last Wednesday, in the morning, for brunch?"

He dropped his eyes to the money clip. "The police," he murmured.

"Yes," I said. "They do perform a valuable service."

"I have been asked..."

"Not to say anything to anybody. Yes, I know." I put the money clip back in my pocket, reserving the fifty between my fingers. I started to fold it.

"But, if as you say, you are..."

"Acting for the late Mr. Laki."

He sighed. Fifty was all that he would get, and we both knew that twenty would have done. "Mr. Laki did not dine with us last Wednesday at any time, unfortunately."

I let him take the bill from my fingers. "Thank you," I said, but he had already glided off to attend to business.

I went to the display of fruit and took an apple—a shiny red Mac—waiting to see if the arrangement would start moving. But it didn't, and I ate the apple in the cab on the way down to King Street.

The King Edward Hotel is pretentious, but it delivers much of what it promises, and I like it. An old hotel, it was done over a few years ago and now wears the pastel shades of the moment highlighted by the flashes of stainless steel and curlicues of chromium that suggest something of arts both *nouveau* and *deco*. Very eighties is the King Eddie.

Elaine was already there, sitting in a tub chair, smoking a cigarette, looking good and perfectly at home. She wore a slinky beige silk thing that had slid completely off one shoulder and which also threatened to open up beyond the thigh at the least provocation. She didn't rise when I approached, but offered me her hand, and when I took it, she drew me down for a kiss.

"I've spoken to Umberto," she said. "About a table."

"Ah," I said. "That's good." She stood up, and we walked toward the main dining room. "You and..."

"Umberto."

"Umberto. You're acquainted?"

"Intimately."

"I see."

"We once attended the same night course in Baroque art. He loved Zurburán—austere monks, skulls, terribly intense—and I grooved on Caravaggio. The bodies, you know. Great rolling masses of muscular bodies."

claimed. And we talked about the detective business. I was still searching for the joy in it, I claimed. Neither of us entirely believed the other, which makes for good conversation sometimes.

And when, later, I was making my way back from the men's room, Umberto accosted me with a slight gesture. "Mr. Laki," he said in an undertone. We were standing close to each other in a narrow hall.

"Yes, Umberto?"

"Mr. Laki did indeed eat here on Wednesday morning."

"I see."

"In the Prince Regent Room."

"Do you happen to know the time?"

"I have told the police. I see no reason not to tell you. He came at nine-fifteen and left at ten-thirty."

"Thank you, Umberto."

He hesitated. "There was nothing whatever... unwholesome in his meal. I assure you."

"I know there wasn't, Umberto. It's a matter of the timing."

"So I thought."

"Umberto?"

"Sir?"

"Was Mr. Laki alone?"

Umberto dropped his eyes. He took a half breath and held it longer than he should have. "No," he said eventually. "He was in the company of a woman. Now, if you will excuse me, monsieur?" And with that return to formality, he strode away and onto the floor of the dining room.

The wallpaper in the hall where I stood had a lightly flocked pattern of red flowers. I rubbed a finger along the edges of one fuzzy blossom. Not now, I thought. The question would keep, and it might mature into something more... well developed.

I went back to finish the champagne and the frivolous conversation.

"How do you like the room?" Guberian was in pink slacks and a red knit shirt with a polo player stitched on it. He held a gin and tonic. I had chosen vodka instead of gin.

"It's overwhelming," I said. And it was. Four or five huge promontories of rough nature invaded the massive sitting area, and the lighting was arranged so that it wasn't always possible to tell that glass protected you from the animals you saw. A great lizard, the largest of the half dozen I could see—the basilisk itself—stretched full-length on a rock not a foot from my feet.

Guberian saw my fascination with the beast. "A Komodo dragon," he said with pride. "From Indonesia by way of Japan. They're protected, of course, so it took a good deal of ingenuity to obtain this specimen, I can tell you. But he's a beauty. Nine feet seven inches long." He straightened up a little, as if the lizard's length somehow added to his own stature.

"Dangerous," I said. It was half a question, half a declaration of anxiety.

"Not really," he said. "There are only three recorded instances of dragons eating people. And in two of those cases they were provoked—their territory was invaded. For the most part, they eat wild pigs or deer. In their natural element, you understand. Here I have to content them with . . . other forms of food. Over there are my monitor lizards." His face lit up. "There's one that should interest you in particular. My Bengal monitor—*Varanus bengalensis*. Six feet long. A beauty. And appropriate in the circumstances, I think you'll agree. Alan Laki's new film was to be called *The Bengal Lancer*."

"I had heard," I told him.

"I was going to call him Lance—my monitor—but I resisted the impulse. I am a serious herpetologist. As for the rest of my animals, they are iguanas, the big ones. I have geckos, of course, and skinks, and one fairly large Thai water dragon of which I am inordinately proud." He gestured toward the other side of the room where other glass cages towered to the ceiling.

The room itself was truly big. A slate floor had been set on a foundation buried deep in the wall of a ravine, and out of the glass windows at the back I could see in the early evening haze the distant lights of the skyscrapers downtown. Hundreds of trees in the ravine waved in the wind, their leaves and branches causing the lights behind them to flicker as if in a dream. Gray leather couches were scattered throughout the room, turned so that sitters could observe the reptiles in their climate-controlled lairs. We sat on the one that faced the outside. The sun was setting against our view.

"Now," said Guberian, and he turned to me on the couch, his owlish eyes wide in his small face. "What is your theory?" The crooked smile was back, letting me understand that the idea of a private investigator's having a theory was amusing.

"I don't have a theory," I told him.

"Theories are remarkably helpful devices," he said, still smiling. "Hermeneutic."

"Confining, too," I said. "Especially when you get them prematurely."

"Yet you came to me. You must have had a reason, if not a fully developed theory."

"You are Alan Laki's partner. You knew him. You had interests that were entangled with his."

"And you suspect that someone tripped, shall we say, in one of these entanglements?"

"It's a possibility."

"It is indeed. But not, I fear, a fact."

"Tell me, Mr. Guberian, why did you relinquish control of the film company to Laki?"

"Now, you see? There, surely, speaks a theory."

"I've heard that he caught you in bed with his wife."

He laughed, a hee-hee-hee sound pitched high. "So you intimated this morning. Camelia is surely a beautiful woman, but alas, the rumor is a canard. Nothing more. And in any event, I fail to see how the event, had it happened, would have provided the basis for the . . . the extortion by Alan that you suggest. I have no reason to hide my fornications."

Somewhere behind me a lizard roared in its confinement, a noisy exhalation that sounded brassy the way that distant thunder will when it bounces off a window.

"You tell me, then," I said. "Why did you relinquish control of Lakipix?"

"I think not. Some matters remain private, even after the death of one of the parties. Don't you agree?"

"Murder has a tendency to publicize things."

"So you think it was murder."

"Did he have reason to kill himself?"

Guberian got up from his seat and advanced a few short steps toward the nearest glass cage. "Everyone has a reason to kill himself. Thanatos and the urge for death...or haven't you read your Freud?" He reached down and opened a shiny metal box, from which he took a white rat by the tail. It squealed loudly and flailed at the air with tiny paws. "Look, Mr. Jantarro," he said, "we can go on this way. Each of us is quite capable of intelligent thrust and riposte." He swept his hand along the transparent wall at his side and found a glass handle for a small glass door. He turned to look at me, the rat still dangling, wriggling, squealing. "My resources are greater than yours, although I do appreciate that you are not dependent upon fees in order to live." He opened the panel and I thought I could smell the hot, fetid breath of the jungle. With a casual glance, he flung the rat inside and shut the panel. "But I should be loath to go to all the trouble and expense of discouraging your interest. I am in all frankness a busy man."

"What do you suggest?" I was determined not to be put off balance by his theater. But I found it hard not to follow the rat as it scurried in search of safety, a patch of innocent white in the dark green vegetation.

"Let me hire you—"

"I have a client."

He smiled at me, and I turned to gaze out at the dusk. Something big stirred behind the glass wall. I willed myself not to turn back and look. "Not really, Mr. Jantarro. You are not employed by Camelia or her lawyer. I have learned this since we spoke. Nor has Randy, that poor benighted fool, attempted to hire you. No, you were at one time employed by Alan, and now, I suspect, you are spurred on posthumously, shall we say, by an excess of guilt or zeal. Or hubris, perhaps. Is that not accurate?"

The noise behind him was disgusting. I swallowed a large portion of my drink in order to drown the sounds. "I have a client," I insisted.

"Very well," he said, and he walked into my field of vision, a swaggering, cruel little monster. Sweet Arnie. "Perhaps we might approach this in another fashion. I never give up easily, you see, Mr. Jantarro. That is the secret of my success."

"What other way?" I asked. I was ready to leave. Or to hit him. And I understood that these were the very reactions he had sought to provoke.

"Let me say—state, if you will—that I did not kill Alan Laki." He waved a small hand. "Now I do not for one moment imagine—there, you have me imagining!—you are an insidious man, Mr. Jantarro." He chuckled in a child's voice. "No, I do not for a single moment believe that this statement will deflect any suspicion you might have been directing my way. Nevertheless, I choose to make it. As well, I shall offer you some food for thought. Something to chew on other than the image of these tiny bones." He tapped his chest with both hands, and he giggled. "Other suspects"—he began to tick them off on his fingers—"might include: first, Laki himself; he was as dry as the proverbial dust on his new film, and what he had shot stank to high heaven; second, Randy Noone—yes, he adopted his sister's stage name, which shows you what a desperately spineless twit he is; young Noone and his brother-in-law were at daggers drawn, because, in the immature mind of Noone, Laki owed him the wherewithal to launch his career as an auteur and yet stubbornly, not to say contemptuously, refused to honor the debt; and third, I recommend to your consideration one Michael Dennis, of whom it is said that incandescent light never sets on his erection; he is—or was—lover to fair Camelia and, naturally, enemy to the man she favored mostly, her boring old husband."

He wound up at the glass cage into which the rat had disappeared. He peered through the glass with great intensity. "I say nothing of myself. There is, apparently, no need." His breath fogged the glass and he wiped at the mist with a hand.

"And Camelia?" I asked. "You've left her out."

"Yes," he said. "Well, honor-bound to spare the lady. Is that not the chivalrous way so favored here in North America? Besides," he said, turning to face me at last, "I've given you Michael Dennis, and surely if you lift him up, out from under will crawl another suspect, I should say."

I put down my drink and began the long passage through the menagerie toward the front door. "Good luck, Mr. Jantarro," Guberian called out after me. "Good luck, and do keep me abreast."

Outside, darkness was unrolling itself. The air had become humid, heavy with trapped moisture, and walking away from Guberian's was like swimming under water. But I had to get to the other shore. Or the monsters would get me.

SEVEN

IT WAS EIGHT-THIRTY on a Saturday night and I was restless, with thoughts running around in my head like molecules in Brownian motion—bumping into each other, going nowhere and everywhere all at once. I wanted someone to talk to, to think out loud with.

But Glenda was busy. She and her client would just now be sitting down to a good meal and a cozy natter about nifty legal things.

I thought about Camelia. She would have eaten the jailhouse swill at five-thirty and would by now be lying on her bunk, shaking with fear, probably, and at the same time experiencing the numbing boredom of incarceration. I remembered how that was, how the two seemingly inconsistent things could go together.

And I tried to think some sense into this case, to force my brain past the ugly images it had taken away from Guberian's house of horrors. But each time I picked a notion as a place on which to stand, it crumbled away beneath me from the weight of my confusion. I told myself that I was blowing it by clinging to the idea that Camelia was...was what? Innocent? Beautiful, yes. Desirable, certainly. But what had either of those wish-born feelings of mine to do with the hard realities of guilt and innocence? Not a single damn thing. Even so, I told myself that I didn't care. That a man has to let himself off the leash of reason every now and then or go mad completely. That even this illogic was right, because Camelia was beautiful, was desirable. *Was* innocent. And round and round I went as I told myself more things than I knew. Until my confusion grew so great that it stopped me from any more telling.

I called my friend JoJo Polifemi from a booth on Bayview, where I'd wound up after my walk from Guberian's. But the phone rang ten times and then I hung up. He'd be out with his new boyfriend, I guessed, some painter he'd met at Willem

Gunder's last party. Willem was settling into domesticity with Sara, so it was no good bothering to call him.

I stood on the sidewalk, wilting in the damp heat but buzzing on the inside.

Then I remembered that Horacio Gutierrez was playing Beethoven tonight at Roy Thomson Hall. If I hurried, I could get in at intermission and catch the second half of the concert. I got a cab outside Pantello's and settled back to watch traffic do its own Brownian thing.

For some reason the seats at the very front of Roy Thomson Hall are always empty. A few couples and I hung in the aisles waiting to make sure that no season ticket holders would claim them, and then just before the concertmaster came on, we plunked ourselves down two rows back and dead center. This is not a good place to hear orchestral music from: you lose most of the woodwinds, and the violins are overpowering. But for listening to soloists the seats are unsurpassed.

I was close enough to read the chalk marks from the shipping companies on the underside of Gutierrez's Steinway. I could smell the polished wood, the faint tang of oxidation from the strings and the harp of the great instrument, the sweat of musical effort all around me.

And then Gutierrez came out, took a quick bow, flipped his tails over the bench, stared for a terrible instant at the ordinary-looking, ivory-covered keys, lifted his bent hands—and we were off. For an unmeasurable time I lived inside Beethoven's Piano Concerto no. 4. Gutierrez was playing for me, and I existed for the music. Or because of it. I'm never able to tell.

Piano music simply *is* music for me. And I firmly believe that if there is a Second Coming, God will arrive to the strains of the finest piano ever built. There might be trumpets as well, or even the thrumming of strings; but I won't be able to hear them. And nor, I believe, will He.

We applauded until our hands were sore, which in my case presents problems. I find I can make more noise by banging a rolled up program against the plastic hand. It also means I can go on clapping longer than most people. Which I did.

I drifted toward a cab and then to bed on a cloud of recalled notes. I had no worries, no spectrally restless client, and no suspects to interrogate. I had only a tiny piece of some truth larger than any question to which it might be the answer.

BUT I DREAMED. And in my dream Camelia Noone was trapped on a movie screen while I sat in the audience. In the sepia tones of very old movies, she was jerked this way and that by the racing frames within the projector. But her anguished face implored me to release her. She would peel herself away from the screen, a larger-than-life cutout, reaching toward me; but then the scene would change and she would be dragged back into the flat plane, compelled to act according to another's script and someone else's direction.

I ran around in the darkened theater, searching for a way to stop the horrible performance. There were rats—Disneyesque creatures that talked to each other and considered me intelligently—in each of the dark and empty rooms of the cinema. And when finally I took a knife and hacked at the shimmering screen, Alan Laki was there behind the arras, warding off my knife blows with long flickering fingers. I tumbled through into emptiness.

And woke, blinking at the ceiling in my room. I got up to turn the air-conditioning higher. It was hotter and stickier than it had been when I went to bed. Before I went back to sleep, I thought of Guberian's dragons and wondered why I was afraid of them.

I HAVE A computer expert. Everyone needs one, especially if he is in the detective business. Mine is a young kid of twenty-two named Ravi Srinivasagam, who immigrated from Sri Lanka four years ago. Ravi is deep in the complicated toils of some advanced university program which promises to release him at the age of thirty with a worldwide reputation and more power than is good for one person to possess.

Soon after he arrived, I met Ravi at the Center for Rehabilitation and Mobility, where they made and still service my arm. They were working on a knee joint for him because his had been shot away by a bullet back home. They are simply the best there is at making prostheses. And I like to go back to the body shop from time to time, not only to get a tune-up but also to show the kids what a fork is and how you pick up peas with it.

Ravi, we quickly discovered, wouldn't leave their computer terminal alone, and in order for them to get any work done when he was around, we had to buy him a computer of his own. After that he never looked back.

"Cagey, sir," he said when I called. Sunday has no meaning to him. Nor does night, so far as I can tell.

"Have you got a moment, Ravi?"

"It is morning, still. Most of my circuits are yet free." He pretends to be a machine because he knows it bothers me. I now pretend it doesn't bother me, because it really does.

"Great," I said. "I want you to do some breaking and entering."

"Contrary to the Criminal Code, is it not, Cagey, sir?"

"Very contrary, Ravi." For Ravi, I soon discovered, all information, whether located in private or government data banks, is public property; he understands perfectly the concept of confidentiality; but he simply does not believe it applies to him, and so he works in his spare time to liberate all this captive information. This is another thing he teases me about.

"Just so long as we understand one another, Cagey, sir."

"Ravi, I'm looking for information about a drug prescription for a tonic composed of iron, quinine, and strychnine. Sometimes called IQ and S. I doubt that it's stored anywhere, even if payment for it was made from a drug plan. But try, will you? And I want to know who the physician is for Alan Laki. I should say *was*, because he died recently. And for his wife, Camelia Noone Laki, and his brother-in-law, Randy Noone. That should be on the health insurance computers."

"Most certainly it will be."

"I can't tell you anything about the prescription, except that it was probably recent—within the last year."

"It is probable, is it not, that the Lakis will have a number of physicians? The wealthy are often ill in many ways."

"That's true, and I'd like the names of any you can find. How did you know they were wealthy?"

"I have a friend who reads newspapers." He sounded disgusted. "She insists to repeat for me all that she reads."

"Is that so bad?"

"Not bad, merely useless for the most part. I cannot forget anything, you know." I did know; his memory is phenomenal.

"I appreciate this, Ravi."

He laughed. "Good-bye, Cagey, sir. I shall contact."

AT ELEVEN I felt free to phone Randy Noone. I got him, as I suspected I would, at the Laki house. "I want to see you," I told him.

"Why?"

"To talk about your sister and her case."

"You should speak to her lawyer."

"I shall, Randy. But I also wanted to talk to you."

"I don't know," he said.

"Don't worry. You don't have to answer any questions you don't want to. But I think you do want to help your sister. Don't you?"

"Yeah, but I don't figure talking to you is the way to do it. We figure you helped the cops put her away."

"Who's we, Randy?"

"Vanstone, her lawyer. And me."

"That isn't true. You saw me and Mrs. Laki. Did it look to you like we were hostile to each other? I was hired by her husband to help her, and I'm not going to let the fact that he's dead stand in my way." I heard myself say the words and I shivered a little.

"I don't know," he said again.

"I can spare you an hour at four o'clock today. It's important," I said.

"I'm going to call Vanstone," he said.

"Good idea. See you at four." And I hung up before he could dither anymore.

It didn't seem possible that a Hamlet like Randy could have poured poison into the king. But he might know something from having hid behind the curtains while the grownups acted out their fates. I would have a better idea after I had spoken to him. And presumably to Vanstone, the lawyer, as well, for I imagined that Randy would try to have him there as protection.

AND I called Glenda. "Wake you?" I asked.

"No. I was just doing my sit-ups."

"How was last night?"

"Fine," she said. "What did you do?"

"Looked at some lizards, went to a concert. The usual thing."

She laughed and I wasn't jealous about her client any longer. "Lizards?"

"You'd like them."

"Lounge lizards are the only ones I like, and I don't like them very much. Speaking of which, are we eating in or out tonight?"

"I thought we'd have cocktails here, unwind a bit, and then go out later. To Giancarlo's."

"Yum. I'll skip lunch. And do another five sit-ups."

"And Glenda, do you know a lawyer named Vanstone?"

"Harvey Vanstone?"

"Don't know what his first name is. Works for rich folks. Takes criminal cases."

"If it's who I'm thinking of, works for rich folks is right. But Harvey doesn't do criminal. Not really. He's more of a...family adviser."

"Sounds like the guy."

"You going to meet him?"

"Maybe. For sure some time. But maybe today."

"Well, watch your cholesterol intake."

"Oleaginous, is he?"

"Like the fat on a pork roast."

"Yum."

"Tell me all about it tonight. About the lizards, too. I've got to go and get in shape."

JOHN SCOTT looked first at the books I was carrying under my arm. Then he smiled briefly at my face. "*The Politics of Hunger* by Paul Vincent," I said. "About the allied blockage of Germany in World War One." I tossed it onto his lap and he grabbed it. "*Galileo: Heretic,* a translation by Rosenthal of the book by Redondi." That one too sailed into his lap, and it was seized as eagerly. "And *Deconstructing Maleness: A Scattering of Bones,* by Gail Etherby." This, too, I tossed, he glared at it, and then he glared at me.

"Do you good," I told him with a broad smile. John Scott had been a friend and comrade in arms of my father. When my dad went back to teaching after the Civil War in Spain, Dr. Subtilis, as he used to call Scott, turned to pamphleteering and doing all he could with his small press to promote the revolution here. When my dad died, his friend entered the veterans' wing of the Sunnybrook Hospital where he fights his crippling arthritis and reads voraciously in hopes of understanding why the revolution still has not come. Since I reestablished contact with him a couple of years ago, we work on the problems together for a bit every Sunday afternoon.

"It will *not* 'do me good,' as you put it."

"Too old to learn new tricks?"

"Bah!" he said. "There's nothing whatever new in feminism. The damn Swedes, for God's sake, understood all there was to know about the 'woman question' at the turn of the century. And any thoughtful person could always have seen that the social order was a degenerate and oppressive hierarchy. But it's class that matters, not sex."

"The deconstruction, then."

"Poppycock."

"That's the idea. Or, I think it is."

"How are you, John?" He managed to move his wheelchair over close enough to extend his hand. I took it and shook it firmly, even though I knew it caused him pain.

"Good," I said. "Uncertain, as usual. But tolerating it better."

He flipped the books onto his nearby bed, wincing with the stabs of pain in his shoulder joints. "And you?" I asked him.

"I'm as ever. Nothing changes."

"Come and live downtown," I said, as I did every single week. "I'll supply you with books and various opiates and more changes than you can imagine. Why, just the other day the building superintendent put sixty-watt bulbs in the hall and now we can see the fingerprints on the wallpaper."

"You and the woman..."

"Glenda?"

"Yes, Glenda. Excuse my memory. It, like the rest of me, is rotting. You and Glenda living together yet?"

"Walkies?" I offered, going to stand behind his chair. "It's hotter than hell outside. The sweat will do you good."

"We were talking about Glenda. What are you waiting for, boy? The anxiety of middle age? The impotence of senescence?" This from a man who never married.

I pushed and together we went out into the beautiful greens of the parklike grounds that stretch for acres behind the hospital. I told him about the Laki case, and he listened without interruption, the way that he always does. I finished by explaining that I had at least four suspects, if I ruled out suicide, which I couldn't say I had.

"The wife," he said.

"Camelia." I thought that perhaps I had gone on at length about Camelia.

"Yes." We were circling slowly back. I was sweating and he was as dry as desert sand. "Wisdom would suggest that you relinquish either your interest in her or the case itself."

"I know,"I said.

"Of course you do. That is the nature of wisdom. To be always and everywhere known—by ordinarily intelligent persons, at least. The question is, do you intend to follow the wise course here?"

I watched a squirrel scamper up the trunk of a great oak and turn on the bark to scold us from a safe position. "I don't think so," I confessed.

"And she holds a great appeal for you?"

"I feel as if I know her," I said to myself out loud. "And as if she knows me."

"You're using her," Scott said.

"I beg your pardon?" Sprays of green oak leaves were falling as the squirrel happily chewed through the succulent new growth near the top.

"John, you are a fully mature man. You temporize and vacillate concerning this Glenda, holding her now at arm's length, now closer. And then you meet this woman—a possible murderer, no less, and involved in a case you have assumed responsibility for—and within minutes you are infatuated. Don't you see that you are merely using her to avoid the question of commitment to Glenda?"

"You're saying I should marry Glenda?"

"Bah!" he said. He wrested control of the wheelchair from me and spun it to face me on the path. "You haven't listened to a word I said. Worse, you haven't listened to yourself. Far be it from me to interpolate myself into your affairs. But if I were your father," he said, and he paused while his glare became a softer expression, "I'd tell you to shit or get off the pot." He turned the chair back again more slowly. "Now," he said, "get me out of this damned heat, if you don't mind."

EIGHT

AGAIN I PRESSED the lighted bell beside the white door, and again I waited while it caused solemn chimes inside the dead man's house. But this time my mouth wasn't dry with anxiety. This time I was eager to get it over with, to find out what Randy had to offer, and to cross him off my list. I was also eager to get inside where it was air-conditioned.

The lawyer opened the door. At least, I assumed he was the lawyer: he wore a gray three-piece suit, with a gold watch chain that curved across his ample pot; his white shirt had cuffs with links in them; and on his face he bore a phony look of greeting on top of a permanent base of worry. He was in his mid-fifties and he hadn't had his face lift or his liposuction yet.

"Mr. Jantarro?"

"Mr. Vanstone."

"Indeed. Won't you come in?"

"Is Randy around?"

"Can I offer you some refreshment? A tea. Or something stronger, perhaps?"

"I did want to speak to him."

"And I'm sure he wants to speak to you. I myself am having a beer. There's a cold Beck's I can recommend."

"That sounds find," I told him, if only to get some relief from him while he went to pour the thing.

But he simple called "Luis," and a Filipino man in whites came and took the order. Vanstone led me down the cool hall into the living room and sat with a grateful noise in one of the soft chairs. On the mantelpiece an ormolu clock I hadn't noticed before rang the quarter hour with the Westminster chimes, and we both turned to look at it while it did its thing. "I represent Camelia Laki," he said, and then he turned from the clock face to mine.

"And Randy Noone as well?" I asked.

He made what I call a legal gesture—an equivocal movement of hand, mouth, eyes.

"Is that a yes or a no?" I asked.

Vanstone sighed. I was putting too fine a point on things. "No, I have not been retained by Randy. But I am the family's lawyer and have been for many years now."

I pretended to look interested. "You did the work for Laki's films?"

He sipped his beer. He swallowed. He licked a tiny trace of foam off his lips. "No," he said, working as much thoughtfulness into the word as he could. "No, he employed lawyers chosen by his film company to do that work. But you, Mr. Jantarro? Turn about is fair play and all. Whom do you represent?"

I considered how to do it, and then with no expression at all I told him, "I'm afraid I can't divulge that information."

He colored. "Really," he said, annoyed. He opened his mouth to expostulate.

But just then Luis came with my beer, the open bottle and a tall lager glass balanced on a silver tray. He poured expertly until the glass was half-full, and then he set the tray down on the little table at my elbow. I thanked him, and then I asked him, "Luis, would you be kind enough to tell Mr. Noone that I would like to speak to him? He is expecting me. My name is Jantarro." It's a Basque name originally, and although my family moved out of the Iberian Peninsula when the Duke of Alba collected them to fight in the Netherlands in 1567, I can give it a Spanish twist when I need to. Something in Luis's eyes let me know I had done it right.

Vanstone thought about struggling to his feet, from where, presumably, he would be better able to control events. But after gripping the arms of the easy chair and dragging his buttocks forward a bit, he gave up the effort and slumped back. "Well, it's not Camelia who you're working for," he said, "that I do know. And neither is it Arnold Guberian. I know because we have spoken recently about you." He gave me the eye to see if this piece of information would cause me to wilt. "And it certainly isn't Randy," he went on when he saw I was unbowed. "So frankly, I'm damned if I can see who has an in-

terest in Alan's death sufficient to warrant their hiring a..."—
he thought better of it—"an investigator."

I smiled at him. "Yes," I said.

And Randy appeared, looking from one to the other of us,
seeking signals that the grown-ups had arranged what part he
would play.

"Oh, Randy my boy," said Vanstone, "I believe you know
Mr. Jantarro, who is a private investigator. He wishes to ask
you some questions, although I am duty-bound to say that—"

"Hi, Randy," I interrupted. "Relax. Have a beer. I'm not
the dentist. And I *am* concerned about your sister."

His tall body swayed between us. He ran a hand through his
thick growth of black hair. For a moment we all thought he
might burst into tears.

"Were there only the two of you in your family?" I asked.
"Camelia and you?"

He looked at me, surprised, and nodded.

"And there must be ten years between you in age. You would
be the long-hoped-for boy, and she the big sister. Right?"

"I..." he said, and it sounded like an animal grunt in that
deep bass of his. "I was an accident."

"But I'll bet Camelia was tickled pink when it turned out to
be a baby brother."

"What do you want?" he said.

I sighed. "I want to find out if you killed Alan Laki."

I had expected great fireworks from him at that, loud pro-
testations of innocent outrage. But instead he nearly smiled,
and then he asked, "Why would I do that?"

Vanstone again came forward in his seat. "Now look here,
Jantarro. I must protest. You are on dangerous ground here.
Randy, my boy, I advise you not to answer any of his ques-
tions. And certainly not to go on the way you've started."

"Vanstone," I said, "cut the crap. For one thing I'm not a
cop, and for another thing, if you keep shielding him I *will* start
to think he's got something to hide. Right now I'm going
through the motions—professional motions; you know about
those, I assume—so that I can drop him and concentrate on
others."

"Even so," said Vanstone, "it is a highly improper line of
questioning."

Randy actually laughed. "Harvey, you sound like a judge already," he said. Vanstone contrived to look pleased and put out at the same time. Randy flung a leg over the side of a chair and swiveled his body in my direction, somehow confident now. "No, I didn't kill Alan," he said to me. "What gave you that idea?"

"I've been told that Alan refused to offer you the kind of help that would have launched your career."

"And for that I'm supposed to have killed him?"

"Your sister has the estate now, the money, and she can help you."

"You're forgetting that my sister's in jail."

"That's unfortunate. But it doesn't mean you didn't kill him. You might have hoped the cops would buy the suicide idea. And you're certainly big enough to have helped him take his hemlock."

He almost smirked. "It's an idea," he said.

"Where were you on Wednesday, Randy? From about ten in the morning to about four in the afternoon."

"Randy," said Vanstone warningly.

"It's all right, Harvey," he said to the lawyer. Suddenly, he was tired, as if he only had the energy for a minute's cockiness. "I've told the police. I might as well tell him." He turned to me. "I was at my place, by myself, until about one o'clock. Then I went out with a friend for drinks. After that—about four—I bought some beer and went home. Where I got drunk. Again."

"No witnesses before one?"

"None."

"Your friend?"

"Mark Alfano. He remembers. We didn't get that drunk."

I switched tacks. "Tell me about Alan," I said. "What kind of person was he?"

"You met him," said Randy, listless once more.

"Only a couple of times. But you, you knew him well. So what sort of man was he?"

"He was a brilliant man," interjected Vanstone. "A powerful man of talent."

"He was a son of a bitch," said Randy flatly. Vanstone looked at him, shocked.

"A son of a bitch," I echoed.

"He was...he was..." Randy sputtered, his vocabulary failing him at the start.

"Mean?" I suggested. "Unfeeling?"

"Damn right," said Randy. With his eyes he dared me to disagree. "Cruel. He was cruel. He'd get strings around you, then he'd make you dance like a puppet. And he'd laugh. It didn't matter if you didn't want to...to...dance. He pulled on the strings and you did it."

Vanstone tut-tutted. "A great director has to, umm, have talents that enable him to get the best out of people. Better than they know they possess perhaps."

"But we're not just talking about actors in front of the camera, are we, Randy?" He shook his head. "What did he do to you, Randy? What dance did he make you do?"

"You can sneer if you want to. Go ahead. But you didn't have to deal with him."

"I'm not sneering," I assured him.

"But you worked for him."

"He's dead now."

"And still causing grief for everybody."

"You haven't told me what he did to you," I reminded him.

He jumped out of his chair, stabbed both hands into his thick hair, took them out, looked at them, scratched at his chest, looked at me, and looked away. "He called me 'worm,'" he said in a low voice. "Whenever I'd come over, he'd say, 'Here's the worm again.' He even laughed when I got eczema on my...my... He said it was from crawling on my belly." He turned his back to us. "It's hard to explain. He humiliated me."

I waited a beat or two. Then I said, "You hated him, didn't you?"

Randy, still facing away, nodded.

"And yet, Camelia lived with him. How was that possible? If he was the cruel man you say he was."

He shrugged. "Maybe it was just me."

"Was it just you?"

Vanstone came out of his stupor. "I must insist. No further questions. Randy, it will not help your sister to go any further with this. I assure you."

"Are you pleading her guilty?" I asked Vanstone.

He looked shocked. "Of course not."

"I take that to mean that you think she didn't do it."

"The one has nothing to do with the other," he said, surprising me by getting it right. "But in fact, as it happens, I do believe that Camelia is innocent."

"And you do, too?" I asked Randy.

He turned with an angry expression. "Of course she's innocent."

"Well, then, gentlemen, who *did* kill Alan Laki?"

There was a silence after my question. Vanstone finally broke it with a small cough. "Emm," he said, "that's not really our problem, you know. My concern—*our* concern—is to raise a reasonable doubt about Camelia's having done it."

"It would help if you could point in another direction. You might even be able to get the cops to switch their aim."

"Are you angling for a job, Mr. Jantarro? Because it sounds like that to me."

"I already have a client. I'm asking for cooperation."

"If, indeed, as you say, you do have a client, what reason do we have to believe that there will be no conflict of interest?"

"I don't think there is," I said. I was doing what Laki had hired me to do, wasn't I? Looking out for her? How could there be a conflict?

"Well, that's no doubt reassuring to you, but it doesn't persuade me."

"I want to see her," I said. "I want to be able to talk to her."

"No," said Vanstone immediately. "No way."

"You can't stop me."

"I can advise her not to see you, and I most certainly shall. I can also arrange for the authorities to be wholly uncooperative."

I thought. I had said so often that I had a client that I believed it myself. And in a way, I meant what I said. It was a matter of honor with me that the murderer should not get away with killing Alan Laki. But there was a chance to get some of the information essential to solving the case, a chance to talk to Camelia Laki, whose spending of thousands of dollars had prompted Laki to see me in the first place. Was I prepared to switch clients in midstream? That was the question.

And the answer to that depended on how I felt about another question: did I believe that she had killed her husband? Because if I did, I couldn't work to free her. Could I?

I heard John Scott telling me about wisdom. Available to all ordinarily intelligent persons, he had said.

"Tell you what," I said to Vanstone. He had been finishing the last of his beer, watching me cogitate like a man who aches when he sees another working. "If I leave my current client and sign on with you, will you let me talk to her?"

"An intriguing possibility, Mr. Jantarro. The question naturally comes to mind: what would you expect to be paid for your services?"

"Nothing," I said. "I've already been paid more than I deserve on this case."

He was flustered. "Well, we can't have that," he spluttered. "I mean, we can't have you employed and not pay you. It wouldn't be...right."

"You work out something you think is fair," I told him. "But I'll get to see her."

"You will, naturally, act on my instructions."

"Let's say, I'll work to find out how Alan Laki died."

"Yes," he said, "well, that's not quite..."

"You said yourself you think she didn't kill him."

"I did and I meant it, but I can't have you rolling around the deck like a loose cannon."

"I'll report to you, and you can fire me if you think the wrong toes are going to get crushed."

"Daily?"

"Twice a week, unless there's something special."

"Twice a week on your own motion and you'll respond to my calls."

"Done."

"Then I think it would be acceptable for you to meet with my client. I'm going to see her myself tomorrow at eleven. I'll meet you outside the Detention Center at ten to eleven, shall we say?" He finally levered himself out of the chair. He was holding out a smooth hand for me to shake.

"I'll want some time with her on my own," I said.

He withdrew his hand. "Oh, I think not," he said.

"There may be things you ought not to hear."

"That can't be right."

"Let's ask her," I said. "Tomorrow. We'll let her decide."

"Very well," Vanstone said. He looked at Randy. "Shall I tell her you'll visit on Tuesday?" he asked.

Randy looked at both of us with some disgust—and, I thought, with some fear as well. And without speaking he turned on his heel and walked out of the room.

"He's under strain," said Vanstone, looking at the door through which his client's brother had vanished.

"Yes," I said. "He is indeed."

"It's only natural."

"I wonder," I said.

NINE

"UMM, NICE."

"It's just a little Burgundy they recommended," I said.

Glenda laughed. "And here I am amused by its pretension. I'm so easy."

"Speaking of which—pretension, I mean—I'm working for Harvey Vanstone. Sort of."

"You'll need more than a little Burgundy, then." She screwed up her face in thought. "Is this the case you were babbling about the other day when you couldn't put a head of lettuce to the sword?"

"It is." I poured her more wine and got up to turn the Chopin off. We would get back to him later, I hoped.

"What's the 'sort of'? You said you were 'sort of' working for Harvey."

"I like to think that it's his client I'm working for."

"And who is that?"

"Camelia Laki."

"Recent star of TV news and the tabloids?"

"Right. The former actress, and currently widow and inmate of the Women's Detention Center."

"Lucky you. She's a real treat to male eyes. I remember her in *Undertow*. She was really good."

I swallowed a good quantity of the Burgundy. "She's still impressive," I said.

Glenda looked at me. "You've met her?"

I nodded. "Before the cops scooped her. I was working for her husband."

She brought her face close to mine and put a finger under my chin, lifting up my head. Her eyes were twinkling. "You've got a crush on her, haven't you?"

I drew my head away. "I don't know what you're talking about," I protested. The strange thing was that I felt indignant.

"J. K. G. Jantarro! You have, you have! Star-struck."
Grinning, she leaned back in the couch, taking her wine-glass
with her and, after a pause of ten seconds, crossing her legs.

Glenda has lovely legs. Glenda has lovely ears, arms, shoulders, teeth, and even lovely feet. Her face is a delicate oval
framed by straight black hair and set with large brown eyes that
shine from her intelligence. Glenda has a style that is her own
and that is compelling. She is self-possessed and eager, ambitious and willing, serious and witty. Glenda is too attractive to
be merely beautiful. And I believed that I loved her.

So I said, "I think I have. A little one."

"Maybe more than a little."

"Maybe."

"How...how often have you ... seen her?"

I blushed, something I don't do very often. "Twice. Once at
a party and once after her husband died. At her house. To
question her."

"Come here," Glenda said. She patted the cushions right
next to her. "Come on, silly man."

Feeling foolish indeed, I did as she asked. She dipped a finger in her wine, and, almost abstractedly, she painted my lips
and then the other features on my face. "Cagey," she said, "I
love you. Shh!" she said, and the wine-finger was pressed
across my mouth. "I really do. And that means...oh, that
means I don't want anything from you that you don't already
give me. I am not a well of unfulfilled longing, for instance,
that you have to pour yourself into, or a frustrated spinster that
you have to marry. And I am certainly not a judge of your
feelings." She inserted the finger between my lips and tapped
at my teeth. "Guilt is something I only deal with at the office."

I bit lightly on her finger and she stuck it back into her wine.
"I wanted to tell you," I said. She smelled lightly of perfume
and more strongly of desire.

"I know."

"It will pass," I said.

"You're worried about her, aren't you?"

"She's in jail."

"Ah yes," Glenda whispered. And she placed a hand on my
plastic arm. "Cagey?"

"Yes?"

"I misspoke, a moment ago." She had a glint in her eye.

"Misspoke?"

"When I said I didn't want anything from you...that I didn't already have."

"Oh," I said.

"Yes."

"Time to fill a well of longing?"

"Well, at least to help," she said.

I got up to put Chopin back on and to be led to the bedroom.

I WOKE in a sweat about six in the morning to find that the relative humidity has risen during the night by a hundred notches or so. Glenda was sprawled like a felled runner as far away on the other side of the bed as it was possible to get, breathing in short puffs as though exhausted. Carefully, I levered myself up on my arm and peered out of the window: everything outside was uniformly light gray, the way it would have been if we'd all been dropped into a bucket of tepid dishwater. Off in the distance I could hear a faint rumble that was either thunder or a jet.

There was the nagging sense of having forgotten something, something that I would need in the day to come. I looked back at Glenda, who was still racing with something inside herself. I considered having a shower to wash off the stickiness, but I couldn't muster the energy to get out of bed. Besides, I thought, the sound of the water would wake Glenda, and she needed her sleep.

My arm was getting tired supporting me in this limbo position I had taken, so I flopped back down and wrestled with the pillow in search of the faint coolness of its underside. When I woke again at seven, I got out of bed to crank the air-conditioning all the way up, and then I drowned myself in a lukewarm shower.

Glenda was sleepily awake when I came back into the bedroom to dress. "Time is it?" she asked.

"Seven-thirty. Almost."

"Making a dawn getaway?"

"Going to jail."

She struggled to a sitting position. "Oh, Cagey!" she said. "You didn't tell me." She swung her legs off the bed and rubbed her eyes. She turned them on me.

"It's not till eleven," I said.

"You have to see Camelia Noone?"

"That's right."

"Are you going to be okay?"

"I'll have to be, won't I?"

"Cagey, Cagey." She stared at me some more. "Can I make you some breakfast?"

I looked at her and smiled. "I doubt it," I said.

She stuck out her tongue at me. "I doubt it, too," she said. "But the machine makes coffee. I'll go talk to it." Barefoot and naked, she padded off to the bathroom and then to the kitchen to manufacture some of the liquid black stuff.

I had not been to a jail since they had taken me to one against my will nearly seven years ago. It had been a nightmare, the hooks of which still caught at me and tore at my fear and rage. Oddly, the brutalizing I had suffered at the end of my incarceration wasn't much worse in my recollection than the numbing four months that preceded it, a hundred and twenty lost days of waiting for visits from my lawyer, waiting for court appearances, waiting for anything that would relieve the despair. Waiting for vindication. Waiting for revenge.

I killed a few people when I got out. In the rehab unit they let us set up dummies and savage them. I was top of the class in that. A little slower in the rest of what they wanted me to learn. Really slow about driving a car again; I still can't do it right for some reason, and I've almost given up trying. And slowest of all about being able to visit the scene of my disaster. The psych folks tried to get me to pay a call to prison, but I would not. Could not. Never have.

Until this morning.

Maybe.

Glenda came in with two steaming mugs. "It worked," she said, beaming. She put mine on the dresser and sipped from hers. "Nice tie," she said.

"You bought it for me."

"I know," she said.

"I'm . . . scared," I said.

"Would it help if I came with you?" She peered at me over the rim of her mug.

"I thought about that," I told her. "I think I've got to do it by myself."

"At least it's the Women's Detention Center."

"I've thought about that, too."

"The walls are concrete block inside. Painted creepy gay colors. Late-fifties upbeat. Pinks, blues, yellows."

"I see."

"The conference rooms are actually okay. Let me think." She closed her eyes. "Pine table, pine chairs. Light pine. Linoleum squares on the floor. Glass blocks instead of bars." She opened them to look at me searchingly.

"Uh-huh."

"Only bars"—she sipped again—"only bars are when you come in. Window in the front door has chicken wire in it. But there're two little guard rooms on either side and the windows there have bars on them."

"It smells, doesn't it?"

"Yes, Cagey, it does."

"Of... of..." I could feel my gorge rising.

"Mostly disinfectant," Glenda said quickly. "Drink your coffee."

"Mmm."

I ran for the bathroom and vomited.

I WAS DUE TO MEET Vanstone outside the Detention Center at ten to eleven, and I was there at twenty past ten. I could feel the brandy that Glenda had urged on me as it slopped around in my guts like battery acid. Although it did no good whatever, I told myself to shape up. I even went so far as to think, Act like a man.

I walked past the entrance slowly, letting my eyes linger on the dark red brick, noting that it was the crummy kind with the scratches in the surface that they thought was stylish after the war, observing that the door opened to let people out as well as in, hearing the fervid rattle of the half dozen air conditioners that had their butts sticking out of the front wall. Heavy, hot clouds oppressed from above, withholding the rain that would surely bring release.

On the second pass I tried to notice other things, but I disappeared somewhere inside my head without being aware I had done it.

I dodged traffic to get to the Gourmet Fast Foods Cafe that was set up across the street next to the Colonel's KFC. The doughnut was stale but the coffee was okay. It was twenty-five till the hour. I ordered another coffee.

Vanstone was tapping his foot impatiently when I finally got back to the jail side of the street. He looked at his watch ostentatiously.

"I know," I said. "A minute to eleven."

"I wanted to have a strategy meeting," he said.

"How about this? We go in together. You talk to her first, and then I talk to her second."

He grumbled and started up the narrow path that led to the front door.

"Sure is hot," I said.

He grunted something. We were actually at the door. It was a steel thing that someone had painted red. Glenda had been right: there was chicken wire in the glass of the window.

"Think it'll rain?" I said. "Sometimes if it does, it only makes things worse. You feel cooler for a while and then it's steamier than before."

The door was open; Vanstone was in the space it made; he turned to me: "Are you all right?" he asked. His plump face was unnaturally white because he had used talcum after he had shaved.

"Yeah," I told him. "Fine."

But of course, I wasn't fine. My face must have gone as white as Vanstone's, because the guard who signed us in kept looking up at me. She seemed worried, as if I might faint. I felt small and very far away. The sounds around me were all tinny, distant sounds, and under the painfully tight muscles of my chest my heart began to accelerate like the TR-7 I used to drive like a maniac when I had a pair of arms.

I don't know what Vanstone and Camelia talked about. It surely wasn't important. I do remember her hollow eyes that kept turning on me even though he was speaking. She had a bruise on her cheek and spots on her face that were angry red from having been rubbed or squeezed. The skin on the back of her hands was already starting to dry and turn flaky. She kept pulling at the arms of her prison dress.

"Jantarro?" Vanstone hit me with his elbow.

"Yes," I said. "I want to talk to you, Camelia."

She turned a worried face in my direction. "Are you all right?" she asked.

"Not really," I told her. "I...I was in jail once myself and..." My mouth went dry. I swallowed. "I didn't like it."

"You can leave us, Harvey," she said to Vanstone.

"My dear, I don't think—"

"I'll be fine. Go and do your lawyer thing. I need to talk to Mr. Jantarro."

He made huffy noises that turned his reassurances into protests. I heard the door close behind me.

"I'm glad you came," she said. "And that you're working for me." Her hand reached for mine and stopped short, as it had to. My plastic fingers lay inert, inches from her flesh.

I tried to gather my thoughts. "I want you to level with me," I said. "First about the money."

"The money?"

"You spent a whole lot of money in the last three or four months. Why?"

She paused and looked away at the dimly lit glass blocks. "I'm sorry you don't believe me. That's going to make things...harder. But the truth is, I didn't spend more than I usually spend." She lifted the hand that was near me and let it fall again. "Maybe it seems like a lot. But it wasn't. Not really."

"How much?"

"I don't know how much," she snapped angrily. "I don't happen to have my books with me."

"A quarter of a million?"

She laughed harshly. "No," she said. "No, not a quarter of a million. Five, six thousand, maybe. Maybe ten."

"So then what was Alan doing?"

"Doing?"

"Coming to me, asking me to find out about your spending, following you."

She shrugged slowly, holding her shoulders hunched at the top, and then letting them subside with a sigh. "I told you. He was...disturbed. About something. Not about me."

"Were you . . . did you have a lover?"

"A lover?"

I could feel an anger of my own welling up, slopping over from the small container I had become. I punched my words at her. "Yes. You know. Sex. Something strange. Your cunt and somebody's cock. Fucking, it's called."

She stared at me, frozen. I glared back. And then she burst with laughter, and I managed to smile. "Oh my," she kept saying in between peals of laughter. "Oh my."

"I'm sorry," I said after she had calmed down.

"You sure do have a way with you, Jantarro. You are a real smoothy, that's for sure."

"It's the place," I said.

She nodded slowly, her eyes still fixed on me. "Yes," she said. And, "I have had lovers. Alan knew. He had affairs as well. We . . . were civilized about it. As disgusting as that sounds, it's true. I don't know . . . how that happened."

"So it wouldn't be sexual jealousy driving him, then."

"Not Alan, no. Not about me. No."

Her eyes penetrated mine, and I felt myself start to float. "You see," she said, "he didn't care . . . didn't love . . . not really. And I tried . . ." She wet her lips nervously. "I kept trying, I suppose—the lovers. But I never found anyone." Again her tongue moved across her lips. "I'm still trying," she said. "You . . ."

A guard banged on the window and held up three fingers. "Our time is almost up," I said, surprised.

She began to rush her words. "Will you come to see me again?" I hesitated. "Tomorrow? Please? Every day, if you can. If they'll let you. And if you can."

I put up a hand to stop her. "I don't know," I said. "I'll try. But now I need to know how come you were at the King Street office at the time Alan died."

"I . . ." she said. "I went to see him because he called me and asked me to. He was dead when I got there. I . . . took one look at him and ran. It was utterly foolish, but I was terrified."

"Why did you lie, then? Why didn't you tell the cops later?"

"Because I didn't kill him and I thought . . . I thought I could get away without . . ."

The guard rapped on the glass again and opened the door. "Time," she called.

"Come again," said Camelia urgently. Another guard came in and stood by her, holding her arms.

"Yes," I said.

TEN

I STOOD on the sidewalk forcing myself to take deep, slow breaths. My heart was still racing, and despite the oppressive heat my skin was still clammy. I held my hands out in front of me: my right hand trembled and the plastic one moved back and forth like a metronome because all my nerves were jumping on their own and turning the myoelectric switches on and off.

I looked for a cab. The heavy clouds overhead rumbled as they fell lower toward the earth. I raised an arm to signal a Yellow Cab that was cruising through the Colonel's parking lot across the way, and as though I had called it down with my gesture, a bolt of lightning flashed fluorescent green. The sudden thunderclap made me jump. An instant later the sky opened up and rain poured out.

Everything seemed to start into hectic movement: birds everywhere flew up; drivers put their lights on and worked their horns; wind drove papers up the road; hanging signs banged against their restraints; and people began to run. I had to position myself in front of the cab and wave my arms to get him to see me. By then I was drenched.

A curious elation overtook me. I had conquered my fear. I had been to jail and I had come back again. And what was more, Camelia Laki wanted to see me again. Never mind that I hadn't had time to ask her half of the questions that needed asking. Never mind that to see her again would mean going back into the prison. And never mind that water ran down my neck and legs as I sat in the cab.

At home I showered, changed, and made myself a hefty Scotch, all to the strains of Beethoven's *Emperor* played at blasting volume. I was crushing sardines onto toast for lunch when Glenda called.

"Well?" she said impatiently.

"Hi," I said.

"Cagey, don't play cool. How was it?"

"It was lousy," I said, "but I'm alive."

"You did it?"

"I did it."

"Oh, Cagey, I'm so glad."

"Tell you the truth, love, so am I." I heard myself call her "love" and I felt just a little perturbed.

"How about we actually make it to Giancarlo's tonight? My treat."

"You're on," I said.

"Pick me up," she said. "Six-thirty, seven."

"Will do."

And we hung up.

I ate lunch thoughtfully. There were a great many things that needed doing. Broderick hadn't got back to me about the movement in Camelia's bank accounts, and I needed to cross that *t* before I could feel comfortable. I should follow up with Ravi about the prescription for the strychnine tonic. I needed to find this Michael Dennis, if only to be able to go back to Guberian and tell him that he was wrong about Camelia. I wanted to have a talk with young Randy about the film that Laki had been working on, the supposedly failing *Bengal Lancer*. And sooner or later I had to brace Elaine Younger with the fact that I believed she'd been the last person to eat with—and maybe sleep with—Alan Laki and ask her why she had lied about it. I could have been wrong, but I thought the maitre d's silence on the subject of Laki's female companion had told me something.

As well, there was still the small matter of figuring out who had caused Alan Laki's death. If Camelia was to be sprung, that was essential.

I brushed the toast crumbs onto the floor, rinsed out the sardine tin and dropped it into the garbage, and put the plate into the sink.

The phone rang again. "Mr. Jantarro?"

"Speaking."

"This is Roger Tarmon, Mr. Broderick's secretary. Mr. Broderick would like to invite you to lunch."

"I'd be glad to accept. When did he have in mind?"

"He's free tomorrow, in fact."

"Tomorrow it is."

"At his club? The Laurier? At one?"

"That would be fine," I told him.

Things were breaking my way, I thought. All I needed to do was to hang around and the solutions to all my problems would invite me to lunch at their clubs. But when, five minutes later, the gods failed to bring me a call from Michael Dennis, I put down my postprandial Scotch and dialed Ravi's number. I got a high-pitched whine that probably meant he was busy undermining the entire phone system. I hung up quickly.

There were seventeen M. Dennises in the phone book as well as one forthright Michael Dennis. I wasn't about to call them all and ask if they knew Camelia Laki, so I decided to kill one bird with two stones.

I CAN'T HONESTLY SAY Elaine was glad to see me. "I come bearing gifts," I told her as I closed the glass door behind me to shut out the noise from the rest of the *Star*.

"Darling, I'm absolutely sure that you do. I can see them from here. But, as Helen said to Paris, 'I'm not sure this is the time for horsing around.'" She didn't get up. She lit a cigarette and didn't bother to put it in her holder.

"Three quick things, then. I see you're busy." I pulled a chair over and sat across the desk from her. "First, for you: Guberian gambles, all right. He gambles and loses, heavily and regularly."

"I see," she said. "This is from the horse's mouth, I suppose?"

"The owner's mouth, shall we say."

"That's all a little cryptic, dear, even for me. And hardly startling."

"Have you been to his house?" I asked.

"His house? Guberian's? Not that I can remember. Why do you ask?"

"You should go. He keeps lizards. Big ones." I stretched my arms wide in the fisherman's claim.

"Really?" she said.

"Iguanas the size of...horses. Make a great feature. 'A man and his reptiles.' Readers would love it. Giant glass enclosures in his living room. Feeds them rats. He'd probably let you watch—take a photographer.''

Elaine was intrigued despite herself. ''Lizards.'' She shivered. And she looked up at me.

''Michael Dennis,'' I said. ''Reputed to be a lover of Camelia Laki and vice versa.'' I saw her relax. She let her chest sag, and smoke came out of her mouth. ''Any idea who he is?'' I asked.

''A small-time actor,'' she said promptly. ''Was with the company at Théâtre Intime. Could still be. Does some commercials. And has his tongue out for film parts and female parts. Though I heard he was bisexual.''

''You have an address?''

''Fuck, Jantarro, I don't go that low. Besides, do some of your own work.''

''Right,'' I said. ''Thanks. And, say, why didn't you tell me it was you that Laki had breakfast with last Wednesday?''

''I—'' She shut her mouth, took out another cigarette, realized she had one burning already, and sighed through clenched teeth.

''Hmm?''

''Look, Jantarro, it was one of those dumb coincidences. I had brunch with him, then he gets killed, and the next thing I know you walk in and start to pump me about him. I mean, what would you have thought if I'd told you I was the last person to see him alive?''

''Last person to see him alive was probably the killer.''

''Okay, okay, don't fuck around. You know exactly what I mean.''

''A coincidence, then.''

''That's all it was.''

''What did you talk about?''

''I don't think I want to say anything more about it.''

''Did you two guys get it on?''

''Mind your own business.''

''You are going to have to go to the cops, Elaine.'' I spoke gently, calmly.

''Says who? You?''

''I'm not going to turn you in. I'm not threatening you. It's just that they'll find out.''

"Not now that they've got their killer."

"The 'really sweet' Camelia, if I remember what you said right."

"Shit."

"Think about it."

"What else do you think I've been doing?"

"So, what did you talk about?"

She saw her hands were shaking and she put them out of sight on her lap. She looked older by ten years. "He was upset about some movie," she muttered.

"Some movie?"

Her phone rang. She picked it up and put her hand over the mouthpiece. "That's all I'm saying," she hissed. "Get out, Jantarro. Go on, before I call security."

"Hey," I said. "Elaine, if you're in trouble, I can help."

"Get out," she said. "Hello?" she asked the phone.

"THÉÂTRE INTIME, bonjour."

"Uh, I'm trying to get in touch with Michael Dennis."

"Oh. He's not here." The voice lost all trace of its French accent.

"Do you know where I can reach him?"

"Have you tried his apartment?"

"Can I have the number?"

And with that it was a relatively simple matter to go back to the phone book and discover that Michael Dennis lived on Palmerston, just north of College.

It was one of those big houses that had once belonged to a single family but now were divided up into four or five apartments. The whole street was like that, a pleasant boulevard with old-fashioned streetlamps and a transient population of would-be yuppies.

His was apartment 3, and I pushed the buzzer and waited. I heard a door open above me and feet descending the stairs. A man of thirty, wearing a maroon velour sweatshirt and brown wide-wale cords with lots of pleats at the waist, opened the door to the vestibule. He had a round face, and open expression, a pug nose, and gray eyes that cowered under very long lashes. "Yes?" he said in a pleasant voice.

"Are you Michael Dennis?"

"Yes."

"I've come from Camelia Laki," I said.

"Oh, my God."

"I'd like to talk to you."

A tic started up over his left eye. He dropped his voice to a husky whisper. "Are you...are you with the police?" he asked.

I let myself laugh a little. "No," I said. "I'm definitely not with the police."

He looked behind himself and then over my shoulder. We were alone. Outside, the puddles were continuing their rise back up into the air in steamy vapors. The sun kept taking potshots at us from behind cloud cover. And cars went by in the street with wet whooshing sounds.

"You'd better come up," he said.

Mahler was playing, a loud, lush stream of music. "The Fifth?" I guessed.

Dennis was pleased. "Yes," he said, "don't you love it?"

"Piano music is my weakness," I told him.

"Yes," he said. And he turned the Mahler off. "I haven't got any piano—"

"It's all right," I said. "I came to ask you a few questions."

"Yes?" He had painted nearly everything in the apartment white, including the light fixtures and the doorknobs. He had white books on his small white bookshelf. And the shag rug was white. Glass tables, one covered red bowl, and a red motorcycle helmet offered the only relief.

I showed him my identification and told him I was working for Camelia. He sat carefully on the edge of a white chair. "I understand that you and she were fairly close," I said.

"I don't know what gave you that impression," he said, trying to bluster. "I've met her, of course. She is most... generous in the way... She's kind to actors like... What do you want?"

"I guess I want to know when you stopped being lovers."

He stood up as if he'd been injected in the gluteus. "Now look here," he said, and, speechless, he pointed to the door.

"It's either me or the cops, Michael. And I'm working for the angels."

"You can't just...barge in here and...expect me to...I mean, this is *private*!" he wailed.

"Not entirely, Michael. Not entirely. And it'll be...utterly—that's the word—utterly public very soon if you don't open the closet door."

"Camelia. You said you were working for Camelia. I mean, how could you want to smear her reputation this way?"

"She's in jail, Michael. Have you ever been in jail? I think that right now she'd accept the tawdriest reputation in the world for the right to suffer under it in freedom."

"But what does our...her past have to do with anything?"

I stood and stared at him. He actually writhed under my gaze and twisted away from it. I reached out—with my prosthesis—and pulled him back. He looked down in horror at the thing on his shoulder.

"We...we were lovers," he said hurriedly.

"When?" I asked.

"On and off," he said.

"When?" I kept my prosthesis where it was, and he was too frightened to touch it.

"This year. The last couple of months. I don't know."

"Was it over?"

"I didn't want it to be. I mean, I loved her. She's so...so *wonderful*."

I let him go and he backed off two steps. "When did you last see her?"

He bit a nail as he regarded me nervously. "Let me think," he said. "A couple of weeks ago. Thursday. It was a Thursday, I'm sure, because I have to rehearse Thursday afternoons. I'm in *Repulse*, you know. And we rehearse Thursdays and Fridays in the afternoons because of the matinees on Saturday and Sunday."

"A week ago last Thursday. That was the last time you saw her?"

"That's right. She said we had to stop. But she was always saying that." His face became twisted. "I know she was seeing other men. I know I wasn't the only one. I didn't mind. Honestly, I didn't."

"Her husband, for one," I said.

"What?"

"She was still going to bed with her husband."

He frowned. "Well, so what if she was? I mean, they were married, after all." He laughed harshly. "You know, you hear all about the man who goes out and fucks his secretary and tells her that the little woman doesn't understand him. Well, I'll tell you, it happens the other way round, too."

"Are you saying that she used to complain about her husband to you?"

"Well, for Christ's sake, why do you suppose she was having an affair?"

"But she talked to you?"

"Some." He was backtracking now. He had stopped shaking and he was recovering his composure. "He was pretty beastly, if what she says is anything to go by."

"Like what?"

"Mental cruelty. He would make her so... so anxious that she'd show up here positively shaking. I'd have to hold her for an hour before she'd stop."

"What specifically?"

"She wouldn't say."

"One more question," I said. "No, two."

Dennis picked up the red bowl and lifted the lid. He looked inside and put the lid back on. His hand still trembled a little, so he pressed the lid tightly shut.

"Where were you last Wednesday?" I asked. "Five days ago. From about ten to four."

"I don't know," he said. "I can't remember. I was here. I work at nights. Actors do, you know. I must have slept until noon. And then I just hung around going over my lines or something."

"Alone?"

"Yes, alone."

"And the second question: did you kill Alan Laki?"

His jaw dropped, revealing gold crowns at the back of his mouth. Then he snapped it shut with a click. I watched the blood rise into his face. His hands started really shaking. He looked at the bowl he was holding, put it down on the glass table with a clatter, and took a step toward me. He had balled up his fists. "You'd better go," he said.

I took a step backward and he came on. "Did you?" I asked again.

"Get out of my house, you sleazebag," he said. And he raised his fists, which were now as white as the points on his cheekbones.

"I'm going, Michael," I said. "But I'll probably want to check back with you on one or two things. And, oh, is there anything you want me to tell Camelia when I see her?"

He blinked and then he took a swing at me, a lazy right hook that I easily stepped away from. I held him for a moment with a look, and then I turned and left, closing the door carefully behind me.

ELEVEN

THEY MADE TWO MISTAKES: they didn't wait until I was completely out in the open, and they got hold of me by my left arm.

The Co-op cab had pulled up the semicircular driveway in front of my apartment building. The cabbie had been grumbling about the weather all the way from Joe Allen's, where I'd had a couple of beers after talking to Dennis. There was a dirty blue Ford that sat squarely in the middle of the drive and right in front of the doorway. "Some people," the cabbie said, annoyed, "don't know their ass from other people's elbows. They just don't give a shit. Know what I mean?"

I was trying to work out the mechanics of this, half in and half out of the cab, fishing in my pocket for the money to pay him.

"Hey!" he said suddenly.

I looked up and through the windshield. Three men had left the Ford and were headed our way. One was a stocky type with greasy brown hair worn in a ponytail, and another was simply big all over and grinning through a jagged mouth in which every other tooth seemed to be missing. These beauties carried wooden clubs as thick around as their wrists and maybe a couple of feet long. I couldn't see the third one clearly or what delights he carried, because he was tight behind the other two.

I flicked a glance over my shoulder. It was clear, and I should have run. But I hesitated. One of them was there already, and he grabbed my left arm by the wrist to haul me out. Another swung. I ducked and he hit the top of the open door.

"Go!" I shouted to the cabbie.

He was paralyzed, his mouth open.

My left arm was now stretched taut. I was braced in the doorway of the cab with my legs against the front seat and my right arm scrabbling at the upholstery. One of them brought his stick down, better aimed this time, and with the strangest cracking sound my prosthesis came away in their hands, broken through at the elbow.

The two attackers lurched back, tripping over the curb and falling into the flower bed beside the driveway. The third man turned to see what had happened to his cronies, and I slammed the cab door shut with me inside. "Go!" I shouted again. "Drive!"

"I can't," the cabbie wailed. He pointed at the Ford blocking the way.

"Up and over the curb."

He looked where I pointed. He looked at the thugs who were back on their feet yelling at each other. He looked at me.

"Do it," I told him in what I hoped was a nearly normal voice. He turned in his seat, put it in drive just as the first club hit the roof of the cab, and, jerking the wheel hard to the left, gave it gas.

We jounced over the curb with a violence that made us both hit the roof. Somehow they managed to get another swipe at us, because suddenly a large part of the windshield went opaque. I saw bushes whip by the side windows, and we claimed the street, narrowly avoiding the big maple that stood at one end of the driveway.

"Jesus Christ," said the cabbie. "What now?"

"Just drive," I said.

"I can't fucking see."

"Do it anyway. Lean over. You can see out of the other side."

Instead, he rolled down his window and stuck his head out. We were swerving all over the road. Cars were blaring their horns at us.

"Call it in," I said. "Get them to send the cops."

"What the fuck did you do?" he shouted back to me, still with his head out the window.

I leaned over and grabbed his mike. I pressed the button on the side. "This is an emergency," I said. "Can you hear me?"

"I copy," said the speaker. "Who is this?"

"We're on Kingman," I said, "about to turn onto Moore. Headed north. Call the cops."

We were picking up speed. The driver was getting into it, teeth bared and blinking into the wind like a dog enjoying the rush of air past the family car. I looked through the rear window. The blue Ford was gunning up Kingman behind us. We made the turn onto Moore too fast and fishtailed through the intersection.

We must have gone through a red a block later at Stowell, because all of a sudden we were hit by another car on the right rear and we sailed twice around in a circle before coming to rest against a light pole on the wrong side of the street. The hood and the trunk were sprung open, and steam was billowing out of the front.

There was a moment of perfect stillness.

Then the cabbie groaned. People began to gather. Someone wrenched open my door, and then someone else got the cabbie out. As I stood up, I saw the blue Ford roar by. The driver and the guy in the back were staring straight at me with worried expressions on their faces.

"Get away from the car," someone advised, "I smell gas." I was led down the street. I heard a woman say in a strangulated voice, "He's lost his arm. Oh, my God, he's lost his arm." And then with a soft whump and a great wave of heat, the cab exploded into flames.

A siren worked its way in our direction. And then another and another began to braid their sounds to the first.

"WHO WERE THEY?" I asked.

Bench peered down at me as I lay on the bed in the emergency ward cubicle. He grunted. "You all right?"

"Yes, I'm all right. I've just got the shakes, is all. Who were they?" There was a graze on the side of my head that stung like acid on the skin, and something on my right leg that hurt as well. I was feeling around to find out what it was.

"Shock," said Bench. "Gives you the shakes."

"Thank you, Doctor."

"We don't know—who they are. I was going to ask you." Bench ran a finger across the ends of the hairs of his little mustache.

I fought back a strange impulse to laugh. "Well, it proves one thing," I said.

"What's that?"

I had found the source of the pain on my leg. There was a gash perhaps three inches long. My hand came away bloody, but I would live. "It proves Camelia Laki isn't a killer."

Bench tried to widen his eyes theatrically. It didn't work. "Oh?" he said. "You figure this was connected?"

"Don't you?"

He shrugged and moved his head a little on his stiff neck. "Can't say. Probably. Maybe. Who knows? Lots of people must have a hate on for you." He saw the blood on my hand and looked around on the enamel trays for something. He found some industrial paper tissues and handed me a bunch. I wiped at the gore.

"Why are you here," I said, "if you don't think it's connected?"

"Attempted murder. That would do as an explanation. Besides, you're just around the corner from my place of business."

"Bullshit."

"Bullshit that they were trying to kill you?" He reached into his pocket and brought out a plastic bag. He dangled it over my face, and I saw that inside there was an open switchblade knife. "Found it next to what's left of your forearm. Your hand. Mind you, the clubs would have stove in your head pretty nicely, too."

"Seriously, Bench, it is connected. And that means it can't be Camelia."

"It's 'Camelia' now, is it?"

"I've got somebody out there worried."

Bench let his eyes travel up and down my sheet-shrouded form, and he chuckled. "Seriously, Jantarro," he mocked, "you've got the hell scared out of me." He put the knife back into his pocket and shook his head. "The connection between this and Laki's murder is remote, as the lawyers say. Only thing connects it is your ego, but that's big enough to connect anything that happens to anybody south of St. Clair. Besides, there's nothing says dear Camelia couldn't have arranged for you to be offed."

"I'm working for her, genius."

"Or that's what she wants you to think. She arranges it so that you're not working too hard against her, and then she decides 'Fuck it' and sets you up. Maybe you stumbled over something she doesn't want touched. Who knows.''

"You guys get a theory and that's it. The brains shut down. Brains? What am I saying? It must be shock. Your jaws shut on somebody and you're programmed not to look any further. Just clamp down and growl.''

"Unlike you, hey, Jantarro? You don't hang on to the notion that your fair lady is innocent. Not at all, hey?''

A woman in white swept through the curtains and glared at Bench and then at me. She had a stethoscope looped around her neck and a little black plastic sign pinned to her chest that said M. ANDREWS. She looked to be sixteen years old. "No visitors allowed in Emergency," she said to Bench.

"Police," said Bench.

"Nevertheless," she said, "I have to treat this man now, and I'd like you to leave. Please."

Bench grinned at me. "We've got your hand and what's left of your arm down at the station. I want to see the rest of you as soon as Florence Nightingale is through with you. We've got some mug shots to look at. And your itinerary for the last little while to discuss." He gave the doctor a small nod. "Miss," he said. And he left.

She pulled the sheet off me, saw my stump, and said, "Oh." She touched it, to make sure she had it correct. Then she looked at me, perplexed. "What's wrong with you?"

"Not a damn thing." I was still scowling at the space where Bench had been. "Not much," I said. I tried to smile at her. "Shock," for one thing.

PAULIE MAC whistled. Well, he made a sound through those bow lips of his that probably would have been a wheeze if they hadn't been pursed. I had gone home, showered, and changed. I didn't think I looked that bad. "You, uh, you ran into some trouble, seems to me." He waited until I had found a chair. "Have some candy," he said.

"No, thanks," I told him.

"Go on," he insisted. "Help boost the blood sugar."

I sighed, got up, and reached for a Belgian chocolate. He smiled and smacked his lips with vicarious pleasure. "So, what happened?"

"Three goons with homemade baseball bats. Oh, and a knife."

He took a chocolate for himself, put it in his mouth, and wiped his fingers on a large handkerchief that lived in his breast pocket. "How come you're here? You think maybe I had something to do with it?" He spoke without looking at me; he was gazing at the little geode I had given him.

"Paulie, why would it be you? No, I wanted to know if you'd heard anything." Part of the win-place-and-show biz he was in involved wishing certain people broken legs; he would have a line on all the useful talent around town.

He shook his head, which is to say he moved his chin a little to the left and then a little to the right. "What did they look like?"

"Bikers," I said. "Only they were driving a beat-up blue Ford. Stolen, probably. One guy about five nine weighing in at maybe two hundred, brown hair in a ponytail, looked like he'd had his nose broken a few times. Another guy, same weight but six one, six two, shaved head and a dentist I wouldn't recommend. Third guy I didn't see too well. Levi jacket over a bare chest, and a tattoo around his neck. A chain, I think. I figure him for the knife."

"Sounds like bikers," he agreed. He was toying with a tiny Rubik's cube. A slim man in a sharkskin suit came in from a side door. "Jerry," he said, "see what Dog's been up to. Who's he hanging out with."

"Yes, sir," said the sharkskin suit, and he left.

"A button under your desk, right?" I asked.

He smiled, and for a moment he looked exactly like an over-fed six-year-old cherub. Then he bent to the serious work of playing with his toys. "Jantarro," he said almost tentatively, "I run a business."

"I understand," I said. "I'm willing to pay."

He waved a fat white hand and made a noise. "Your money doesn't interest me," he said.

The problem was that I was running out of things to trade. He wouldn't be too excited by the fact that Guberian kept lizards. He probably knew that anyway, because Guberian probably bet heavily on the Mexican iguana races or something.

"Our mutual friend," he said. He'd got the Rubik's cube all white on one side. I used to get that far myself. "Our mutual friend might be in some financial trouble, I would guess. What with Laki dead, and Laki being the real movie man and it being a movie company and all."

"It could be," I said. "Although, doesn't Guberian Enterprises do stuff other than movies?"

"Hard to say," he said. "On paper they do all sorts of things."

"Oh," I said, understanding. "I was going to need to find out anyway."

"That's nice," he said. He now had one side of the cube red as well. I hadn't thought it was possible to get only two sides the same color. "I'll be in touch," he said.

"Me too," I told him.

"That's nice," he said again. Now everything on the cube was motley once more. He sighed and put it down.

"OH GOD," I said as soon as I got back to my place and opened the door.

"And a pretty wrathful one at that," said Glenda. It was getting on for eight. I had forgotten our date.

"I'm sorry," I said lamely. "I ran into some difficulty."

"Lord, Cagey, you did." Now she was all concern, and it only made me feel worse. I could have called.

"How long have you been here?"

"Two martinis."

"You mixed them yourself?"

"Are you all right?"

"You mean all these years I've been doing it for you, and you could have done it by yourself?"

"Cagey! Tell me what happened." She was fingering the gauze they had applied to my head at the hospital.

"Make me one, and I'll tell you."

"You don't drink martinis."

"Tonight I do."

"What about Giancarlo's?"

"Are you hungry?"

"Well," she said, "underneath this alcoholic glaze I think I'm starving."

"I'll call him. Maybe he can still fit us in."

Her eyes were on my empty left sleeve. Sometimes when my plastic arm has to go in for a tune-up I wear the old wooden one with the hook at the end. And sometimes, like now, I just tuck the sleeve of the jacket into my pocket. "Are you really all right?"

"I really am," I assured her. "So let me call, we'll go eat, and Giancarlo can make me a martini."

Which is what happened, and all that happened—only because I fell asleep in the cab on the way home and Glenda insisted on tucking me in alone for a good night's rest. I tried to protest, telling her I really needed comforting and cosseting.

"Nonsense," she said.

"You're so tough," I mumbled, and then I dropped off the edge of consciousness.

TWELVE

THERE'S A DANCE they do—in the Philippines, I think—which involves hopping up and down while two crouching people clap bamboo poles together down around your ankles. I was hopping, and Glenda was clapping—at both ends of the poles, somehow. And then it was a pair of Camelias who were holding the sticks, grinning as they went faster and faster after my feet. My toes turned into piano keys, and as I banged at the ground, I played chopsticks more and more frantically until the black key-toes fell off. I stumbled, the sticks connected, and my left foot came away.

I am so used to losing limbs in dreams that even asleep I know what's happening and—usually—how to deal with it. It's a case of ignoring the illusion, of relying on the stump, until either the dream is over or the limb returns. So I kept hopping on the short leg.

And woke in pain.

I had scraped off the dressing on the gash on my leg and I was bleeding all over the sheets. By the faint light of dawn I hopped, dripping, into the bathroom to make repairs.

I WAS AWAKE and moody. So I did what I usually do when the day starts too early with the tendrils of night matters still curled around my consciousness. I set the coffee machine to spitting on the grounds; I retrieved the morning paper from its place on the mat outside the door; and I started on Bach's *Well-Tempered Clavier*, those twenty-four pairs of preludes and fugues—meditations, it seems to me—that run the gamut of tones and feeling from C to B minor.

I have an old Soviet Melodiya set of recordings with Sviatoslav Richter on the piano that requires a second or so over two hours and two minutes of playing time to lift me gently through the steps from moodiness to my own more usual C major approach to life. In the smallest of steps Bach takes the aspirant in you all the way to the half tone below C and then gives you a push and says, "Go on, take the next half step on your own."

But as with all real journeys, it seems to me, you only get where you want to go if the trip itself is engrossing. And together, Richter and Bach grant me glimpses from window after window in a winding tower that together reveal a meaning—satisfying, complete, inexpressible in language—I can only find at their hands. They reconnect me to life.

So I listened, and along about the sprightly PreludBin D major I remembered the coffee and poured myself a cup. I read in the paper about a man who had been killed in a brawl. It wasn't me, and I felt good about that. I thought of Camelia and was cool enough to recognize that, if it made sense to her, she was perfectly capable of arranging somehow to have me beaten. To have me killed. She was wealthy, strong-willed—perhaps ruthless. What did I really know about her?

I knew that she was enchanting.

I turned the pages of the paper, drank my coffee, and felt the sore spots on my body throb. It might have been Guberian; he, too, was capable of it, I thought. And it might have been the boyfriend, Michael Dennis, who had come close himself to hitting me. It could even have been the restless and emotional Randy.

The helix of music turned and I turned with it. Another coffee. More rustling of newsprint. From major to minor and back again in measured paces. The bridge column went on about psychic bids. They sometimes work, it said. But they were unpredictable. I laughed. It must have been during the A major fugue. The timing would have been right.

"CAGEY, SIR, how very good of you to be calling."

"Ravi. How are you?" It was still early, but he wouldn't notice.

"Everything functions, Cagey, sir, so I must be well."

"About that business of the Laki doctors, the prescription. Have you had any luck yet?"

"Oh, I right away discovered what you are seeking. Almost instantly. If you were only to let me install a simple computer and a modem I could inform you with such ease at the very moment and even now you would be knowing."

"That's all right, Ravi. Perhaps another time."

He laughed. "I would make you diagrams," he said. "Which switches to throw and in what order."

"I wouldn't understand," I told him. "What did you learn?"

"I am calling it up." I pictured his brown classical features intent on a magic spell, a magician's top hat on his head, perhaps, as he called things up from the ether. "Ah, here I have it. Alan Laki's general physician is one Robert Baxter of 667 University Avenue; he has also a urologist, Thomas Nattress by name, practicing at Mount Sinai Hospital. Once he contacted a psychiatrist. This is Vanadia Prescott of 1112 St. Clair West."

I was scribbling all this down. "And for Camelia Laki?"

"Michael B. Hofernes." He spelled the name. "This one is her general physician and can be found at 2376 Yonge Street. And a gynecologist, to be sure. Anne Regully of 98 Castle Frank. But for her, only those two."

"And for Randy Noone?"

"For him only one and that one is a psychiatrist. A Marion Friedman of 56 Heath Street West."

"Thank you, Ravi. I'll put a check in the mail."

"But, Cagey, sir, you are forgetting."

"Forgetting what?"

"The prescription."

"You managed to find a prescription for that strychnine tonic?"

"Three of them in the last year for the city. Will that be satisfactory? I must say that it is conceivable that there are others I was unable to find." He sounded annoyed, but I was elated.

"More than satisfactory. Dare I ask how you found them?"

"Perhaps you ought not to be daring."

"Tell me what you found, then."

"The oldest, prescribed on February thirteen and filled the same date, is for a patient who is called Jean Gavriel and who lives at 4763 York Mills Road. The next is for a person identified only as U. N. Denman of 973 Victor Avenue. This was prescribed on May twenty-four and was being filled two days later. The last was prescribed on June nineteen and filled that very same day. The patient was Michael Dennis of 112 Palmerston Avenue."

It was as easy as that, I thought.

When you knew someone who knew how to break into private systems and steal confidential information unhampered by the requirement of having a search warrant obtained on reasonable and probable cause—*then* it was as easy as that.

"Would you like the names of the physicians who were prescribing these medicines?"

"I would, Ravi, thank you very much. I would indeed," I said.

IT WAS as easy as that, I thought.

But I made myself wait. And think. Confrontation was what came first to mind. I would go to Dennis, lay this on him, and watch as he crumpled into a heap of confessional remorse.

Then it occurred to me that it might not be quite so simple. And if it weren't, I could blow it badly and offer him a chance to escape. Or kill me, if it came to that. I needed more information, a way to bracket his guilty body so that no matter how he squirmed he would be unable to evade me. Maybe I could try and talk to his doctor.

Camelia's freedom was riding on my choices, and I couldn't afford the luxury of going with my first impulse.

I actually considered the conventionally wise course of sharing what I had found with the cops and with her lawyer. But I decided that, too, required more thought. And so I paced and I thought.

"YOU LOOK like hell, if you'll excuse my saying so." William Broderick, the financial expert, was laboriously counting out sixty-three cents, alternately looking up at me and down at the coins in his hand.

"I could make change," the waiter offered.

"That's all right, George. I have it here." He was in the process of paying the last of the tax on a cigar that had already cost him twenty-five dollars. He had had no difficulty at all with the bills.

"Thank you, sir," said George.

"You wait all through lunch to tell me that?" We were at the Laurier Club, an Edwardian barn of high ceilings, shiny dark wood, and hushed conversations.

"I didn't want to spoil my appetite by asking you what happened and getting an answer," he said. He had the correct change at last, and he tipped it into the waiter's palm. "There," he said, with what I thought was an inordinate sense of satisfaction.

"Well, how about we swap? You tell me about Camelia Noone Laki's money and I'll tell you about J. K. G. Jantarro's brush with the forces of evil."

"I must say it doesn't seem to have affected your mood." He was deploying a gold-plated tool that made a special cut in the end of the cigar. He held a flame under the other end, sucked it up into the tobacco, working his cheeks like a hungry baby, and then with great pleasure sighed out a bad-smelling cloud. "Plutocrat" was the word that came into my mind.

"I've cracked the case," I told him.

His eyes twinkled. "Good for you," he said. He waved his cigar. "The cops seem to have got there just a bit ahead of you, though."

"Don't believe everything you read in the newspapers."

"Ah," he said, leaning forward. "I must confess," he said, "I've been speculating on how it might have happened. Suicide. Murder. And by whom. It did seem possible that he had taken objection to her trips to the well, and that she had...iced him, I think you people say." He grinned at me. His well-manicured tones were pulling my leg.

"Trips to the well?" I asked.

He nodded, dumb for the moment because of the way he was savoring the Havana. Then his perfect white teeth came free again. "Six in all," he said. "Three rather blatant ones—and I gather it was these that you first learned about. One for...let me see..." He put his head back and blew smoke toward the high ornate ceiling of the lounge. "Eighty-six or so. Number two for one-oh-one, and the third for the rest. Of the two-seventy, that is."

The rest of the two-seventy, I thought. My mind was racing around one central point like an animal staked out: she had lied to me. I was dizzy and perhaps a little nauseated. That might have been from his cigar, but I couldn't be sure. "No," she had said to me. "Not a quarter of a million." And she had laughed at the very idea. What kind of fool did she take me for?

"You're certain of this?" I asked Broderick.

He frowned at me. "Are you sure you're all right?" I had questioned his command of financial data.

"How much more?"

"Beyond the two-seventy?"

I nodded.

"Well," he said, "it was pretty well hidden, according to my people—the cops are pawing at her books now, but I wouldn't bet on their finding it—not without help." He considered the ash, decided it was long enough, and with great care worked off half of it into the silver ashtray. "We estimate she drew on another two-fifty."

"Two hundred fifty thousand?"

"Only round figures, you understand. A bit complex. Flow-through from Lakipix to a company called Japonica and from there to . . ." He sucked on the cigar, blew smoke, waved at it. He went on in some detail.

I sat there and pretended to listen. Inside me a hot anger was fusing everything I thought I knew about this case into a slag of stupidity. My stupidity. My credulousness. Like a corrupt gem in this ugly setting, the hard fact of Camelia's betrayal glowed dull red in my guts; and I struggled to prevent Broderick from seeing the flush of shame I felt at having been used so easily. I scarcely heard a word the man was saying. All I could hear was the roar in my ears, and all I could feel was the powerful urge to confront her with her lie, to confront her, to see her face when I told her, to see her face. Surely, she would have some explanation, I thought; and I was stunned by the idiotic persistence of my wish to be near her and to believe her. I felt sick.

SWEAT WAS BEADING on my forehead and I wiped at it yet again. "Your arm," she said, noticing it for the first time. "Are you all right?"

"Forget the arm, forget me, just answer the question."

"Mr. Jantarro—" She laughed. "I can't keep calling you Mr. Jantarro. What's your name?"

It was hopeless. I didn't like jail and I never would. I couldn't concentrate, couldn't maintain a constant course of thought. I sighed. "John," I said.

She laughed again. "Well, Johnny, you sure look pissed off. How come you're pissed off at me? What do you imagine gives you that right? I like you. More than that. There's something"—she wagged a thumb between us—"chemical going on. But, hey, that doesn't mean you can put the boots in anytime you want. I'm not bent that way."

"You lied to me," I said.

"Poor baby."

"Yeah."

She reached into her prison gray blouse and brought out a pack of Camels. She knocked one out of the pack and tamped it on her thumbnail with a few sharp raps. She saw me looking. "I'm getting into the part," she said with a smile. "The delicate young society matron turns butch in jail; her family is more horrified by this than by her crime; no one has suspected that she harbored these crude propensities." She even lit the thing with a big Zippo.

"I forget you used to act."

She plucked a stray bit of tobacco off the tip of her tongue. My chagrin amused her. "Let me tell you something about the movie business, my sweet ugly hero. About movie people. Never believe a single word they tell you. About anything. From the grip to the producer, they practice mendacity." She gave the word its Big Daddy southern twist. "*We* practice mendacity. It's all film-flam." Bitterness rose like a blush to her lovely face.

"So tell me some lies about the money," I said.

"They say that poison is a woman's murder weapon," she said, blowing smoke into my face. "Do you think that's right, Johnny my love?"

"Listen," I said. "No one's going to say 'It's a wrap,' Camelia. Not on this. This one's for real." I wanted her to stop this acting. I wanted her to come clean.

"Yes. So Harvey keeps trying to tell me. Should I fire the old fart? What do you think, Johnny? I think he's not up to murder. Don't you?"

"The money?"

"You won't abandon me, will you?" It was more of an observation than a question. "I didn't kill him, you know."

"The money."

She sighed and stubbed out the Camel. "Let's work with this script idea," she said. "We now work it so that I took the money, but for a good cause. It has nothing to do with Alan's death. No one believes this except the lone private eye. And why he persists in believing this, no one can understand."

"What was the good cause?"

She shook her head. "Go with this version. Can you do that?"

"Do I have a choice?"

She got to her feet. "No," she said. "Nobody else has choices. Why should you?" She tried to wink at me but got it wrong. We would have to do another take.

I HAD the answering machine working again and had managed to get the tape in the right way around. It only took me ten minutes of fumbling to make it play me back my messages.

Glenda was checking up on me: Was I all right? Did I want tucking in again tonight?

An underling of Bench's wanted me to call back as soon as possible: there were mug shots waiting for me to look at.

Harvey Vanstone's secretary wished to remind me that her boss would be expecting a call from me either later today or first thing Wednesday morning.

And Paulie Mac wheezed into the tape for a good thirty seconds before he managed to tell me that I was indeed looking for a biker named Dog, who had once ridden with the Motor Scum but who now was apparently employed in the theater trade as a stagehand and gofer.

I poured myself a Scotch and put away the albums of Bach I had left out this morning. As I let my eyes run along the titles of the records in my collection for something stronger than the morning brew, I told myself I really had cracked the case. Camelia was right: the money was irrelevant. It was Michael Dennis who had got Laki to swallow the strychnine, because it was Michael Dennis who had the tonic prescribed for him in the first place, and because it was Michael Dennis who had sicced Dog on me. They were both in the theater and they were both bikers—I remembered the red helmet in Dennis's white room. It was Michael Dennis because he wanted Camelia. He would do anything for her. Even kill for her. It was that easy.

So why was I uneasy?

I picked some Jelly Roll Morton and some Fats Waller from the rack. Then I got myself a refill from the Scotch bottle. And last of all I called Glenda. I waited until her message was through and after the beep I simply said, "Yes, please."

NO COST! NO OBLIGATION TO PURCHASE!

PLAY "LUCKY 7" AND GET AS MANY AS THREE FREE GIFTS . . .

HOW TO PLAY

1. With a coin, carefully scratch off the silver area at the right. This makes you eligible to receive as many as two free books, and a surprise mystery gift, depending on what is revealed beneath the scratch-off area.

2. You'll receive brand-new Mystery Library novels. When you return this card, we'll send you the books and gift you qualify for absolutely free!

3. And afterward, unless you tell us otherwise, we'll send you 2 additional novels every month to read and enjoy. If you decide to keep them, you'll pay only $3.50* for each book with the added convenience of Free home delivery! You must be completely satisfied, or you may return a shipment of books, at our cost, or cancel at any time simply by noting so on your shipping statement.

4. As well as The Mystery Library novels, we'll also send you additional free gifts from time to time.

*Terms and prices subject to change. Sales tax applicable in NY.

FREE SURPRISE MYSTERY GIFT
IT COULD BE YOURS FREE WHEN YOU PLAY "LUCKY 7".

THE MYSTERY LIBRARY "NO RISK" GUARANTEE

- You're not required to buy a single book—ever!
- Even as a subscriber, you must be completely satisfied, or you may return a shipment of books, at our cost, or cancel anytime.
- The free books and gift you receive from this "Lucky 7" offer remain yours to keep—in any case.

If offer card is missing, write to: The Mystery Library Reader Service, 3010 Walden Ave., P.O. Box 1867, Buffalo, N.Y. 14269-1867

THIRTEEN

THERE WERE four things I had to do in order to set up Dennis. And I needed to get help from Groper on three of them, so I phoned him at ten the next morning and arranged to meet at the Parkdale Tavern.

"Why there?" he said, with complaint in his voice.

"What's wrong with the Parkdale?"

"It's . . . it's dangerous, Cagey. There's bikers there."

"It's okay," I promised him, "I'll protect you."

"Sure," he said reluctantly, "right." There was some skepticism in his voice.

Groper and I go back to when we were thrown together—pretty much literally—in jail. He was in for passing bad checks, which is what they call it when you don't forge signatures well enough. He had recounted his entire life history to me at least twice then, and I had listened. For that I had earned his friendship. I, in turn, had explained how I had been framed, and he had listened to me. For that he had earned mine.

He's a little guy. Smaller even than Guberian. Which is why he's "Groper," because you have to grope around to find him. And because he's small, I think of him as a pilot fish in the world of crime, hovering at a careful but constant distance from the big boys, picking up whatever they disdain.

We sat in a booth, which is how he likes it, because he tucks his legs up underneath him when he sits, and people have been known to make fun of him for doing it. It's a practice easier to hide in booths. Ours was as dim as they come and located in the corner of the big, dirty drinking room at least fifteen feet from the nearest light. The tabletop was sticky with spilled beer.

"Geez," he said, his strongest oath.

"Not like home," I agreed.

Groper looked nervously over his shoulder. There was only one other couple there this early in the day, a very drunk, very large man with a skinny woman whose fixed gaze and pasty face suggested that she was one of the walking wounded from the Mental Health Center just up the road.

"Drop four," I told the waiter, and he took four glasses of draft from his tray and slammed them onto the table, slopping the top inch off each as he did so. I paid. "Keep the change," I said.

Groper regarded the beer as if it was the devil's work. He drinks rye and coke, and very little of that. "So," he said, "how's the boy?" It's his invariable opening.

"Working on this Laki thing," I said. He likes me to impress him. Hell, I like it, too. But this time his little brow knitted. "The movie director," I prompted. "Died last week?" It stayed knitted. "He was a rich guy," I said didactically, "who made a pisspot of money out of movies. Somebody got him to drink poison."

He shivered despite the fact that the air-conditioning in the Parkdale hasn't worked since 1972. He pushed the nearest beer glass away. "Poison," he said. "That's for women." Women frighten him more than any instrument of death. I decided then and there not to tell him about Camelia.

"Listen, Gropes," I said, "I need your help." He straightened up in his seat. I heard his oxfords scrape around on the bench. "First, take a look at this." I shoved across the table a copy of an old search warrant that I'd altered to suit my present needs.

"Geez," he said.

"Is it really bad?" I asked.

"It's awful," he said. "Look, here's where you used white-out. And the ink is different. This is thick and this is fine ball-point. Bet you used a felt pen."

"Yeah, but would Joe Citizen buy it?"

He held the warrant at arm's length and then closer. "Light in here is terrible," he said. He rubbed a finger over the surface. "Paper's wrong," he said. "You can even see where the fold marks are." He looked at me, pity suffusing his face: "How soon you need this?"

"It's only got to fool this guy."

"How soon?"

"Real soon," I said.

He sighed. "You got the original?" I gave him the search warrant that had once been used on me. He made to go.

"There's something else," I said. He stopped moving. "I need a message delivered and I need"—how to put it?—"some muscle."

"How soon?" he asked again.

"Let's talk timing," I said.

I walked with him to his car, a giant 1979 Grand Prix. We agreed to meet again at two, when he would have some friends along, one of whom could deliver my message. While the message was on its way, I would take the warrant to Dennis's doctor, and use it, if I had to, to get a statement out of him about the strychnine prescription. Then the fun would begin at the Parkdale Tavern, and Groper's other two friends could watch my back.

He stood beside his car, a mahout beside an elephant. "I can't be there," he said. He looked uncomfortable.

"Sure," I said. "You'll have done all the work by then."

"It's I got to see my aunt."

"Sure, Gropes. No sweat."

"She makes me see her every day almost."

"Lonely, I guess."

He looked up at me to see if I was taking all of this as seriously as I should have been. "It's not like I got any choice."

I reached down and clapped him gently on the shoulder. "Hey," I said, "a man's gotta do what a man's gotta do." I could hear him repeating that to himself as he clambered onto his beast and rumbled away to forge my document.

"Heck, I don't know." Dr. Resnick had a waiting room full of sniffling children and sniffling mothers, his supply of old *Time* and *Reader's Digest* magazines was in tatters, and his receptionist had the look of someone about to do something desperate.

I smiled at the doctor and stood stolidly in his office, letting him decide whether he wanted a fuss or wanted to help me.

"I'm kind of busy," he said. He was a middle-aged man of rumpled appearance who oozed ineffectualness. He had buttoned his white coat on the wrong buttons.

"This won't take a minute," I said.

"Didn't think they had one-armed cops." He pointed at the empty sleeve, tucked neatly into the pocket of my blue, downscale, coplike suit.

"I mostly gather information. Can't chase the bad guys." I smiled even more broadly, on the theory that strong sun will loosen up a man faster than the fluster of wind. Thus far I had managed to avoid actually saying I was a cop; I like to keep my illegality at this low level as much as possible.

"Yeah," he said. "Balance. If you have to run, I mean. But you could get a prosthesis," he said. "They make really good ones now."

"Got one," I told him, "but it's in for a tune-up."

"Oh." He looked down at his desk and then past me, into the chamber of rhinoviruses that was his waiting room. I thought for a minute he was going to ramble on about the common cold, but all he said was, "Close the door, will you?" I put the phony search warrant back into my jacket pocket and did what he wanted.

"Michael Dennis," I reminded him, still smiling.

He grunted. "Hate doing this. Giving away confidences." I nodded sympathetically. "What exactly do you want to know?"

"When did you prescribe it? How often have you prescribed it? Why? That sort of thing."

"It won't hurt anybody, you know. Perfectly harmless. Heck, you used to be able to get it over the counter, you know."

"So why did you prescribe it?"

"It's a tonic." He leafed through Dennis's file in a desultory fashion. "Michael used to be a sickly kid—young man, really. I thought this would pump a little more iron into him and make him feel better at the same time. The strychnine does that, you know. It makes the muscles feel good. More the placebo effect than anything else."

"How long's he been taking the stuff?"

"Oh…" Resnick leafed through the file. "On and off for ten years."

"That's a long time."

He gave me the look of a dog that's just been kicked. "Not really," he said defensively.

"You prescribed it last on..." I consulted my little black notebook, bought expressly for the purpose. "June nineteenth of this year."

"Yes, that's right," he said. "How did you know?"

I renewed the broad smile I'd started with. "When was the last time before that?"

Resnick sighed and consulted his notes once again. When he looked up, he seemed more confident. "September of last year. Been trying to wean him off it," he said, as if tasting how that line would sound if he got in trouble for supplying Dennis with too much of a good thing.

I tapped my pen on the notebook the way I'd seen Bench do it years ago when he didn't have note-taking minions. "You ever prescribe straight strychnine for him?"

Resnick looked genuinely shocked. "Are you crazy?" he said. "That's a deadly poison. Of course not. I wouldn't in a million—" He stopped and I watched as two and two made four inside his woolly head. "Oh," he said. "Is he...? I mean, has he...? But how?" He wiped his brow on his sleeve. "Oh my!"

"Just one more question, Doctor. You've been most helpful." The wattage in my smile was making my cheeks hum. "Do you happen to know where he had the prescription filled?"

"No," he said, and shook his head. He was still coming to grips with the possibility that one of his patients was either dead or a killer. "As you know, that isn't... I mean, it's up to the patient where he..."

"Sometimes," I said, "when I renew a prescription I ask the doctor to phone in the authorization. Could you take a look?"

He nodded slowly, and one more time fumbled with the papers in the file. "Yes," he said. "Here it is. You were right. It was Hashmall's Drugs. I have the number if you want it."

"Thanks," I told him. "That's all right." Everyone in the waiting room glared at me as I stood in the office doorway, preparing to take my leave. I smiled at them, but that only seemed to make more babies start crying.

"There isn't..." said Resnick, coming up behind me. "I mean, is there anything...?"

I shook my head, snapped the notebook shut, and shoved it into my side pocket. "No," I said, grinning with anticipation, "nothing. Nothing at all." I had time to make the visit to the drugstore before my appointment with Dennis.

"You," said Dennis.

"Not Dog," I agreed. "Just me."

"But the message said—"

"—that Dog wanted to meet you. I know."

We were standing at the back of the Parkdale next to the booth I'd been warming for the last couple of hours. Groper had supplied the three men, all construction roughnecks in jeans and white T-shirts. I'd sent the smallest of the three with the message to Dennis that Dog wanted to meet him in the Parkdale Tavern at four. The other two were now sitting across the way, drinking, flexing their muscles, and doing a half-assed job of pretending they weren't interested in us. But Dennis was too startled to notice.

"Take a pew," I said.

He looked down at the bench and then up at me again. "What's going on? Where's Dog?"

"Please," I said. I sat. "I'll answer all your questions."

Dennis looked around the place, as if he expected to find Dog at some other table. With a bewildered look on his face, he sat down. "What do you want?" he said. "How do you know Dog?"

"Oh, really, Michael. Dog and I were once very close to each other. You know that."

"I don't know what you're talking about." He grabbed a beer off the tray of a passing waiter and poured half of it down his throat. "Look," he said, "I don't know what this is, but I don't like it. I'm due at rehearsal soon. If you've got something to say, say it." He kept casting his eyes about the room, looking for Dog.

"Let me lay it out for you." I'd thought about how to proceed, and I'd decided on the quick and hard approach. "You killed Alan Laki. You did it with strychnine. You mixed powdered strychnine—which you stole from Hashmall's Drugs on July seventeenth—into your iron, quinine, and strychnine tonic, and then you shoved the shit down his throat." I had spoken to the drugstore owner, who had told me about the theft. "Only things didn't go exactly as you'd planned, because Camelia got arrested for the murder." As I heard myself say it, I realized that there was another way it could have been. "Unless, of course, you'd planned it so that she'd take the blame—an act of revenge for the fact she'd refused to leave her husband for you."

Dennis was goggling at me, openmouthed. I waded in with the second series of punches. "The next thing to go wrong was that I started nosing around. I found out about you and Camelia. And that was too much. So you hired your old biker buddies, under the leadership of that fine knife artist, Dog, to put me off—off the planet, if it came to that. Except that it didn't work. It's all gone wrong," I said confidently, "ever since you killed Laki."

Dennis tried speech and came out with a noise in his throat. He tried again. "You're crazy," he whispered hoarsely. He wasn't looking for Dog any longer. I had his complete attention.

I shook my head. "It's you who's crazy. Killing people is crazy. Maybe that's the line your lawyer will take. A few years up at Penetang with the criminally insane. Maybe you could even deal for it."

"You really are nuts. I didn't do any of that shit. What are you trying to do?" There was a quaver in his voice that would have done a better thespian proud.

"Oh, come on, Dennis. Grow up. It's all there in black and white. Item: Laki is killed with strychnine mixed with that IQ-and-S elixir you have prescribed for you. Item: more strychnine is needed, so it's stolen a month ago from the same drugstore that made up your tonic. Item: I'm investigating the case and just after I see you I get beaten up by a biker called Dog; you and Dog are buddies—that's why you're here, remember? Item: you and the dead man's wife are making it; you were jealous of her husband."

I refreshed myself with a swallow of ale. "It's all there," I said.

Dennis set imploring eyes on me. "You've got it wrong," he said. "It's all wrong. I didn't do any of that. Sure, sure, I used that tonic shit. But I never poisoned anybody with it. You can't.

I could drink the whole bottle and it wouldn't hurt me. Besides, somebody ripped it off. A month ago. They cleaned me out. You've got to believe me."

"I wouldn't believe you if you raised your right hand and swore on the *Boy Scout Handbook*." He was supposed to be crumpling by now. I pressed a little harder. "And the cops won't believe you either. Have you ever been in the slammer, Dennis? Hmm? I have. It's worse than your worst dreams. Even if you swing both ways, like you do. It's the worst thing you can imagine, Dennis. Only thing to do, the way I see it, is to dump it out, empty the whole thing right now. I take you down to the cops and you cooperate like a crazy man. And like I said, maybe you plead insanity. Even cut a deal for murder two."

He was shaking his head, flinging it violently from side to side, a child's gesture that sought to deny that the words were even being spoken. Then all of a sudden he erupted from the booth. He smashed a glass across the side of my head, and I slipped beneath the table in a private blaze of flashing lights and a cold baptism of beer.

He kicked me, connecting painfully with my ribs. I scuttled away into the dark, stinking corner beneath the booth. Shouts and sounds of broken glass erupted throughout the room. Surely, I thought, my construction workers would be there by now. Like a turtle, I stuck my head up a couple of inches past the tabletop, retreated, and came back up again, a few inches farther this time.

The place was in riot. It was a real bench clearer. Anyone who could wield a bottle was in the fray, flailing away at the nearest person. I thought I saw Dennis on the floor, arms over his head like a soldier after the grenade bounces in. But my vision was obscured by the legs of the brawling mob. I got to my feet and inched out of the booth. As soon as I had a chance, I'd pull him out of the scrum and drop him off at police headquarters.

One of my bodyguards made his way to my side. "You okay?" he shouted. I nodded, and the lights went on inside my skull again. "Let's go," he said, and he grabbed my arm and started pushing me toward the broken exit sign at the back.

"Dennis," I said. I pointed at the melee. "The guy I was talking to." I had to shout into the man's ear. "I want him out."

My muscle started back toward the fight, and then he stopped. I heard it, too. It was a thrumming noise, a rhythmic whirring like the sound a falling helicopter might make. We looked around in the dim light. And then I saw two toughs in leather swinging things in circles over their heads. One of them connected with a chair, and pieces of wood flew in all directions. I realized that it was bike chains they were using. There were grins on their faces that made me wish I had never set foot in this place.

People fell away from their gleeful onslaught. My bodyguard looked for his buddy, and then grabbed me again. He had a small, snub-nosed revolver in his hands. "Come on," he bellowed, and he cocked his head toward the back door.

"Dennis," I shouted over the din.

My man shook his head, and with a smooth motion he picked me off my feet in a fireman's carry and rushed at the door. My heels knocked it open, and suddenly we were in fresh air and sunlight brighter than my eyes could tolerate. Without much ceremony, he dumped me a couple of paces up the alley and ran back into the tavern.

I got to my feet unsteadily, still dizzy after the blow from Dennis's glass. I heard what sounded like a shot. And then another. People started bursting out of the back door like popcorn from a hot pan. Then my bodyguard came out at a run, followed by his friend, who was nursing an injured hand.

"Dennis," I said.

They grabbed me and hustled me up the alley to where their car was parked. I tried to resist. One of them tapped me, and I folded into the backseat, falling asleep before I landed.

FOURTEEN

"DEAD AS A MACKEREL." Bench glared at me, his pug face pushed aggressively into mine. "More like a flank steak, really. A couple of those chains caught him good and damn near cut him through in half a dozen places."

I felt as though my stomach was dropping lower than my feet, and my head floated dizzily away. What was left of me in the middle felt a sense of guilt as leaden and corrosive as any I'd known.

"You didn't know he was dead?" Bench backed off a few inches and examined me out of cold eyes.

No, I didn't know that Michael Dennis was dead.

"Bah," he said, not waiting for my answer, "I shouldn't bother asking you. Why should I trust anything you say?"

"I don't lie," I managed. I thought of Camelia. This could be very bad for her.

"Yeah. Great. And you don't tell the truth either." Bench went behind his desk and dropped into his chair. He undid the button on his jacket and then did it up again. "Jesus, Jantarro. If you'd told me about Dennis, if you'd told me about these bikers, he'd be alive today."

"I didn't kill him," I said. I sank into the other chair, numb and hurting at the same time.

"You mean I can't charge you with his murder? No, I can't. But, Jesus, I'd love to."

"I'm pursuing a legal investigation. I'm only able to report to my client."

"Big fucking deal. You're pursuing your ego, that's what you're doing. Jantarro's going to wrap this one up all by himself. He's going to be in on the kill. Well, you missed the kill by maybe a minute, and it's me who's got to do the wrapping—me and any relatives that Dennis might have had."

I was damned if I'd give Bench the satisfaction of seeing how bad I felt. "Look," I said, and I had to stop to swallow.

"Look, you had it all figured out. There was no way you would have followed up on Dennis even if I'd spilled my guts. You had the wife in the can, and so far as you were concerned, that was that."

"You were supposed to come in and look at some mug shots. I distinctly remember telling you to do that."

"So I identify a couple of the guys who tried to rough me up. Are you telling me you'd have gone after them?"

"Sure. Eventually."

"And meanwhile Camelia Laki sits in the slammer."

"Where she probably belongs."

"Probably?"

"Where she belongs, until a judge decides different."

I had my mouth open to continue the argument, but I stopped. It was too easy. Too easy to pick a fight with Bench and dump my anger onto him. Too easy, that way, to escape from looking at the role I'd played in Dennis's death.

"Okay," I said. I straightened up in the chair. "Let's talk about that. About Camelia." I wanted him to see the reason-ableness of my view.

"Nothing to talk about," said Bench.

"But there is."

I had thought there wouldn't be. I had thought that Dennis would crumple. And even when he didn't and I was rescued from the fracas—whether I wanted to be or not—I had thought that with what I had on him the cops would pick him up and Camelia would be sprung. I hadn't thought any further than that. But now that they'd picked him up in a body bag, it was time to use my head. Well past time.

"Like what?" said Bench, adjusting the fall of his tie so it lay exactly on the row of buttons on his shirt. He sneaked a cou-ple of fingers between his belt and the end of the tie, just to make sure he'd done it right when he'd put it on in the morn-ing.

"With what I've got on Dennis, you've got to give up on Camelia Laki." That seemed to be the nub of it. My reason-able position.

"What you *had* on him."

"No." I shook my head and it still hurt from the dead man's beer glass. "I still have it. You have it. It was his prescription that was used to kill Laki. The strychnine was stolen from his drugstore. Hashmall's. I spoke to the owner today. And Dennis was Camelia's lover, so he had a motive.''

"Circumstantial," said Bench.

Without warning—and despite my best efforts—I lost my temper. "For Christ's sake, Bench, all your evidence is circumstantial. You told me that yourself, remember? *You* don't have an eyewitness. *You* can't connect her to the stuff that was shoved down his throat. *You* don't even have a decent motive. Don't give me that circumstantial shit." I was starting to shake and I could feel that the skin on my face was tight.

Bench took my display in stride, even, I thought, nodding a fraction as though he'd finally pushed the right button and obtained the reaction he'd been seeking. He spoke calmly. "What I meant was, nothing you've got makes me think we were wrong. He didn't confess. He can't confess now. So I've got poison—poison that she had access to because of her lover, according to you. I've got her fingerprints—recent fingerprints, mind you—at the scene of the crime. And I've got an eyewitness that puts her there near the time when he was killed."

"Fingerprints, for God's sake. It was her husband's office. Of course there're going to be her prints all over the place."

Bench shook his head. "It's the timing that's critical. And I told you that."

I made myself breathe slowly and deeply. If I couldn't command my emotions, maybe I could get simpler things under control, like the in and out of the stuff that keeps you alive. "You've got to admit that there's reasonable doubt," I said. "Now you know it was Dennis's stuff that went into Laki, his pharmacy that got knocked over, you've got to say that there's a reasonable doubt. At least."

Bench let his chair come forward abruptly, flinging himself at his desk. He swept the area in front of him clean. "Look, Jantarro. I shouldn't need to tell you this. Maybe you're too...I don't know...too close to this. You're fucking up. I shouldn't have to tell you that reasonable doubt is for the courts. I don't give a fuck about reasonable doubt. I've got a damn good case against this lady, and I'm going with it. You want to give her lawyer all this shit about Dennis, you figure it'll be a big reasonable doubt number, that's up to you."

"And about Dog? That's just one big coincidence, too? Let the courts handle that? Because you're all right? I mean, he tries for me, and it turns out he just happens to be a buddy—maybe a butt buddy, but you'd have to work to figure that out—a buddy of Michael Dennis. And that doesn't move you an inch, because you're all right. You've got a sucker and that's it."

"Which is it, Jantarro? Dennis fucks sweet Camelia or he fucks the dirty Dog. You're all confused."

A kid in uniform stuck his head into the office and took it out again hastily when he heard Bench's tone. Bench waved at him impatiently, and he came all the way in. He handed Bench a computer printout. Bench started to read it, looked up at me halfway through, and then went back to reading it. When he was finished, he put it on the clear space in front of him and smoothed it out with both hands. "Yeah," he said.

"Yeah?"

"Michael Dennis reported a break-in at his apartment on July nineteenth this year. Two uniforms go round. The usual. Stereo, TV, some gold chains. And"—Bench stabbed a stiff finger down into the paper—"*and* they cleaned out the medicine cabinet. Got some tranks, maybe some ludes—who knows, right?—and they got—it says here they got—'a bottle of prescription tonic.'"

"So he says."

"Said."

"Easy to say. To set it up."

"Go home," he said. "Get out of here."

"It doesn't prove anything, Bench."

"Proof is for the courts, Jantarro. I told you. Go on, get out of here. I've got work to do."

And so, I thought as I found my feet, so had I.

"DO YOU WANT to talk about it yet, whatever it is?" asked Glenda.

"Not just yet," I said. We had just finished a dinner at the Brasserie les Artistes that might as well have been held instead at the Necropolis, the nearby cemetery. The Brasserie's a loud, loose place, but the noise had swirled around the two of us as ineffectually as wind-driven leaves around a pair of tombstones.

"You're not getting away," she said.

With the small part of me that was still noticing such things, I recognized that it was a perfect night. Not too hot, not too cold. And a gentle breeze imported scents exotic to the city. We were walking the first part of the way to my place.

She wasn't going to let me get away. "I'm not going anywhere," I said. That evening it didn't seem possible for me to move at all. I didn't even know how I was managing to walk.

Again and again I rehearsed in the small metal cylinder of my mind the arguments that made me responsible for the killing of Michael Dennis. And each time that the weak, fleshy part of me dared to raise a counterargument, I shut it off ruthlessly. I was going to imprison myself before I'd let Glenda get a chance to intervene.

"Is it us?" she asked. She had stopped in front of an antique store, and, largely unseeing, I stared at a big wooden weathercock that was spotlit in the window. The point of the vane would swing around and accuse me if we stood there long enough, I thought. "Because it doesn't feel like us," she added.

"How do we feel?" I asked.

"Oh," said Glenda, with a careful casualness, "we feel . . . real." She laughed quietly. "That sounds so trite, doesn't it? Expectant, then. Expectant and potential. Ongoing, parallel, continuing, emergent. Cagey, talk to me!" She grabbed my good arm and shook it.

"I can't," I said. "I feel dead."

"Oh, Cagey, how sad." She put a hand up to my neck and ran it into my hair. I put my arm around her.

We walked some more. Slowly. Cars went by, I suppose. And people passed us. The sidewalk and the brick walls beside us seemed exceptionally dirty to me, and I felt an urge to clean them—to have them cleaned—an urge that only grew in strength the more I understood how impossible the task would be. I retreated back into the simpler task of castigating myself. From time to time, I was actually aware of the supple movement of Glenda's hip under my hand.

"I was up in front of Walker today," said Glenda. We had turned up Sherbourne. It was the first time either of us had spoken since we'd walked away from the antique store. "The prick who used to practice insurance law and now thinks he knows everything about everything because he's a judge? You remember," she said, "I've told you about him before. Well, today he surpassed himself in assholism. He starts to get sarcastic in the middle of my cross of the main defense witness. Now, it's a pretty complicated case of stock manipulation, if I do say so myself; but Walker, he doesn't see what all the fuss is about. 'We can do without the indicating, Mizz Redway,' he says for starters. 'Indicating?' I ask. 'The flounces,' he says, 'the batting of the eyelashes.' And of course that's it. He doesn't like women in his court. In or out of it. Well, it goes from bad to worse, until he winds up tearing a strip off me and accusing me of fucking up the case right in front of my client. 'Gross misconduct' was the phrase he latched on to. Worked it to death." Glenda sighed.

"He's wrong, of course," she said, "but it took me a good hour of indicating after court to get the client to trust me and not Walker. And anyway, the client trusts me and so what? It means an appeal because of Walker and I don't know if he's going to go for an appeal. Wouldn't surprise me, if we lose he'll turn around and slap me with a writ for professional negligence.

"I'll go see him in chambers tomorrow—Walker, that is. See if we can work out a truce. Sure hope we can, because the bank is leaning on us. Ann tells me the manager wants to see us tomorrow afternoon about our line of credit. She thinks maybe he's considering reeling it in. Which is bizarre, because after all these years we're just starting to take off into the big time. The bottom line doesn't show it yet, and that's the problem. But some of the top lines are looking real good. But bank managers can't lift their eyes to the horizon, let alone to the top lines.

"And tomorrow I see my gynecologist. Routine. So I know what she's going to say. She's going to say that nature's clock is ticking ever more faintly and it's getting on for five to midnight. And do I still have this fantasy about giving birth to more of the human race, because if I do I'd better quit the dry humping and get more than my feet wet."

I found my voice. "Glenda," I said, "if you want to talk about getting—"

"Shut up," she said quietly but firmly. "I got a letter from my dad yesterday. His usual style: 'I'm fine, your mum's fine, hope you're fine.' But I've been getting letters from him for twenty years so I can make 'fine' judgments, and reading between the 'fines' I figured he was telling me that my mother's not doing any better. Sounds to me like she's going downhill pretty fast, in fact. I really want to go visit them, but I don't have the time, and even if I did, there's too much to be faced. If Mum does die—*when* she does die—Dad'll last about three months. On his own. Maybe anyway."

We had arrived at Bloor Street. Glenda waved at a cab that was stopped in front of the subway station. It did a U-turn and pulled up in front of us. I opened the back door, and Glenda moved in front of me. "I'm sorry," I said.

"Don't be," she replied. "I wasn't intending to make you feel sorry."

"No," I said. Glenda got into the cab and reached for the door handle.

"Good night," she said. And she closed the door between us.

"Oh." I looked at her through the open window. "I've been leaning too hard, haven't I?"

She shook her head. "Not really." She struggled for a moment to formulate a longer reply, and then she sighed. "Your fair maiden is still locked up in the tower, isn't she?" she asked. I nodded. "Well, you'd better kill the dragon and get her out." She leaned toward the cabbie and I stepped back. They drove off.

I may have stood on the sidewalk for half an hour. Or it may only have been a minute or two. I felt angry with her, but I wasn't. Not at all, really. I had done what I always seemed to do. I had wandered off on my own, wandered so far away from her and from all other real people that the only things I could see were the churnings that went on inside me.

Bench had said it, too: I was pursuing the edges of my rapidly inflating ego. And now that it had been cut down to size, I was beached in a very lonely, very dry place.

I waved at a cab of my own and gave the driver my address.

Kill the dragon, she had said.

Maybe this time I'd just arrest it, I thought.

FIFTEEN

THE EGGS FELT COOL and smooth in my hand, and the orange juice tasted like nectar. For some reason everything was special this morning—bright, fresh, and expressive of intimate concerns. I tried to crack the eggs into the pan with the one-handed move that chefs use but only managed to crush them as usual; and so I spent a couple of minutes picking bits of shell out of the forthcoming omelet. When it was done—a bit too crispy on the outside—I flipped it out of the pan onto a plate which I stuck in the oven to keep warm. I found a forgotten jar of guava jam at the back of the fridge and slathered it thickly on an ambitious stack of toast.

With a slice of this tropical confection in hand, I went to the window and chewed reflectively while the brewing coffee slipped its fragrance into the air. The big red maple below, the empty playground across the way, the concrete egg carton of an office building that dominates the skyline hereabouts—all were present with a visual smack that was partly the result of the low, early morning sunlight. But the chiaroscuro didn't explain everything. It was as if all my senses had been reborn overnight. I thought of Michael Dennis, who wouldn't be using his senses anymore, and I wondered about how exactly death and rebirth were related and about how guilty I should feel.

For a change, I put the breakfast together on the dining room table, even going to the trouble of getting and folding a paper napkin and letting it lie under my fork for the thirty seconds it took me to sit down. Mozart kept me company. I ate with relish.

I was back at the beginning, I decided. In this snakes-and-ladders world, I had lost my footing and needed to start up the rungs again. I thought of my first client, the first dead man. Alan Laki fretted in my mind's eye, framing with his long, artful fingers the scenes of his worry, the blind spots of his uncertainty, and perhaps—just perhaps—the prefigurations of his death. My wife is spending money, he had told me. Great amounts of money. Find out why.

And what had I accomplished for him? I had verified his suspicions. No. I had proved him more right than he suspected. Twice as right; for Camelia had gone through half a million in the months before he died, not the $250,000 he had feared.

But beyond that, what had I done? I had been so bedazzled by her that I had actually been satisfied with her explanation: she had used the money for good purposes; I had to trust her. That was a snake to slide down if I ever saw one.

So one thing I had to do was to find out why the money had been spent, why it had been pulled with a curious mixture of boldness and secrecy from the various accounts and companies that Laki and his wife had set up.

I filled my cup one last time and wandered back to the window. The sun was higher now, and the world below me presented itself in the full, flat, ordinary guise of reality. A teenaged boy chased a teenaged girl around the playground; they teeter-tottered for a while; then she pursued him to the jungle gym. I would send flowers to Glenda. It was a typical thing, a trite thing even, for an insensitive male to do on the morning after a misunderstanding; but it was what I wanted to do, and I thought that perhaps she would understand.

And then there was Elaine Younger and her guilty secret. She, too, had come close to bamboozling me into ignoring her role in all of this. I had to find out from her what it was that she and Laki talked about at his last brunch.

Maybe when I had the answer to these questions I'd be able to persuade Bench that Michael Dennis had been a murderer. And if it turned out that this made me feel better about having been involved in his death, well, that wouldn't be a bad thing either.

My cup was empty. I put it in the sink with the dish and the cutlery. I wiped the table, catching most of the crumbs and putting them into the sink, too. I slipped into my jacket, turned off Mozart, tucked my flat left sleeve into the left pocket, and smoothed the whole thing down. And then at the doorway I paused. I wouldn't say I was afraid. Not exactly. It was just that two men had been killed, and the image of Dog and his friends was hovering at the back of my mind.

I don't like guns. I almost never carry one. For one thing, you can hurt somebody with a gun. For another, that some-body is likely to be yourself. But they do make a bang, and sometimes loud noises are just what you want when the other guy won't listen to sweet reason.

Dog had carried a knife, I remembered.

With a sigh, I took off my jacket and fetched the little .38 Chiefs Special I kept for moments of insecurity like this one. It straps on under my left armpit, and when I'm not wearing my prosthesis, it feels as if I've got two stumps. Deformed. Which is a good way to feel if you must carry a weapon, I suppose.

My .38 and I strolled a couple of blocks in the sun, getting used to each other; then I caught a bus down to the waterfront and Elaine Younger's office.

SHE WASN'T IN. "Called in sick. Again," a harried-looking man with wild hair and jerky gestures told me. There was more than a suggestion of grievance in his tone. I asked him for her home address. He shot me a suspicious look, so I gave him my trust-worthy face, the one that Glenda says makes me look too ugly to be anything but stupid and, therefore, perfectly harmless. "Tcha!" he said. "Ask...ask..." He spun around, stabbing the air for a victim. "Ask *her*," he said, fixing on a young woman who looked up from her desk, surprised. He raced away through the obstacle course of desks and machines.

Elaine had a house on Withrow, a semidetached, two-story affair faced with pale slices of ugly phony stone set in a creamy gray mortar. Concrete steps led up to a porch of more con-crete, rimmed with a black wrought-iron fence. Old-fashioned venetian blinds on the inside of what used to be called a pic-ture window were shut tight against the sunlight. I banged on the beige steel door. A neighbor stuck her head around the partition separating Elaine's side of the porch from hers. "Hi," she said. She was wearing a pink tank top; her gold hair was up in curlers.

"Hi," I said. I knocked again.

"You want Elaine?" she asked.

"Yes," I said.

The woman inserted a long fingernail under one curler and scratched at her scalp as she considered me. I saw her observe my expensive suit and then the empty sleeve. She smiled at me. "You a friend?" she asked.

"A friend," I agreed.

The hand came down from the bird's nest on her head and lingered as it passed her breast, brushing it slightly. She widened her smile, revealing a wealth of regular white teeth. "Is she home?" I asked. She leaned farther across the railing and strained the tank top.

"She is and she isn't," she confided. "If you get my meaning."

"She has company?"

"You might say that," she said. "She's in bed with Johnnie Walker." She winked and her tongue explored a corner of her mouth.

"I didn't know," I said. I drink; you drink; she drinks: it's the basic grammar of urban life. I wasn't particularly surprised to find that Elaine was into hyperbole.

"Come in and I'll make you a coffee and you can phone her from my place. Maybe she'll hear the phone. She usually does."

"Thanks," I said, "but it's kind of important."

She looked at me and than she sighed. "Yeah," she said. "Well, look. She never locks the door." Her shoulders moved under the thin pink straps. "Some people don't have the sense they were born with. I mean, this is a big city and there's lots of... well, you know... weirdos out there."

"Thanks," I said.

"No sweat," she replied.

I MADE IT through the tiny front hall and into the dingy corridor that ran beside the main rooms before I sensed that there was something wrong. At first I thought it was simply the disorder or the stench. The place was a squalid mess, with clothing lying haphazardly about; soiled plates and cups covered every surface; and a heap of old papers and magazines loomed in the shadows.

If I believed in ESP, I would have said that I sensed the presence of an intruder. Hairs rose on the nape of my neck and my scalp prickled. I let out the breath I had been holding, and

I slid my gun out of its holster. I put a round under the hammer. Holding the tiny piece of metal in front of me as if it were a talisman that would ward off evil, I pressed forward into the bad vibrations.

There was nothing but more filth on the ground floor. I knew that there wouldn't be. I knew that the trouble was upstairs, and I caught myself glancing up at the ceiling from time to time as I stalled. Still, I persuaded myself, I had to be thorough. So I opened closet doors and poked into dark corners. There was something terribly pathetic about the disintegration all around me, the broken crockery in the cupboards, the crumpled liquor-store bags stuffed under the sink, the rotting food in the refrigerator. I had thought she was secure, and I caught myself muttering that she deserved better than this.

I took the stairs one at a time, placing my feet on the treads where they butted up against the wall and wouldn't be so likely to squeak. It was about as useless as a superstitious gesture; whoever might be here would have heard me come in the front door, would know I hadn't left yet, would be waiting for me at the top of the stairs.

I stopped where the stairs took a turn and a landing gave me room to breathe. Above me a weak shaft of light probed dust-laden air in a dispirited way. My heart was making a racket in my ears and rocking me slightly even though I tried to hold still. The gun butt felt slippery in my hand. I strained my ears to hear any sound that might betray an intruder, but all I could make out were the noises of a day going on outside without me.

As I stood there, hesitant, I was surprised to find that a sadness overtook my fear, a feeling of profound sorrow for all of God's creatures and for me as well. I shook my head, to free me of this luxury, and without further thought I walked up the few remaining steps and into the only room open to the hall.

Elaine was sprawled sideways across the bed, her beige satin nightgown rucked up past her hips. A water glass lay on the floor beneath her limp right hand, which drooped toward it off the edge of the mattress. Above them both on the bedside table, an upended liquor bottle held a drop of amber fluid improbably suspended on the rim of its mouth, a drop that might never join the pool of whisky that had long ago sunk into the rug. I bent over her and put a pair of gentle fingers on her neck;

her flesh gave way beneath them like Plasticine. Her mouth was slackly open and her thick tongue lolled in the inside of one cheek. No breath moved in or out of her. Her eyes were rolled back so that only whites met my gaze. The skin of her face was as cold as ice and shot through with fine cracks as though it had been shattered.

As I moved to draw her nightgown across her pubis, I saw that she had soiled herself. I reached for the sheet and, untangling it from her blue wrinkled foot, I pulled it all the way up over her. I gathered her stray hand, held it for a moment, and made to place it with the rest of her under the shroud. I must have felt the tiniest resistance, because I was suddenly seized with the belief that she wasn't dead. I whipped the sheet off her head and put my cheek in front of her mouth. I still couldn't feel breathing. Again I searched for a pulse in her neck. And this time I imagined I found one—thready, feeble, inconstant.

I phoned for an ambulance, and then I kneeled in the whisky pool beside the bed and pushed my breath into her with the rhythm that imitates life.

I HELD ON to a strap inside the ambulance as we careened around curves. The attendant was radioing ahead, and the crackling voice from the hospital sounded as far away as all those imaginary places I had overheard as a child on my short-wave set. We would never get there in time. Even under the lashing of the siren we would never get there.

I looked at the attendant. His eyes lifted momentarily to mine. "Will she make it, do you think?" I asked him.

"Think?" he said. He shook his head. "I never think. Not on this job. It doesn't pay."

We braked going into a jammed intersection and everything slid forward and then back again. I couldn't stop thinking.

"Oohh," she groaned. Her eyelids fluttered and her dry, cracked lips worked at the air.

"I won't stay long," I told the nurse. They had pumped her stomach and shot her full of whatever it is they use to counteract booze and barbiturates. She was coming back slowly from the soft shores of death.

"It's all right," said the nurse. "I'll be getting her up in a few minutes anyway. She's got to stay awake and walking around." The woman's face was hard, and her words were edged with a trace of cruelty. I looked at her levelly for a minute. "You the...husband?" she asked. I shook my head. The nurse sighed. "I can't feel sorry for them. The suicides." She tilted her chin in Elaine's direction, just so there would be no mistake as to whom we were talking about. "They take up beds other people need. They take up...medical attention other people need. And for what? So we can get them strong enough to do it right the next time."

"You want to wait outside?" I said. She shrugged and then she left.

Elaine groaned again and tried to turn. I got a piece of cotton wool soaked in water and wiped her lips. Her tongue came out and took up the moisture. She opened her eyes. "Jantarro?" she whispered. Then she closed them again and nestled her head deeper into the pillow.

"Elaine," I said, and I slapped her gently on the cheek. "Elaine, wake up."

"Jantarro. Fuck," she said in her dream. Her words slurred away into meaninglessness.

"Elaine, Elaine, it's important."

"Oohh. Was going to stop. Did stop. Swear to God." And again she tailed off in a slurry of sounds.

"You almost died."

She opened her eyes and began crying. "Don't want to die," she said very quietly.

"Why the barbiturates, then, Elaine? Why?"

Her big wet eyes tried to focus on my meaning, on my face. "No bar— ...no bar— ...bar—" she attempted.

"There was an empty pill bottle by your bed, Elaine. A bottle of barbiturates."

"Oh no," she wept. "I didn't. I didn't. I didn't." A hand reached out for my face and fell short. It flopped like a doll's beside the bed. "Did I?" she asked pathetically.

"I don't know," I told her. Someone had laced her booze with pills. Of that there was no room for doubt. But whether it was she herself, or someone else who had done it for her, I didn't know. "Tell me about Alan Laki," I said. Her eyes were shut again and the tears already drying on her ravaged skin. Once more I slapped her softly on the cheek. "Tell me what you talked about, Elaine." But she didn't hear me. She was sleeping with a quiet snore. So I left to get the nurse.

And to make a phone call.

SIXTEEN

BENCH THANKED ME for the information. Said he was glad to see I'd come to my senses and was reporting in like a decent citizen. I had the pay phone at the limit of its cord as I strained to see across the waiting room and through the little windows in the doors to the ward. When they started walking Elaine, I wanted to be there.

I told him he'd better get someone over to her place to look for signs of intruders. They should ask the woman next door, I advised.

All I could see through the tiny rectangles of glass was a red fire extinguisher clipped to the wall and a cart covered with a white cloth. The rest of the corridor was empty.

Bench grumbled that he was busy. Someone should be stationed outside her room, I explained to him. He told me I was crazy if I thought there were enough cops to spare a baby-sitter for a drunken newspaper reporter. I told him he was crazy if he didn't do what I suggested. We hung up on each other.

I swung open the doors to the ward. There was no one in the hall, so I let them swing shut again, grabbed a service elevator, and dropped down to the lobby. On my way to admitting, I got myself a coffee from one of the vending machines. It gave me extra powdered cream and extra sugar even though I didn't ask for them.

The woman behind the counter in Admitting ignored me for as long as she felt able, then she took off her glasses and lifted her eyes to mine. "Yes?" she said. "Can I help you?"

I showed her my license. "I'm the one who brought in the drug overdose about an hour ago."

"Which one?"

"Elaine Younger."

She looked down at her computer terminal and then up at me again. "That would be Emergency, wouldn't it?"

"She's been admitted," I explained.

"Yes, but she came in through Emergency."

"Does that make a difference?"

"It depends."

"On what?"

"On what you want."

"I gave the wrong name," I said.

She looked at me with a mixture of suspicion and hostility. "You gave the wrong name," she repeated tonelessly.

"I had thought her name was Elaine Younger, so that's what I told the people here when they admitted her. But I've found out that it's not. Her name is Elaine Franklin." If Bench wouldn't put a guard on her—and I couldn't really blame him for not doing it—changing her name in the records might at least slow down someone trying to find out where she was.

She tapped out something on her keyboard. "We don't have an Elaine Franklin," she said.

"I know that," I said. "But you should have."

"If they screwed up in Emergency," she said, "you'll have to speak to them there. We don't have any responsibility for Emergency here."

"Do you have an Elaine Younger?" I asked.

She tapped some more and nodded, snapping her gum. "Elaine Younger."

"How are you spelling Younger?" I asked her. She narrowed her eyes and spelled it for me. "That's not the right spelling," I said.

"How is it supposed to be spelled?"

"F-R-A-N-K-L-I-N."

She started typing a letter at a time, and halfway through she looked up. "Hey," she said.

I pushed my license toward her again. "It's official this way," I assured her. She gave her gum one vicious snap, and with a shrug she hammered the last letters into the electric mind.

"I'm not taking responsibility if it's wrong," she told my back as I was leaving.

Upstairs a nurse and an orderly were parading a very limp Elaine between them. "Come on, honey," the orderly was saying. "Come on, baby, you can do it." The nurse was prodding Elaine's slippered heels with her own white shoes.

"I'll take one arm," I told them.

The nurse looked up at me. "It's all right," she said. "We can do it."

"I just thought I'd free you up for...other things." The orderly looked back and forth between us, a frown creasing his brow.

The nurse inhaled a deep breath and let it out slowly. "Look," she said to me, "I'm sorry about...back there."

"Don't be," I said. "I'm glad to help." Elaine was studying the floor, swaying from her supported shoulders like a rag doll.

"It's just that I had a friend once who—" The nurse let a spasm of annoyance distort her face. "Oh hell," she said. "Here." And I took her place at Elaine's side.

"Come on, honey," said the orderly, and we began to move in a curious dance up the polished hallway.

When we reached the end and turned to come back, I asked her, "What did you talk about with Alan Laki?"

She lifted her head and let it fall again. "What did I do?" she said quietly. "Tell me, Jantarro, what did I do?"

"It looks like you tried to kill yourself." I could feel the orderly stiffen right through the medium of Elaine's slack body.

"Why would I do that?" she asked the floor.

"I don't know."

"Come on, babe," said the orderly nervously. "Move the feet." We set off in our slow shuffle.

"Do I hate myself that much?"

"I don't know."

"You don't know much, do you, Jantarro?"

"Not much," I agreed.

"Me either," she replied after three or four slithering paces.

"Elaine, you've got to tell me what you and Laki talked about."

"I've got to go to sleep," she said.

"No sleep," said the alarmed orderly. "No sleep, honey. Sleep's bad, babe. Bad for you right now."

"I already told you," she said after a few more steps.

"What?"

"What we talked about. When you came to my office." Her voice was tired.

I tried to remember. "You said he was upset about some movie."

"Yes." She had halted her forward motion and was falling asleep on us.

"Wake up, Elaine," I said, and I gave her a shake. The orderly urged her on. "What movie?" I asked her. "What movie was he upset about?"

"Can't remember," she mumbled.

"Was he upset about *The Bengal Lancer*? Was that the one?"

"His movie?" she managed from the edge of consciousness.

"Come on, Elaine." I practically shouted in her ear. "It's important."

"Not his film," she said. "Not...his...film." She was fully asleep now. I looked over her head at the orderly. He shrugged at me, an anxious expression on his face.

"Let's go find the nurse," I said. "Maybe she should rest."

"We'll give her half an hour," the nurse said. "Then we'll get her up again." She looked at me with a considering gaze, and I saw that she was a good-looking woman behind all that anger and weariness. "Thanks for your help," she said.

I shook my head. "No," I said. "I'm going to have to leave now. It's you who has to stay for the long haul. Thank *you*." The color rose in her cheeks and she looked away. Then she smoothed down her uniform and swept out of the room. I bent over and gave Elaine a kiss on the forehead. She stirred and smiled.

I NEEDED TO SEE Guberian or Randy Noone. Either of them would surely know about Laki's film, why he might have been worried about it, and what Elaine might have meant by "not his film." And although I would have relished another crack at Sweet Arnold, I figured that I might get further with Camelia's awkward younger brother.

"Harvey Vanstone's looking for you," Randy told me straight off when I phoned. I owed the lawyer a call, I realized—probably two by now, according to our agreement. "He wants to talk to you."

"And I want to talk to you, Randy."

"What about?"

"The movies. Think you can help me with that?"

And of course I had him. As suspicious as he was of me, he was even more proud of his knowledge of film. Which is why I was sitting in an airy, light little room that he called his office. It was a converted bedroom at the back of his sister's house.

"This is nice," I told him. I meant it. There was something about the room that made you feel peaceful, thoughtful. Even creative. It wasn't the kind of place I'd have thought this over-aged adolescent would have chosen. I would have figured him for a black hole of angst papered in posters and churned up by the machine noise of pop music. I began to think I'd settled for too superficial a view of Randy Noone.

"Thanks," he said in his basso profundo, looking down at his shoes as though all his spoken words fell to the floor. "It's not really mine. Cammy set it up for me a couple of years ago." He wrestled with his shoulders and produced a shrug. "I...I'm using it now...to keep an eye on things while she's..." He flapped his big hands helplessly.

"In jail," I finished for him. He glared at me: I'd said the accursed word. "I saw her," I told him. "Day before yesterday."

He practically toppled in my direction. "How was she?"

"Bearing up," I said. "As well as anybody could under the circumstances." I watched him soak up this information. "She's a pretty tough lady," I added. He nodded absently. "You're worried about her, aren't you?"

He turned to look out of the window at the bright green treetops that waved in the summer breeze as carelessly as if nothing at all were wrong with the world. "What do you want?" he said.

"I want to know about movies," I told him.

He turned back to face me, drawn in despite his reserve and his suspicion. "What about them?"

I wriggled a bit on the chair. This was the problem. I didn't know what I wanted to know. Not precisely enough. I would have to fish around. "I want to know what can go wrong with them."

He looked down at me from his superior knowledge as though I were mad. "Wrong?"

"Yes, wrong," I said. "I mean, if you're making a movie, why would you get upset? What could go wrong?"

He laughed, and genuine laugh lines sprang up around his eyes. Maybe he'd make it into adulthood after all, I thought. "What *can't* go wrong?" he said, still laughing.

"No, I mean more specifically."

"You name it," he said, "and it can go wrong."

"Like what?"

"Like what?" He was on his feet, pacing great strides in the small room. I was struck by a resemblance between him and his brother-in-law, a resemblance I was sure he wouldn't be happy to recognize. Perhaps he'd picked it up unconsciously in spite of the fact he'd hated Laki. "Like what?" he repeated. It seemed my questions had exasperated him. "Like money, for one thing," he said, still pacing. "No money, no movie. And money has a habit of disappearing just when you need it."

That made sense. But it also didn't seem like the kind of thing that had been Laki's problem. He had left enough wealth behind to have made half a dozen more movies. "What else?"

"Distribution," he said. "Distribution can really fuck you up."

"I was thinking more of what can happen before the film is finished," I told him.

He looked at me and shook his head: how dumb could I be? "You set up your distribution before you start shooting," he said. "Before you start the script, for God's sake. No distribution, no movie. What the hell's the point? Unless you want to make an art film that sixty people are going to see."

"But," I objected, "I hear about movies that get made and never get released. If the distribution is set—"

He interrupted me. "Most films never see the light of day. They get buried in the can. You can't lock in your distribution. You can't force them to show your film. They can change their minds anytime they like. But you don't start putting together a product without at least a promise of distribution."

"That wouldn't have been a problem for Laki, would it?" I asked him.

He went stock still. I could see it in his eyes: in his enthusiasm, he'd actually forgotten what this whole thing was about. "No," he said stiffly, "it wouldn't have been a problem for the great Alan Laki. They would kill themselves for a chance to distribute his worst outtakes."

"So what would have been?"

"For brother Alan?" I nodded. "Oh, I don't know," he said, and it was clear he was lying. Clear to both of us. He tried to cover up. "Schedule fuck-up, maybe," he said hastily. "He was financing a whole lot of *Lancer* on his own—"

"His company was."

"Right. Lakipix. Same thing."

"Except for Guberian. He's in Lakipix, too."

Randy's face closed down. "If Laki makes money, Guberian does, too. No conflict there."

"Maybe," I said. Then I asked, "What causes a schedule fuck-up, as you put it?"

"Anything. The talent gets difficult. The script sounds like shit when you hear it on the set and you've got to rewrite. The weather is wrong. Even something like the weather can put you so far behind you might never show a profit."

"Was that happening to *Bengal Lancer?*"

"How do I know?" he said. "His fucking majesty wouldn't tell me anything."

"But I heard you tell Camelia when we first met that you could finish the film. So you must know something about it."

He looked stricken. His eyes darted around for some safe place to land. His Adam's apple bobbed spastically. "I don't know what his problem was," he said eventually. "I really don't. I was just talking. Trying to be the big man. You know. Step into the great man's shoes." He had his fingers entangled in his luxurious, black curls. "Besides," he said in an imploring tone, "I've got my own project. I don't really want to work on his. And I don't have the time anyway."

I wasn't going to let him get off that easily, but I didn't yet know which way to tug the line so the hook would be set deep. I smiled at him and nodded. "So how far along was Laki anyway?"

"How far along?"

"Yes. Had he started shooting? Was it...in the can? What?"

"He was over halfway through the shoot."

"So there's some film."

He frowned. "Film?"

"Yes. If he'd shot some of the movie, there'd be exposed film, wouldn't there?"

"You mean the rushes."

"If that's what it's called."

"Well, sure. There's thousands of feet of rushes."

"Can I see some?"

He looked genuinely puzzled. "You want to see the rushes of *Lancer?*"

"Why not?"

"Well, I mean, it's a pain in the ass. And I don't know if I could get my hands on them. They don't belong to me. The Lakipix lawyers probably have them locked up somewhere. Besides, what do you want to see them for?"

"I don't know," I said. "Just to see what he was doing, I guess. Get an idea of what was happening in his life when he was killed." I knew the film was important somehow, and it seemed to me that it just might have to do with what was going on *in* the film. It wasn't completely unreasonable to suppose that a filmmaker would be upset about what was happening in the movies.

Randy was very reluctant indeed. And that made me even more eager to see the rushes. "I don't know where the shooting script is," he objected.

"Is that important?"

"Well, shit, how are you going to know what you're looking at without a shooting script?"

"There must be one around," I insisted.

"I could see," he said hesitantly.

"Let's do it," I said, standing up. Looking out of the window, I could see all of the trees at the back of the garden. They were still now, but closer to the ground the air was moving, because the flowers in the big beds were bobbing with excitement.

"Now?" he said, astonished.

"Your sister's in jail," I reminded him. "She doesn't have anything but time to look forward to. I think she'd like us to hurry."

He looked around his quiet little room, but there was only one way out. I helped him to take it.

SEVENTEEN

By six that evening we were at the King Street offices of Lakipix, the place where Laki's body had been found. The offices consisted of a dozen rooms of various sizes on the first floor of an old warehouse, all of which were meant to be used for one or another practical aspect of the filmmaking enterprise. Lakipix did its money work and publicity out of a flashier suite of rooms in one of the big bank towers on Bay. "This was sort of his private studio," Randy explained as he led us down the hall nervously jingling a crowded ring of keys. "He'd hide out here, do some work on scripts. Maybe get a bunch of people together for a bullshit session. Mostly he'd edit film here." His eyes slid left as we went past the room where he had died.

Randy had been as tight as a bridge cable all afternoon. We'd driven all over town, from the Bay Street office to a warehouse in Agincourt and back down to Guberian's place on Bloor; and I'd let him organize the whole thing, staying in his classic '56 Buick convertible listening to the radio and thinking while he did the running around after the script, a copy of the rushes, and the permission to view them.

His tightness, I thought, resulted from a blend of excitement and anxiety. He was definitely scared about something; what we were doing was dangerous somehow—for him, or for his sister, perhaps. I couldn't tell. And his nervousness forced me to realize that Michael Dennis hadn't been the only actor in this tragedy. It set me to wondering, in fact, whether I might not have been completely mistaken about him. But it was Randy's barely suppressed excitement that really made me think. He gave off the feeling of a kid about to do something forbidden, about to release something powerful that had been welling up despite an ironclad repression. I made a note to myself to keep him where I could see him so I'd be ready when the release came.

Now I stood back while he searched among the keys for the right one to open a glass-paneled door at the end of the quiet, dusty hall. His hands shook, and bits of brass jangled against the pale wood of the doorframe. A key went in and the door opened.

"The editing room," he said. His voice, overloud, boomed in the big high-ceilinged, windowless room. It looked unfurnished, plain—shoddy, in fact. "Yeah," he said, catching my disappointed expression, "all that slick cutting out of this crappy shop. Hard to believe, but *Griffin* was cut here. So was *Inkblot* and *Yours Truly*." He sighed and ran his hands up and down the sides of his jeans as if there were sticky sweat on his palms.

The security guard, an old man in a blue uniform rubbed pale at the edges, came puffing into the room behind us, his arms loaded down with boxes containing reels of film. "Here you are, Mr. Noone," he said. He had carried them in from the car for us.

Randy and I helped him put them down on a big table against the far wall. "Thanks, Jeff," Randy said. He took a twenty out of his wallet and the bill disappeared into the old man's hand.

"There's the script box still to come," the guard said. "I'll go and get it right now."

"That's okay," said Randy. "I can get it."

"No trouble." The guard hesitated. "I was real sorry," he said, "about...about..."

"Thanks," said Randy.

"I mean, I didn't want to say nothing, but"—he shrugged helplessly—"it's my job after all. And anyways I did see her." This, I realized, was the man who had spotted Camelia here at the time that Alan Laki had died.

"I know," said Randy.

"Always liked Miss Noone. A beautiful lady." He was in confusion, and Randy's embarrassment wasn't helping him.

"A terrible thing," I said.

The guard's eyes fell on me gratefully. "Terrible," he agreed. "I took some time off after. Had it coming, understand. Back vacation time." He shook his head. "Just couldn't understand it."

"No one does," I said. "Tell me. When did you punch in that day?"

"Wasn't supposed to be here till twelve, like. They don't have security until then." He let his eyes wander around a bit. "Cheap, I guess. Anyways, I was here a bit early. 'Bout 'leven forty-five. Just dumb luck."

"You didn't check in on Mr. Laki then, by any chance?"

He shook his head. "I don't disturb nobody, less I have to."

Randy was getting restless. "Professional," I said.

He nodded vigorously in agreement and then altered the motion so that his head was shaking again. "Terrible, terrible thing," he said again. The guard, now released from his burden of guilt and embarrassment, looked up brightly. "Glad to see you're moving in," he said to Randy, and he pointed at a machine along the wall to our right.

"Yes," said Randy neutrally. "I'll come out with you and get the script box."

When he returned, I asked, "Moving in?" I gestured at the machine the guard had identified.

Randy made a dismissive movement with his head. "Just storing some stuff here. Until everything gets sorted out."

"Uh-huh," I said.

Randy tried to stare me down, not an easy thing to do. "It looks like this one," I said, pointing at another machine of the same kind along the opposite wall.

"It's a Steenbeck," Randy said. I raised my eyebrows in a question. "A flatbed. An editing machine," he explained. "I've got an old one. Sixteen mill." He shrugged. "Can't afford the new thirty-five." He looked at Alan Laki's machine.

"So you've actually made movies," I said.

"Of course," he said. He tried to smile. "But only kid stuff."

"But you've got one in the works now, right?" I pointed at a pile of reels stacked on a shelf near his Steenbeck.

"Nothing really," he said. "An old piece of stuff. Don't you want to see *Lancer*?" He took a reel box off the stack the guard had brought in and began to undo the buckles on the straps that held it closed.

I walked over to the pile of film cans near his machine, picked up the top one, and read the label. "Meridiem Productions?" I asked him. He had the first reel of the *Lancer* rushes out of its can and was fitting it to a spool on the big Steenbeck.

"Yeah," he said without turning around. "Fancy name for my company. Noone, meridiem, as in *ante meridiem*. A.m. and p.m. Get it?

"I'd like to see it," I said.

"Well, I almost got it set up here."

"No. I mean, your film."

"It's nothing," he said.

"Still. I'd like to see."

"Can't do two things at once. You wanted to look at *Lancer*."

The Meridiem can I was holding didn't seem old. It was shiny, unscratched. But then maybe like the silver screen itself this material didn't tarnish. I popped the lid. Elaine had said, "Not his film." Not Alan's film. Randy's, then? Was that what was bothering him when he was killed? But why would one of the best-established, most successful auteurs in the business worry about the work of an immature twenty-five-year-old?

"I'd really like to take a look at your film."

He straightened up slowly and tried to appear simply annoyed. "I don't like people looking at my work," he said. But I could see that he was badly frightened, and I realized that we were balanced on the very ledge that he had been anticipating all afternoon.

I took the reel out of the can, and he started forward protectively. "Please," I said.

"Put it down."

"Randy."

"I mean it."

"What's the problem?" He wanted me to see this film of his. I was convinced of that. And when I did see it, something awful would be revealed; I was convinced of that, too.

"It's private," he protested. We were standing toe-to-toe with only the reel of his film between us.

"Too late, Randy," I said, as sympathetically as I could. "It's all gone too far, hasn't it? Much too far to have any privacy left."

"I don't know what you're talking about," he said, and he put his hands on the reel I was holding, but it was a protective gesture rather than an attempt to take it from me, a caress, perhaps, for something dear that was about to be lost.

"Two men dead. A woman in prison. And another woman fighting for her life."

"He was a shit. He deserved everything he got." His eyes were glazed over; he was only hearing half of what I was saying.

"And Michael Dennis and Elaine Younger? What did they deserve?"

He tried to focus on me. "I don't know anything about them."

"I know," I said, even though I knew no such thing. "That's why you've got to stop pretending and help me."

"It's my film."

"I'd like to see it."

"It's good. Really good. It will be."

"I'm sure."

"I won't talk to you. I promise. I won't talk," he warned me.

"Let's start with the film."

"I'll kill myself before I talk to you."

"Perhaps you won't need to say anything. Let's just see this." I'd taken the reel and was fitting it to one of the spools on the sixteen-millimeter machine, the way I'd seen him do it with Laki's film on the larger machine. My clumsiness must have got to him, because he pushed me out of the way and took over the task, threading the film through the Steenbeck and flicking the switches that caused it to come to life. A small screen the size of a television set perched at eye level in the middle of the thing began to glow dully, and suddenly images danced across it in soft color.

"There's no sound," he said. "I haven't done the dub yet."

I sat in the chair in front of the screen and watched as two men in overcoats struggled together in a long, tiled corridor that I recognized as a pedestrian tunnel in a subway station. Beside me I could feel his body bend with those of the little figures fighting on the screen. We cut to their faces: they were long-haired, handsome young men; one of them was bleeding from a cut over an eye, and the blood streamed down across his cheek.

We cut again, this time to a pool of blood in which blond hairs were floating, and as the camera pulled back, we saw the head of a dead woman and then the rest of her awkwardly positioned body. "You hear them still fighting," he said quietly over my shoulder. "Everything echoes off the hard tiles."

One man managed to wrest a hand free, a hand that held a wicked-looking knife, and with a great underhand loop he drove it up to the hilt in the other man's belly. I thought of Dog and the fact that he carried a knife. The dead man hung in the air for a moment and then crashed silently to the floor. We saw the killer's feet pelting noiselessly along the corridor, around corners, and up more tiled halls. "I'm going to try intercutting shots of the bodies," Randy told me. "This is only a first cut, you understand."

"What's it about?" I asked him. We emerged from the empty subway station with the killer, still viewing him from a very low angle, so that as we came up the steps into night, we shot up the sides of the brightly lit skyscrapers in a dizzy, almost exhilarating rush.

He let out a sigh. "It's about betrayal," he said. I felt energy pour off him.

But on the screen there was simply the busyness of a pair of women's hands as they pushed and pulled at a piece of pink tulle that seemed to be twisted into a bow. It flashed as it caught light, and I felt I could reach out and touch its recalcitrant stiffness. "It rustles," he said. "You can hear it." His voice was high and breathless.

The hands continued to pet and preen, and as they did so, the woman being dressed emerged beneath them as though they were the hands of a creator. Finally, we could see her from the back. Her heels, dyed to match the dress, were too high and she wobbled a bit. The dress had too many pleats and ruffles. Her hair was too stiffly coiffed. And I began to feel acutely uncomfortable for her. The dresser was fat and slovenly, and the camera followed a cigarette from her overred mouth to an overfull ashtray. "There's music in the background," Randy whispered. "Eddie Fisher."

I was shocked even before the woman in pink turned around, and when she did, it took me a full thirty seconds to understand why.

I was face-to-face with Camelia Laki—or rather, Camelia Noone the actress who had given up acting. "Now you see," said Randy, his voice thick.

"Yes," I agree. "Now I see."

Randy flipped a switch and the image of Camelia's face, lovely even through the thick, sad makeup, lingered frozen on the screen until he killed the light behind it and she died.

But what had I seen? What did it mean for the death of Alan Laki? I pushed my chair back from the Steenbeck and stood up. Randy was halfway across the room, his back to me. "She agreed to act for you," I said.

He nodded.

"Even though she was terrified of acting."

He whirled to face me. "It was that asshole of a husband of hers that made her scared. She only got terrified when he was pushing at her. I was able to make her relax, even to enjoy it. To be a great actress again."

And then a piece fell into place. "She gave you the money to make the film."

He opened his mouth and then closed it again. But it didn't matter. I knew I was right. This was the "good cause" she had spoken of. "Did he know?" I asked. Randy's mouth was pressed tightly shut in a childish determination not to do what he wanted to do.

If he'd known, I asked myself, why had he hired me? Hired me with the vague kind of suspicions he'd come to me with? He might have suspected, suspected that she was acting in a movie that she was trying to finance, but if so, why hadn't he told me as much? He must have known at the end, though, for him to have talked to Elaine about the film.

I thought about taking the reel of film with me so Randy couldn't destroy it, until I realized that there was no way on earth that he could be induced to destroy this work of his. It would be safe with him, even if it implicated him and his sister in Laki's death. Whether or not it did implicate them was something I needed to discover.

"I'll get back to you," I told him, and he stared at me wide-eyed.

"I'm not talking," he reminded me.

I smiled. "Not now, maybe. But soon, Randy, soon, because time is running out. Anyway, your silent screen has done enough talking for one day."

He looked over at his film and blinked back tears. His fists were clenched. His excitement had drained away, leaving only the residue of fear and despair in him.

I shut the door softly behind me and walked out of the movies into the bright long rays of the sunset.

EIGHTEEN

VISITING HOURS were over, but I went to see Elaine anyway. The elevator carried me to an artificial dusk of dimmed lights, hush, and emptiness. Here and there along the hall I could see the ghostly blue glow from TV sets that leaked out of nearly private rooms. Everything was still enough for me to hear the air-conditioning breathe through the building with its steady hiss.

I waited patiently at the nursing station, an island of unnatural golden brightness, but a deserted one. Urgency came and went silently in the flickering little red lights on the bank phones in front of me. On a shelf behind the counter one of those silly ducking birds dipped and bobbed with maniacal regularity into a beaker of water. Someone named Suzie was having a birthday, according to the stand of cards on another shelf. A Saint Christopher medal lay on the desk under a pooled silver chain.

A figure in pale yellow emerged from a room at the end of the hall and disappeared almost immediately into another room. I waited for her to come out again so that I could attract her attention. And when she didn't reappear after a few minutes, I decided to cast off and make my way through the zone of tranquillity on my own.

Elaine's door was slightly ajar, and a faint light escaped from the opening. She would be sleeping, enjoying a natural, drug-free sleep, I hoped. I would just look in on her and leave more talking to the morning.

But a very old woman was in the bed, tethered to life with a web of pale plastic tubing and thin lead wires. Her mouth was wide open, and, toothless, she gaped at the blank walls of the hospital room. There was the smell of the approach of death.

A belligerent fat man lay in the room beyond, his mouth around an apple, his eyes lifted from a book. "The fuck are you?" he asked, spitting bits of fruit at me. Choler raised all the veins in his neck like snakes. "Get out," he told me.

Even as I shut his door, I knew. The sinking feeling inside me left me with no doubt. But I had to be certain, so I entered the room on the other side of the old woman's chamber. Two empty beds under taut sheets thrust themselves at me.

I stood in the hall, striving in vain for no thought, no feeling. The nurse in yellow came up to me, prepared to remonstrate. She saw my expression and blinked. "What do you want?" she asked.

"I want Elaine Younger."

She frowned and led me back to the nursing station. I noticed that she was reading Alice Munro's *The Progress of Love*. The paperback lay facedown, spine cracked, in front of her chair. She moved it farther under the counter and tapped at the keyboard on her computer. "I don't show any Elaine Younger," she said.

"Try 'Elaine Franklin,'" I suggested. It wouldn't do any good. I knew that with a certainty.

She looked at me. "Franklin?"

"Her married name. I think."

She stared at me; I stared back. Then dutifully she consulted the electronic scorekeeper, and when I saw her eyes veer away from the screen, I knew again with a new certainty. "Elaine Franklin died at seven o'clock today," she said. "I'm sorry."

"How did she die?" There was an anger in my voice that spilled out onto her, and she winced.

"I'm afraid I can't tell you," she said stiffly.

"I mean, was it a result of her... her illness?"

"I've told you. I can't tell you. I didn't come on until eight. I don't know anything about it at all."

"Her chart," I said loudly. "It must be on her chart."

She glanced nervously behind her. A younger woman in white came up and looked anxiously between us. I let out a breath that had been held for far too long. "I'm sorry," I said. "It's just that she was... doing well when I was here earlier today." They looked at me. "I brought her in," I said lamely.

The one in yellow looked at my empty sleeve and something changed. "Oh," she said. "You. I mean, you spoke to Betty this morning. She told me about you. That was the suicide."

I was going to argue, but it wasn't the time or the place. "Yes," I said.

She flicked through the papers in a file drawer beneath the counter. "Cardiac arrest," she announced, reading from the file. She looked up. "Barbiturates and alcohol.... Her heart was weak, I guess." She smiled a wan smile of sympathy.

I thanked her for her trouble. And then I left.

AT HOME I poured myself a large Scotch. I hunted for some music, settling for Mussorgsky's *Pictures at an Exhibition* played by Arthur Ozolins. And I missed Glenda. Neither of my anodynes worked to relieve me of the sadness I felt at Elaine's death. Or of the anger, either. The whisky tasted flat, and music was too uncertain about what it wanted. Glenda's absence loomed like a hole down which I didn't have the guts to jump.

Had Elaine killed herself? I didn't think so. No. I was sure that she hadn't. But how well did I know her? She and I were simply paths that crossed, favors that got exchanged, possibilities that never explored each other the way that they should have. Perhaps she had been so unhappy that death was welcome. Hell, I hadn't even known she was a lush. Not for sure.

In the middle of my second tasteless Scotch I called Glenda. Her message is a nice one, a sensible, unkitschy one; but I didn't want to talk to a machine, so I dropped the receiver back into the cradle. There was a killer out there, *the* killer. And his presence outraged me.

I called Bench even though it was nearly eleven. I let his line ring a full ten times. He answered on the eleventh, just as I was about to hang up. "What are you still doing there?" I asked.

"My job. What is it, Jantarro?"

"Elaine Younger just died."

"I'm sorry to hear that. You and she close?"

"That's not the point. She was the last person to see Laki alive. I've told you."

"Yeah. And you've told me that you think someone tried to off her."

"He succeeded."

He sighed. "Maybe," he said.

"Have you been to her place? Have you sent someone?"

"Jantarro, listen. I got six active homicide cases and I'm pumping away like a goddamn madman just to keep them afloat. And if that gets boring, I got thirty-six inactives stretching back to sixty-four that could sop up a million man-hours of work. And just in case I think I got the time to take a shit or catch a few zees, three cops in the burbs are piling up the messages here because they think maybe I can help them out of *their* troubles. So I got to say that I'm sorry about your friend, but there's no way on God's earth I'm going to snap to attention and run around like your personal robot. Do I make myself clear?"

I told him that he did. I wished him luck, and I hung up, knowing that I'd have to go back to Elaine's house in the morning and do what I could myself. Then the Scotch hit me and I lost the will to stand upright.

I dreamed a lot that night. Pleasant dreams, surprisingly. It's always a wonder to me how the night side of my life seems to have an existence with only the most inscrutable ties to the rest of me. At one point I was swimming in body-temperature water with an effortless grace I haven't managed since I lost my arm. There were mermaids in the water with me—at least I think they were mermaids, because whenever I dived to have a look below, their nether regions disappeared in a wavy haze of indistinctness. There was no Esther Williams synchronized swimming routine about this: these Nereids lolled and sank and played as if they hadn't a care in the world. They ignored me until I called out, and then one of them broke away and moved in my direction. She was beautiful; and if such a thing were possible, she had a face that combined the features of Elaine, Camelia, and Glenda. I fell in love with her on the spot and devoted the rest of the dream to paddling after her in a vain attempt to achieve submerged connubial bliss.

I woke with the sun streaming in the window, and I lay there in its gentle heat, conjuring up the lady of my dreams until the consciousness of what had to be done today bore in on me too strongly to let the dalliance continue.

I showered. I made toast and coffee. And I strapped on my gun.

THE DOOR to Elaine's house was locked. I stepped across the railing between her porch and her neighbor's, and I banged on the neighbor's door. She opened it. This time there were no curlers in her hair: it ran riot in a frenzy of improbable twists and spirals. She wore no makeup and her eyes were washed out and hard, like bleached shells from a beach. She was wearing a gray sweatsuit. "Yeah?" she said. From behind her came the odor of marijuana.

"I'm Elaine's friend," I said to remind her.

She tried to focus, but her muscles weren't doing her bidding. "Yeah?"

"From yesterday?"

Slowly, memory returned to her. "Oh sure!" she said, and she laid an arm on my chest as she moved in close. "Well, hey. Come on in, soldier."

"I wonder if you've got a key," I said. "Her door is locked."

She looked over at Elaine's door. "Hey, she went in an ambulance, right?" She was still staring at the door.

"That's right," I said.

"She okay?"

"She's dead," I told her.

"No shit," she said. She was still leaning into me. "That's too bad."

"Have you got a key?"

"A key?"

"For her door."

She blinked and looked at her arm on my chest, as if it had just then arrived there. Then she brought her gaze up to my face. "Come in," she said, and she grabbed my tie, pulling me after her. With her other hand she gestured at the smoky air. "Going through a rough time," she said. "You wanna toke? Or *something*?"

"Just the key, thanks."

"'Just the key, thanks,'" she repeated in a mocking tone. "I offer the guy my body and everything and what does he want? The fucking key." She gave my tie a jerk and then let it go, disappearing into the back of the house. She returned dangling a key from a piece of string. With her other hand she pulled the waistband of her sweatpants away from her belly; she let the key hover over the opening. "I could make you dive for it," she said.

"Please," I said, holding out my hand.

"Yeah," she replied in a subdued tone. "I wouldn't fuck me either." She dropped the key on my palm, and retreated into herself so far she didn't hear me thank her or say good-bye.

Elaine's house seemed to be just as I had left it yesterday, although if six people had tramped through the detritus of her life I doubt I would have noticed it. Up in her bedroom I took out the half dozen or so plastic zip-lock freezer bags I had brought from home, and into the first I put the overturned whisky bottle. Her glass went into another. And the prescription pill bottle—label made out in her name—went into a third. There's a lab I use that does my technical stuff; they would test these objects for prints. But it was foolish to expect that any useful ones would be there except her own. Even so, I had to do something. I owed her that much.

I took her hairbrush from the bathroom and disconnected the telephone handset from the instrument on the hall table, and both of these went into a bag to provide samples of her own prints, so that any alien ones could at least be identified as such. I'd have to arrange to get the cops to have her corpse printed before I could be certain.

Then I walked slowly around the bedroom trying to see what was there that might have been out of place, or foreign, or telltale in some way. I felt like a primitive Sherlock Holmes without even the benefit of a magnifying glass. It was hopeless. The only hairs on the pillows were hairs that looked like hers; the junk in the wicker wastebasket was all junk that she might have thrown away; and under the bed there were nothing but tumbleweeds of dust.

I left no wiser than I'd been when I arrived.

VANSTONE WAS FURIOUS in a pompous sort of way. He'd known children more reliable than I, he said. He reminded me I'd agreed to call in every other day. He talked of firing me. He spoke of professional integrity. He struck poses I could hear over the phone.

I let him harrumph and bluster for a while, and as he did, it occurred to me that he was frightened. He wasn't really a criminal lawyer. "When's the preliminary hearing?" I asked, cutting into his barrage.

"What?"

"The prelim. When is it?"

"It's Tuesday morning, if that's of any interest to you."

Four days from now. I took a deep breath. "I'll have this thing wrapped up before then, or I'll quit," I told him.

"You've got something? Tell me what you've got. I instruct you to tell me, Jantarro." He fell on my boast like a starving man on a hot meal. If he only knew how lacking in real substance the promise I'd made was. But I needed him in order to get to Camelia. And I needed her.

To get at the truth.

"Do you hear me?" he was shouting. "You're working for me. This . . . this secrecy is impertinent."

"It's not ready yet," I said.

"Ready? Ready? What do I care if it's ready. Tell me what you do have."

"Well, I care. But I'll have something concrete for you by . . . say, tomorrow or Sunday." Where were these airy promises coming from? I wondered.

"You'd better," he said, and he receded into half-mumbled imprecations.

"I need to see Camelia," I said.

"Oh, I don't know, Jantarro."

"Today."

"What can she possibly tell you?" That she hadn't told him, he meant.

"If I knew," I said, "I wouldn't need to see her. Can you arrange it?"

"Give me something in return," he demanded.

"I told you. Sunday, maybe."

"Now, or you don't get in to jail."

I thought about it. Then I told him about Michael Dennis.

Five minutes later I put the phone back on the hook and stepped out of the small plastic booth. Two elevators led up to Glenda's offices: according to the little lights on top, one of them was up at the tenth floor and the other was up at the seventeenth. I sighed, squared my shoulders and pushed the button to call them down. Things would break, I had promised. Maybe they would break my way. Maybe Glenda would have lunch with me. It would be a start.

NINETEEN

"NOT THAT I CARE," said Glenda, picking delicately at a breast of chicken diablo, "but are you ever going to get your arm back?" We were at Cassie's, sitting on the terrace in the sun.

I had filled her in on what was happening even though she had protested that it was none of her business and that I didn't need to talk about things if I didn't want to. I was feeling too good to eat, so I toyed with my sole and drank more than my share of the Chablis. "I'd forgotten all about it," I said. It was the truth, more or less. The prosthesis is both a boon and a reminder of better days. Sometimes I'm minded to forget. "What did the bank manager say?"

"Ann managed to get him on her side. Don't ask me how. And I was there." Glenda was relaxed, happy. She smiled at me between mouthfuls.

"And your mother? Have you talked to her?"

A frown came and went, the way the fluffy clouds above us scudded across the face of the sun. "Yes," she said. "She's in good spirits." She shook her head. "I don't know."

"Can you take some time off? Go and see her?"

Glenda deliberately speared a baby carrot, put it in her mouth, and chewed. When she was finished with it, she said in a thoughtful tone, "Maybe. I've spoken to Ann about it. She says no sweat. We'll work something out."

I poured her more wine and filled up my own glass.

"Well?" she said, with a big smile.

"Well?"

"You've asked me about everything else I dumped on you on Wednesday, was it? Aren't you going to ask me about what the doctor said?" Her smile was more enigmatic now.

"Some things are private," I protested. I had in fact forgotten she had been to the gynecologist. "If there's something—" My mouth must have fallen open, because she began laughing at me. "Glenda, you're not . . ."

She shook her head, still laughing. "Pregnant? No, Cagey, I'm not." She had to cover her mouth with her napkin, she was laughing so hard.

"I don't think it's so funny," I said.

"I know," she managed between bouts of glee. "I know."

"I guess you're not still mad at me, huh?" I asked when she seemed to have calmed down. But that only set her off once again. I was a bit browned off. It felt wonderful.

"YOU CAUGHT ME just in time." The diminutive Guberian reached up and without actually touching my back shepherded me into his office. "I was on the point of decamping even though it is only three in the afternoon. You have kept me honest, Mr. Jantarro, and for that I am grateful." He installed me in a chair on the visitor side of his desk and then wheeled around to the business side from where, standing, he regarded me somewhat owlishly through his thick lenses.

I had been putting off seeing Guberian all week. I fancied he was an evil little man, and being in his presence made my flesh crawl. "I've been to the movies," I said.

He beamed and gave a stiff little bow. "We at Guberian Enterprises thank you—at least that part of Guberian Enterprises in which films are made. Moviegoers are important people."

"Speaking of enterprise," I said, "what does the rest of the company do when it's not financing movies?"

"A bit of this, a bit of that. Look, Mr. Jantarro, I'd love to dally and chat all day with you, but other matters press." He took off his glasses, and his black eyes were reduced to pinpoints; he rubbed the sockets delicately with the thumb and forefinger of his other hand. "Let me see if I can hasten things along," he said. "You still think it possible that I killed Alan Laki. Despite any evidence. Despite any motive. You came here hoping that I shall wither under your steely gaze and divulge to you this sordid secret." He took his hand away from his eyes, put his glasses back on, and gave me a fearsome grin. "Alas, I'm going to disappoint you. I did not kill Alan. And I won't say I did just to suit you. I won't even say it in order to assist Camelia, however much I should like to see her freed from prison. And I'm afraid that's the extent of our business."

I stayed seated. "When I was at the movies, I saw a great actress."

"Oh?" His face was expressionless.

"Yes. Camelia Noone."

He raised his thick eyebrows. "I hadn't realized any of her pictures was running. *Undertow* was showing at one of the cineplexes a while ago. But then, there are so many revival theaters in town I could easily have missed it. To tell you the truth, Mr. Jantarro—and this is just between us—I'm not the inveterate movie watcher you might imagine I should be. So which one was it? *Devil's Glen? Westfall?*"

"It doesn't have a name yet."

"I beg your pardon?" I could have been imagining it, but I thought his mouth tightened. He caught himself looking down at his hands, and he put them out of sight behind his back.

"In fact Meridiem hasn't finished shooting it. Or cutting it."

"Meridiem?" He frowned. "Randy—" He spoke the name and then stopped. For a split second he gave off waves of anger without any visible effort. Then all was calm again. "Don't tell me Randy has persuaded his sister to act again. He always talked of . . . doing just that. My goodness."

"Indeed. My goodness."

"I see you appreciate the kind of feat that would be. The box office would be considerable for a new Camelia Noone picture. Provided it wasn't a complete"—he closed his eyes and sought the right phrase—"hash job." He brought one hand out from behind his back and allowed his fingertips to run along the edge of his polished desk. "Whether Randy is capable of meeting those rather minimum requirements. . ." He shrugged, drawing the hand off the desk. He examined his fingertips.

"You knew nothing of this?"

He shook his head slowly. "I might speak to the boy. It would be a shame to see such a noble comeback ruined because of youthful incompetence."

"But you did know that Randy had a company called Meridiem."

"He talked of making films, of course—real, feature-length films. He probably used the name in my hearing." He set those hard eyes on me. "Perhaps Alan spoke of it."

"Was Camelia bound by a contract to Laki or to Lakipix?"

Again he shook his head, even more slowly this time. "I'm afraid I don't know. I should have thought not. It has been—what?—six years since she had acted. Any contract would have expired by now. Surely." He took in a breath, held it, and let it out over a minute's time. "Why don't you ask her, Mr. Jantarro? I understand you're working for her now. I'm sure she'd be glad to tell you."

"You're well informed," I said.

"One must be in order to compete successfully. Don't you agree?" He smiled, more relaxed now, as if some transit had been successfully negotiated. "Besides, in this case the answer is simple. As it usually is, if I may say so. Camelia told me herself that you were working for her."

"You saw her?"

"No indeed. Nothing on earth would persuade me to enter a prison." He gave a delicate shudder. "I have a fear of enclosed places," he said. "No, she sent me a letter. Via her lawyer . . . Vandenburg? Van-something-or-other. Two letters, in fact. You needn't look so shocked, Mr. Jantarro. She is the wife of an old friend, after all."

"She didn't happen to mention the film Randy's making, I suppose."

"She certainly did not. She was always a . . . private person. But this is taking things a bit far. It's a wonder they could do it under Alan's nose. Perhaps . . . But then, that's your business, not mine, isn't it? That sort of speculation." He regarded me with a self-satisfied expression.

I got to my feet. "Do you want her out of jail?" I asked him. "Camelia."

"I assure you, Mr. Jantarro, nothing would please me more."

"It doesn't look that way. I'm working on it, and you're too busy to talk. I come up with a problem, and you shrug it off. Hell, you even leave the inferences pointing her way. I've got to say, if you do care about her, you've got the strangest way of showing it that I ever saw."

He came around the desk and moved past me to the door. He put a hand on the knob and turned to face me. "May I recommend, Mr. Jantarro, that you pay less attention to appearances and more to intelligent reason. Surely, it has occurred to you that what you have uncovered about Michael Dennis—at my suggestion, if I may remind you—will certainly raise the reasonable doubt that will result in a verdict of not guilty. I really am in regular contact with her and her lawyer, as you can see. I am assured that Camelia will be free soon enough." He wagged a stubby finger at me. "That is what I care about. But you, Mr. Jantarro, you seem to be pressing the inquiry further than Camelia's interests would deem prudent. You seem to be bent on discovering who killed Alan Laki." He opened the door. "You do take my point, Mr. Jantarro, do you not?"

"WAS I GREAT?"

"You had too much makeup on, and you were only this small." I spread my hands—plastic and real—to the width of the screen on Randy's Steenbeck. The newly refurbished plastic one didn't shake, but the flesh one did. I could feel the press of the walls, the sucking of the despair in the place.

Camelia laughed delightedly for a few seconds, and then she looked away toward the glass-block window off to her left and lit a cigarette. She had given up the tough con act. I didn't yet know what role she was playing this afternoon. Tragic heroine, perhaps. It wouldn't have been out of place.

"Poor Randy," she said, seemingly to herself—but with actresses, you never know.

"Poor little rich boy," I said. She brought her head around. "The kind of money you dumped on him is more than a whole lot of people ever piss away in a lifetime." She shrugged delicately under the ill-fitting prison blouse, and then she looked down at her nail-bitten hands, blowing smoke over them as if to vignette them for a shot.

"He can be good," she said. "*Is* good."

"I hope so for your sake, because your comeback is in his hands."

She looked at me and smiled. "You sound like Sweet Arnie."

"Is that what he said when you told him about Randy's plans?"

The smile disappeared. "Don't try to get cute with me, Johnny my lad," she snapped. "It's what Arnie said when I told him Alan was pressing me to act again." She took a deep drag on the cigarette and butted it out in the tin ashtray. "Way back when. Way back at the beginning. When the world was first formed. When Alan and I were happy." She tried a tentative smile. "Most of the time. When I didn't know what kind of a shit he was. But Arnie did. He knew. He warned me." She shook her head to rid it of the memory. "So you're a fan now, are you, Johnny? A Johnny-come-lately."

I shook my head. "It's not the screen image I like, Camelia. It's you."

She wrinkled her nose and looked faintly embarrassed. "I know. I realized that about you right away, Johnny. When you came to that party—to spy on me. I realized you had no idea who I was. You were the only one there who didn't know me—or think they did."

I felt myself go soft inside and I wondered whether I would ever be free of this woman's charms, whether I would ever want to be. Promise seemed to linger around her like the scent of an intoxicating perfume, even here, in the worst possible place I could be. Even in jail.

"Alan," I said, "did he know about you and Randy?"

"The film?"

"Yes."

She shook her head. "He suspected something. That's why he hired you, I'm sure. But he never connected the money with Randy. He never figured out what was happening." She lit another cigarette and smoke curled slowly out of a crooked smile. "It must have driven him crazy," she said.

I told her about Elaine Younger. How she had told me enough about what she and Alan had discussed at brunch ten days ago to make it likely that Alan had indeed known what was up. How Elaine had died. She frowned. "What does it mean, Johnny?" she asked.

"I was hoping you could tell me," I said. "One way to look at it is that Alan found out, confronted you, and when he threatened you somehow, you killed him. Another way is ditto and Randy killed him."

She looked at me sadly. "That's not much of a choice."

"It could be that we're both right," I said. I didn't know how much I believed it, but it was important to say it right then. "Assume it goes this way. You're right in that Alan doesn't know for sure, not until just at the end. But I'm right, too, and he does learn about the flick—when it's too late for him to do anything about it. It's too late because Sweet Arnie kills him.''

"Why?'' she asked very quietly.

"Why does Sweet Arnie kill him?'' She nodded. "Money,'' I said. "It'd have to be money to motivate that man.''

"I don't understand,'' she said. "How would he make money by killing Alan? I'm the one who inherits from Alan. Or will, when I beat this rap.''

"Are you sure?''

"Have I seen the will, you mean? No, but I'm pretty sure. Besides, Alan didn't have any family. And anyway, I think you're being too hard on Arnie.''

I shook my head. "I think he's a creep. How do you see him?''

"He's...he's...'' She hesitated and gazed at the glowing tip of her cigarette for inspiration. She sighed. "He's a survivor. Like me.''

"That's a funny way to describe two of the world's most successful people,'' I objected.

She gave a snort of laughter. "Look around you, big boy. This ain't exactly the Ritz. No, what I mean is—forget about me—it's that he was an immigrant. He's short. He's got lots of fears. He's driven by his fears, you know. And by all sorts of compulsions.''

"Like his gambling?''

"You know about that? Yes, that's what I mean. And in spite of all this he's...he really can be sweet, you know. Thoughtful. Considerate. I sometimes think of him as one of those porcelain dolls. Partly because he's small, I guess. But also because he's hard on the outside, but there's really nothing hard at all inside. And if you drop him, he'll break. Into a thousand pieces.''

I shook my head. "So which script are we running with now?'' I asked her. "You. Or Randy. Or Guberian. Help me out here, Camelia.''

She thought for a minute. "That's not the movie we're making, Johnny. The movie we're making is about getting me out of here. Who killed Alan is for another show.''

Twice in one afternoon I'd been told I was digging too deep. I must be getting close, I thought. Soon I would know. And one of my clients, at least, would be satisfied. Truth be told, I would have preferred it to be Camelia rather than the dead man.

"Vanstone won't like it."

"Does he need to find out?"

"Cagey, are you suggesting I adopt a devious course of action?" Glenda threw a leg over me and put her face an inch away from mine. We were at her place. For a change.

"That would be practicing law without a license, and I wouldn't do that," I said to her lovely eyes. She licked my nose. I threw her off and wiped away the wet. She went after my ear with her tongue. And we wrestled for a bit. She only has a double bed, while mine is king-sized, so the wrestling was more intense than usual.

When the bell rang, we went to our separate corners and lay panting.

"Sleeping?" I asked quietly after a while.

I could feel her shaking her head on the pillow. "Uh-uh," she said. "You?" And she giggled. She took hold of me.

"Insatiableness, thy name is woman," I said.

"I think you mean 'insatiability'," she said.

"Spell it."

"I've already spelled you. It's your turn again."

I didn't think it was possible to agree with her, but apparently it was. She pulled on me and I followed.

"It might already be filed," she said suddenly. I was in her and kissing her neck.

"What?" I was startled into stopping.

"The will. It might already be filed for probate." She urged me forward again.

"Glenda! How the hell can you . . . ?"

"Do two things at once? Just versatile, I guess."

"That's perverted."

"Ooh, Good. Why don't you just concentrate on the one thing, and leave the versatility to me?" She was rocking me from underneath, and I was losing the ability to concentrate in any sense. "Good," she said again, and she put her hands on my ass and pulled me in tight. "Because, if it is, I'll be able to get a hold of it easily. Nice. Nice. Wills... aren't...my...thing...but...oh..."

TWENTY

GLENDA ANSWERED IT. I rolled over and fumbled for my watch, but it was still strapped to my prosthesis over on the other side of her bedroom. The clock on her side of the bed had it as somewhere between seven and five after—it wasn't digital. She was frowning at the phone.

"It's for you."

"Me?"

She handed the thing to me and lay back, groaning. The cord cut across her breasts, and I sat up to lift it. "Yeah?"

"Jantarro?" It was Bench.

"How did you know I was here?"

"Listen, Jantarro. I thought you'd like to know. Your place was broken into."

"Broken into?"

"Actually, I called mostly to see if you were still alive."

"Alive?"

"Wake up, will you?"

"Where are you?"

"Where the hell am I always? I'm at the office. A couple of uniforms from Fifty-five are over at your place. I got the call when Nansen spotted it. He thought I might like to know. I thought you might like to know. Now you know." He hung up.

I stared at the instrument in my hand. Glenda grunted the question from the depths of her pillow. "Got to go," I said.

"Hmm?"

"My place got broken into."

She opened her eyes. "Is your stuff all right?"

"I don't know," I said. But it wasn't my stuff I was worried about.

THE UNIFORMS introduced themselves. One was called Gilbert and the other Cameron. "Three places in all," said Cameron, who was the taller of the two. "One on the floor below and another one four or five doors down." He consulted his notes. "Vlasic," he said, and he looked at me.

I shrugged. I didn't know my neighbors. The place was a shambles. The front door was sprung off its hinges and there was broken glass from the stereo cabinet all over the carpet. Books were flung around on the floor and half of my records were bent in their covers or broken into pieces of black vinyl.

Gilbert saw me take all this in. "Yeah," he said, echoing my unspoken thoughts. "Least they didn't shit in the bathtub or on the floor. They do that a lot. Had one over on Balmoral where they shit on the dining room table—" His buddy cut him off with a hand on his arm. "Yeah," he said again.

I could see from where I stood that stuff from the kitchen shelves was strewn around. My receiver was missing. The color TV would be, too. Then I thought to ask, "The other places, do they look like this, too?"

"No," said Cameron. "That's the funny thing. Clean jobs. Took the usual stuff, but kept it clean." I nodded my head. "Maybe they were looking for a big score and by the time they got to your place they were pissed off," he said.

"*Real* pissed off," said his partner. He crunched across the broken glass and vinyl and stuck his finger in a nice round hole in the living room wall. "Thirty-eight slug came out of here."

"There's another one in the hall," said Cameron calmly, gesturing toward the bedroom. "That's what we wanted to ask you about. About whether there's something going on here, Mr....Mr...."—he consulted his notes—"Jantarro."

Gilbert stood stiff, a hand near his holster, and a piece of glass snapped under his heel.

I THOUGHT ABOUT calling Groper again for some backup, but I decided against it. His kind of help was too hard to control. They'd have treated me like one of the mob bosses and would have made me spend my time on the floor at the back of a big car covered with a hot, itchy rug or, worse, with their own sweaty bodies.

It was Dog again. He or his buddies. And after a couple of feeble passes at nearby apartments for cover, they'd come looking for me with the intention of putting me out of harm's way in a permanent fashion. Because I was digging too deep. Because I was exhuming the body of Alan Laki.

It would have been a death in the course of a robbery. A neutral piece of data to be lost among all the statistics of life in a big city. Too smart for Dog to have thought up on his own.

I called my insurance agent and told him to get his ass over as soon as possible and not to worry about a key. Next I surveyed the ruins of my music library and decided that I'd needed just this push to make the move into compact disk. Then I wandered off to Mike's Open Kitchen for some coffee and grease. It was getting down to endgame, and I'd better make sure it wasn't me that got toppled.

After two eggs over easy, bacon, toast, home fries, and three cups of coffee, I phoned Glenda. No answer at home. But she picked it up at the office. "Cagey. Are you all right? What happened?"

"Just a burglary. But I could use an invite to dinner tonight and for the next little while. They messed up the place a bit."

"Sure," she said.

"And Glenda? Follow up on Laki's will, okay?"

"Sure." She thought for a minutes. "It's not connected, is it?"

"Could be," I said.

"I'll do it right away."

"Call you later."

I paid Mike and walked out. It was already hot.

THIS SATURDAY Guberian Enterprises was locked up tight. Through the big double glass doors I could see the receptionist's desk, neat as a pin, the magazines all fanned out on the tables like a perfect hands of cards, the potted palms with the dull shine of plastic plants. Farther back, the pale lighting fell off and there were only shadows. I would try him at home.

I told the cabbie to wait for me, and I practically ran up the walkway to the front door of Guberian's house. I heard Camelia telling me again that I'd figured the guy wrong, that he was considerate, misunderstood; and again I simply didn't believe her. Someone was gunning for me, and I wanted it to be this particular little runt.

No one answered the doorbell. I stepped into the bushes and peered through the front windows. Dim shapes stood immobile in the gloom. I went back to the door and banged. Nothing happened.

He was probably traveling, I told myself. A man of enterprise travels a lot. L.A. New York. Paris. London. He doesn't wait around at home for Jantarro to arrive and abuse him. He glides away to pleasure himself while Dog and the boys take care of the trouble here in town.

I stood in front of his door for a couple of minutes, trying to regain my perspective. Then I made myself shrug and saunter back down the walkway to where the cabbie, sucking on a coffee and leering at the soft porn page in the *Sun*, was waiting for me.

THE GUARD in the lobby of the Conrad Tower was looking at the same page of the same tabloid. "William Broderick," I told him.

"He expecting you? Sir."

"Yes," I said. I had called from a pay phone on the way downtown. The guard punched in the numbers, and looked between me and the *Sun* girl, while the phone rang. "Jantarro," I told him. He nodded.

He passed the name on to whoever answered upstairs, and I was pointed in the direction of the elevator.

Broderick himself met me as the doors hissed open on his floor. "Jantarro," he said. "What a nice surprise." He was in startlingly white shirtsleeves, and a pair of gold-rimmed half glasses were perched halfway down his nose. He peered at me over them. "To what do I owe the honor?"

"I hate to ask," I said, "but I need a favor. Another one."

"Anything at all," he said, and he began walking us back to his office.

"This will put you one up."

"That a problem for you?" He looked over his shoulder and smiled.

Papers were scattered all over his desk. He saw me looking and grinned. "Saturday," he said. "When I really work."

"I'll be quick. What I need to find out is how Guberian Enterprises is doing. What Guberian is into, roughly. And how well he's doing."

Broderick made a note on a pad. "Shouldn't be too hard," he said. "Is there a rush?"

"I'd take a rough picture if I could get it faster," I said.

"Understood," he said.

I got up and left. This time he didn't show me out.

"GOOD THING you called," Glenda said. "I was just about to knock off."

"It's only noon."

"And it's Saturday."

"Lawyers," I said.

"You lesser breeds have to slog it out. I'm going home to guzzle gin and await the return of the native. When shall I expect you?"

"Hard to say."

"Right. I'm going to guzzle gin in my underwear, if that makes it less hard. Wait. I didn't express that well."

"Lawyers."

"I did discover one thing, though, Cage. The Laki will hasn't been filed for probate yet. And let me tell you, I had to call in a few favors on this one. It's Saturday and the court offices are closed, you know."

"I didn't know."

"Well, they are. But I called Jimmy Vesper, an admirer of mine who toils in the jungle of official file cabinets every moment of his life."

"An admirer?"

"He's sixty-five if he's a day, Cagey."

"Right."

"So he checked. No will filed for probate yet."

"Is that unusual?"

"How should I know? I'm a specialist. I'm now going home to become dissolute. Enjoy." She hung up.

I WENT HOME, TOO.

There was a piece of plywood cut to fit my doorway and a combination lock on a hasp that held it firm. I went in search of the superintendent. He babbled on about all the excitement of the last twelve hours as he came back up with me to reveal the secret of the combination. I told him that I'd be sending someone around to pick up a few of my things, and that until the place was fixed up I'd be staying with a friend.

Inside, there was a note from my insurance agent pinned to the plywood. It explained all the problems that might exist, given the nature of my contract, the particular cause of the damage, and the involvement of the police. It seemed he was especially put off by the presence of bullet holes in my walls.

Before I became self-employed—back in the days when I could fumble a football with either hand—I was paid every two weeks by an insurance company. I know more than it is fitting to know about the workings of that industry, and I smiled as I read between my agent's worried lines.

I called and left a message on his machine to the effect that if I did not receive a check for a named sum within two working days, I would take a series of steps which I described in detail. I bet myself that I'd have it by Monday. Then I called a man I know and arranged for him to come and get rid of the mess, have a new door installed, and deliver a few things to me at Glenda's. He asked no questions, which is why his business was doing so well.

Finally, I poured myself a Scotch and wandered out to the balcony to think. No will filed. Someone still trying to put me out of commission. Camelia more content to sit in jail than she should be. Laki dead and unmourned. Elaine killed, I was sure. I added it all up this way and that. And then I added it all up that way and this. Even after a second Scotch I couldn't get my sums to come out right.

BENCH WAS WORKING on Saturday. Surprise, surprise. "I thought you'd have scared it up," I told him over the phone.

"We did. But it's no big deal."

If I'd had any brains at all, I would have realized a whole lot earlier that Bench would have gotten the will, filed or not. Sometimes my anger slows me down. Sometimes it's my eagerness. Other times my curiosity. But I eventually get there.

"Okay, so what's in it?"

"Everything to charity."

"Huh?"

"You heard me. Everything goes to charity. Old actors' homes. The film department at York University. MS and cancer. That sort of crap."

"Great motive there."

"That's what we figured."

I scratched my head. "So tell me again. What *do* you figure as her motive?"

"I'm only going to say it one more time, Jantarro: we don't need a motive. You know that, for Christ's sake. She hated his guts maybe. Or he looked at her cross-eyed. He was pissed off that she was stealing him blind and she got scared, so she popped him. She didn't know about the will. You pick one."

"Yeah," I said.

And I took my third Scotch on the tour of my wrecked place while I tried to pick one that I liked better.

LUIS ANSWERED the door at the dead man's house. "Señor Jantarro," he said, as he pronounced it with a Spanish *j*.

"I'm looking for Randy Noone, Luis."

He placed his hooded eyes on my face. "He is asleeping, señor." It was three in the afternoon by then. But film people...

"You don't need to wake him, Luis," I said. "I'll do that." And I moved forward.

"Señor," he protested.

I stopped. "I do need to talk to him. No harm, Luis. I'm not going to hurt him."

"You working for Señora Noone."

"That's right," I told him.

He nodded slowly, thoughtfully. "He is sleeping too much," he said, and then he grinned a quick grin.

I sat on the edge of Randy's bed. He stirred. I gripped him by the shoulder, and his eyes came open. "Talk to me, Randy," I said. "Tell me what I need to know."

"Wha—?" He came awake slowly. Then he jerked toward a sitting position, but my arm bounced him down again. He shrank back into the soft bedding and his eyes tried to run out the door. I heard Luis outside in the hall, pretending to dust or something. Staying near in case I broke my promise.

"It's over, Randy. I'm pissed off. This is getting out of hand and you're going to tell me all about it." He began to jerk his head from side to side, and I positioned my plastic hand under his chin. When he realized what was holding him, he froze.

"I don't..." He swallowed. "Nothing..." He swallowed again. "I don't know what you're talking about," he finally managed.

"People are trying to kill me, Randy. And when that happens, I get really upset, and then I'm likely to do anything." I hoped I was menacing. I'm usually not very good at it. Glenda always laughs if I try it when she's in the vicinity. I pushed at his shoulder and his head. "You know what's happening, Randy. I know you do. I can see it in your eyes."

He closed the traitors. Water leaked out of their corners, and his face went a sickly white. "I can't," he breathed.

"What? I can't hear you, Randy."

"I can't."

Now I did know I was right. I took a plunge. "Laki knew about you and Camelia, right? He knew about the film. Isn't that right?"

My plastic hand was too tight up against his throat, and he coughed, so I backed the pressure off a bit. He was crying freely now. "I can't, I can't, I can't," he was wailing. I growled and leaned over him. "I promised," he said. "Can't you understand?"

"Who did you promise? Your sister?" There was no particular reaction. "Guberian?" And that got him. He screwed his eyes shut and tried to shrink out of existence.

TWENTY-ONE

"YOU ARE a most persistent man, Mr. Jantarro." Guberian had a pair of Zeiss binoculars in front of his eyes and was pointing them in the direction of a bunch of horses. As far as I could tell, nothing special was going on with the horses or with the small group of men who were standing around them. But then, for me, horses were things your parents pointed out to you when you were a kid and everyone went for a ride in the car on Sunday. They were something like cows, only different.

"And you're hard to get hold of."

"Not hard enough, it seems. How did you find me?" He was riveted to the binoculars. I squinted across the field to where one horse was being separated from the pack; a particularly short person was holding it by the bridle. I thought they were probably racehorses, which, I gather, are even less like cows.

"It wasn't easy, if that's any comfort. This place"—I waved my arm to take in the four-hundred-acre farm, with its manicured meadows and miles of white picket fences—"is a well-kept secret." Hiding that much land is a trick that only great sums of money can accomplish. Randy knew half of the secret, however: that Guberian owned racehorses and that he kept them on a place just north of King City. And a friend who runs a newspaper in this rural redoubt for the horsey rich was able to guess that one of two farms would be his. The first turned out to be owned by an Arab who had never been there. The second, although listed in his records as being owned by a numbered corporation, proved to be the Guberian homestead.

"I should like it to stay that way, if you please."

"Depends on how pleased I am with what you have to tell me."

Now he lowered his binoculars and turned to look up at me. It was early evening, and although it hadn't really cooled off yet, he was wearing a lavender silk jacket that had a blue stripe down the sleeves, heavy twill jodhpurs, and sturdy brown shoes. What with his diminutive stature and his fancy dress, he managed to look like a jockey, which I guessed was the general idea. Only his glasses detracted from this image, and he focused a lot of anger on my face through their thick lenses.

"Your inquisition, Mr. Jantarro, will have to wait. I should prefer it to be postponed indefinitely. However, that may not be possible. But it *will* be postponed until after I have finished my business here." With a jerk of the field glasses he indicated the dirt track which ran around the field in front of us.

"Going to have a race, are we?"

"No, Mr. Jantarro. Not in the way you imagine, at least. We are running a time trial. My two-year-old, Gandy Dancer, will race against the clock."

"Ah," I said. "But the horse is over there and you're here."

"I will not be riding—" He stopped and tightened his mouth. "Your attempt at humor is offensive. I am perfectly capable of riding a horse, I assure you. I wear this because these are my colors and it is expected that I wear them here."

"I see," I said.

"I very much doubt that. And now I must ask you to confine yourself to the role of silent observer." With that he strode away and left me, one Bally up on a white fence rail and the other on a hummock of what I hoped was only dirt.

Guberian was nervous, that much was clear to me. But whether it was because of the time trial or because of my presence, I couldn't tell. I let myself hope that he could see how keyed-up I was and that it would unsettle him. Randy had spilled the beans, and although some things were clearer, others had become far more obscure. I needed Guberian to help me with this second lot of things, whether he wanted to or not.

I trudged after his little lavender shape and we arrived at the horses at about the same time. There were four of them, and they were a whole lot bigger close up than I had expected. They snorted and stamped and swung their big dangerous rumps around. I kept my distance.

Guberian, unafraid, went right up to the horse that must have been Gandy Dancer and fondled its head. "It's clear," I heard him say to the two men standing next to him.

"Clear from here, too," one of them replied. "What about him?" He nodded in my direction.

Guberian looked at me briefly and then turned away. "He's not important," he said. "Tell Charlie to lock the gates and get up to the rise. If he takes the pickup, Peter can take the van. It will be dark enough soon." The man to whom he had given these instructions removed himself a pace or two from the others and spoke into a walkie-talkie.

"Walk 'em around," another man shouted, and slowly the four horses, handlers and their heads, began to mill in a large circle like beasts involved in a strange rite.

"Won't it be too dark to see anything?" I asked Guberian. He tossed me an irritated glance.

"That's the whole idea, Mr. Jantarro. We do our time trials either very early in the morning or just after the sun has set. There are people who would be very happy to be able to discover how fast Gandy Dancer really is. In this fashion we are able to keep the information to ourselves."

"How can *you* tell?"

"We have infrared equipment. Now, Mr. Jantarro, no further interruptions." I wondered what made him think that the spies weren't similarly equipped; but perhaps Charlie and Peter and others were supposed to patrol the marches for these interlopers.

Things went quite quickly after that. The horses were mounted and ridden onto the track, where they walked off into the dusk for a circuit or two. Then they were ridden faster—that loping thing that horses do—for another circuit or so. Whereupon footlights were turned on at the base of all the fenceposts and the ground glowed softly. Disembodied hooves and lower legs flailed at the dirt; the horses drew abreast of each other right in front of us; and suddenly everything changed. I could feel the drumming through my soles. The noise was exciting. I found myself leaning forward over the fence, straining to see what was happening. Thunder receded, approached, and then there was the blur of leg bits in lighted dust. Everyone was shouting and cheering. And it was over.

Guberian went around pounding the others on the back just like a regular guy. Voices were raised in mutual congratulation. The horses came back and everyone crowded around Gandy Dancer. The jockey dismounted and there was another round of back slapping.

Even in the faint light of evening I could see that when Guberian finally came up to me he was grinning from ear to ear. Maybe Camelia was right. Maybe I had misjudged him. He looked not at all evil now. He looked, in fact, like a happy little boy. But then, if Randy hadn't just been confabulating, I'd got a fair bit of rethinking to do generally.

"It went well?" I asked.

"It did indeed!" I thought for a second he would try to pound me on the back as well. "This is a magnificent animal, Mr. Jantarro, let me tell you. He will bring great honor to the colors."

"Great money, too?"

"Beyond doubt. Beyond doubt." The thought seemed to sober him. But then his bonhomie returned. "We are having a small celebration up at the house. You are welcome to join us, Mr. Jantarro."

"That's very kind," I said. "And perhaps after that we can talk."

"Perhaps," he said. "Perhaps."

There was champagne, of course. Pol Roger. I accepted a glass, drank half of it, and waited for the headache that I always get from bubbly. The farmhouse was a large, rambling affair, and Guberian had obviously turned a designer loose inside it. Everywhere I wandered, there were calculated effects, most of which were intended to suggest a long, worthy, and English heritage. While the horsemen popped corks in what would have had to be called the drawing room, I ran a finger along the rows of leatherbound books in the "library." Macaulay was there and so was Carlyle. Gibbon and Mill, Burke and Bentham. I was blowing the dust off a volume of Disraeli's writings when Guberian entered.

"A first edition, Mr. Jantarro. Take care, I entreat you." His face was flushed and his beady eyes shone like bits of anthracite. He had discarded the satin jacket to reveal a Viyella shirt in a subdued Prince of Wales check.

I put the book back. "I know about it," I said.

He continued across the carpet and hoisted himself into the desk chair, which was raised to put him at normal sitting height. "About the purchase of the Suez, Mr. Jantarro? About Gladstone and Queen Victoria?"

I settled into a leather wingback chair that faced his desk. "I spoke to Randy. He was..."

Guberian sighed. "Forthcoming? I suspected that something like that had happened. It was always a risk. May I say, you must never play poker, Mr. Jantarro. Take it from an expert. You would be cleaned out in half an hour. Your face is a dumb show of your thoughts, so to speak."

"So naturally, I came to you," I said, crossing a leg over my knee.

"A drink?" he asked. I shook my head. "I will," he said. He pushed a button on his desk and a man came in. "A cognac, Peter," he said. "Nothing for Mr. Jantarro." Peter left as quietly as he had come. Guberian looked at me for a moment. "What can I tell you?"

"Randy makes pictures," I said. "Words are not his strong suit. I want to hear it from you."

He sighed again, took off his glasses, and polished them with a cloth he brought out of his shirt pocket. "A sordid tale, is it not, Mr. Jantarro? But a tale not without its ironies. Where would you have me begin?" He held the glasses in front of the green shaded lamp on his desk, checked for imperfections, and then, apparently satisfied, put them back on his face.

"Why don't you start with your resentment of Alan Laki?"

"Resentment? I should rather have said hatred. The man was malevolent, overbearing, cruel—and arrogant to the point of psychosis. Yes, that would not be an incorrect diagnosis. He delighted in finding weaknesses and bearing down on them until the owner was at breaking point. And of course he had the psychotic's infallible sense of where others were vulnerable."

"In your case, that would be your gambling."

Guberian made a dismissive gesture with a hand. "My obsession with gambling, my vanity about my height, my insecurity at being a Mediterranean immigrant, my desire for acceptance." He turned away. "My love for Camelia," he said quietly. "I am not without self-knowledge, you see, Mr. Jantarro. He rode these and other of my flaws the way that Bruce rode Gandy Dancer tonight. Skillfully and with only the lightest touch of the whip."

"He got you to give up your controlling interest in Lakipix."

"He did indeed. I had essayed a wager that proved to be disastrous. He loaned me the wherewithal to cover my bet and promised that I should have the time necessary to repay him. Had he given me time, I would have been able to repay him, and, of course, he knew this. So he called in the loan within a matter of weeks. It was a formal loan. Supported with promissory notes. I was over a barrel. No, that suggests some room for movement. I was fixed. The sole asset I had—the one he required—was my controlling interest in Lakipix. And so he obtained it."

"And that was enough reason to kill him."

Guberian straightened his shoulders. "Please, Mr. Jantarro. Such a reversal would have been merely an annoyance. No, I put it too lightly. It would have been a source of chagrin and no small amount of anger. But it was the way in which he delighted in my discomfiture. The way in which he dissembled and persisted to the end in maintaining that he had been without choice. It was his cruelty, Mr. Jantarro, that merited death."

"So you formed judge and jury and sentenced him."

"Originally, it was to have been more subtle than death. Originally, it was to have been a movie. And wouldn't that have been delightful? A movie, you see, in which his wife, the celebrated and lovely Camelia Noone, played a leading role. He would have been shamed, mocked. And not incidentally, the movie would have made money. May still make money."

There was a gentle cough behind me. I turned to look past the black wings of my chair. Peter had returned with the brandy and with a shotgun. He pulled back the hammer, and with me as the center, he made a big circle to get to Guberian's desk. He put down the balloon glass and turned his full attention on me.

"This would be very stupid, Arnie," I said. "Lots of people know I'm here."

"Yes," he said. He turned to Peter. "Put the hammer down and sit over there." He said to me: "Peter is protective. And I must say, I am uncertain as yet about where you stand. This causes me some…anxiety." He smiled a self-depreciating smile. "Yet another flaw, I am afraid."

Peter did as he was told, and I breathed a little easier. The tiny .38 under my armpit felt as though it was throbbing. "Let's finish the story," I said, "and then we can talk about my standing."

"A commendable openness of mind, Mr. Jantarro." Peter let the muzzle of the shotgun drop; I moved my hand two inches closer to my left side. "Where were we? Oh yes. The movie. He discovered it just before the end. Perhaps I was naive to imagine that it could be made under his nose, so to speak. Nevertheless, he discovered it and began immediately to take certain steps to ensure its ultimate failure. He would have stopped at nothing, you understand. And however good a film may be, however popular the talent, making a movie successful is never guaranteed. His death was then the only option."

"You were all agreed," I said.

"Oh yes. Camelia and Randy and I were as one. Camelia the most fervent. She was for killing him from the first, perhaps because the prospect of acting once again—even under her brother's direction—was simply too frightening. And when she broached the matter with Randy, the man was galvanized. He begged for the chance to be the one who actually did it.

"However much he had harmed me, he had hurt them so much more. Particularly Camelia. He was incapable of having children, you know. Perhaps it was God's way of stopping his corrupt line. But at the first, Camelia wanted so to have children. She pleaded with him to let them adopt. He would tease her with the prospect of his consent, and then always he would change his mind just when she thought there was a chance of success. He broke her heart in this way."

"Why didn't she simply leave him?"

"I begged her to do just that. But at the beginning she was too much his creature. He had forced her into fame, you know. And in many senses he owned her. And when finally she surmounted the role of victim, revenge was uppermost in her mind. She would leave him by his death. That was what she wanted."

"So what went wrong?" I asked. Peter's gun was now pointing at the floor; he was following the words as they poured out of Guberian. I had my hand halfway up my chest and could feel the bottom of the holster.

"I wish to God that I knew," Guberian said. "It was to have been later that day. We were to foregather and Camelia was to go in to lure him out, to a spot along King Street we had picked. Randy was to have clubbed him from behind. It would have looked like a mugging, a robbery. All our alibis were set.'' He turned his hands palms up on the desktop and stared down at them. ''But things went wrong from the beginning. I was delayed, arriving late. The others were frantic, practically hysterical. I calmed them both down, and Camelia went in. A minute later she came running out. 'He's dead,' she was screaming. 'He's already dead.' And so, of course, he was.'' Guberian turned his hands over and pressed them hard on the wood.

I slipped my gun out of its holster. ''Drop the shotgun, Peter,'' I said. Startled, he let it clatter to the floor at his feet. ''Kick it away,'' I instructed him. He did as he was told.

''Think!'' said Guberian, leaning toward me across the desk. ''Only think! Turn me in and you seal Camelia's fate. Is that what you want? Is it?''

''If she killed him, it is,'' I said.

''But she didn't. That is what I have been telling you.''

''She came out and said she found him dead. Maybe she killed him while she was in there.''

''There wasn't time. I assure you, Mr. Jantarro, I have gone over this in my mind many times. When you have done so yourself, you, too, will see. There wasn't time. She wasn't in possession of the poison. She was carrying nothing in which it could have been concealed.''

''They could have killed him before you got there.''

It seemed that the thought had never occurred to Guberian. ''Oh no,'' he protested. ''She was shocked beyond measure by the discovery. Of that I am certain.''

''You certainly went out of your way last week to push me in their direction. Why should I believe you now?''

He made a quick nervous gesture with his hand. ''Mr. Jantarro. You were dashing around like a rhino. You would have explored all those possibilities anyway. And most important, I had to keep your mind off any possible...collaboration among us.''

I stared at him. ''Well, one of you did it,'' I said.

He sat back. ''Not necessarily.''

"It would be too much of a coincidence," I said. "No. One of you jumped the gun."

"But which, Mr. Jantarro? If what you say is true. Which of us? And more to the point, was it Camelia? Can you be sure of that? Because if not, you will only seal her fate in ignorance."

It was my turn now to lower a gun. I took the shotgun from the floor, broke it, and took out the shell. As I went through the laborious process of making my plastic arm do my bidding, I thought. What Guberian was urging was wrong. I should have called Bench from here. Even if they denied everything, Bench would have been able to squeeze Randy the way I had, and he'd roll over for them as obediently as a pet. But I didn't know which of them had done it. And until I could prove that it wasn't—or that it *was*—Camelia, I would only be handing the cops the means to put her away for a long, long time.

"All right," I said.

"Good," said Guberian. "Good! You've done the right thing for her. I'm not going anywhere, so you needn't worry on that score. My horse is here." He smiled at me. "Oh," he said, "you won't easily be able to get a taxi up here at this time of night. Peter will drive you home." He saw my look. "You may sit in the back, if that will make you feel better."

He came with me to the door. "Find out who did it, Mr. Jantarro. If that's what it will take to settle your mind, then find out who did it. That is what will be best for Camelia."

TWENTY-TWO

THE STRANGENESS of Glenda's bed woke me early Sunday morning, and I lay quietly in the perfume of her room, mulling over what I had learned the day before. But after half an hour or so of drifting this way and that, my thinking ended where it had begun: any of the three of them could have killed Laki. I sighed and rolled over.

Glenda stirred. "I thought it was you," she said sleepily. "It felt like you." I had made Guberian's Peter drop me off blocks away from where Glenda lived, and had taken a taxi the rest of the way. Glenda had already been asleep when I let myself in.

"Bagels, cream cheese, lox," I said. I kissed her hair.

"Mmm. What happened to coffee?"

"All right, all right. You win. Coffee, too."

She struggled to a half-sitting position. "Where?" she asked.

"Moishe's Dairy," I said. "It's near Edwards Books, and I want to get something for John Scott to read." Sunday was the day for my visit to my father's friend.

"Right," she said. She ran her hands through her hair and made all the waking-up moves she usually makes.

"And Glenda?" I said. She stopped on her way to the bathroom. Her body was lit by the morning sun and it shone like something gold. I sat up myself. "Some advice, too."

"Giving or taking?" she asked.

"You giving," I said, "and me taking."

"Bagels, cream cheese, lox, coffee, *and* advice. You're asking one fuck of a lot, Cagey." She pretended to frown and it only made her look lovelier.

"There's more," I said. "Come with me to Sunnybrook."

She widened her eyes for just a second. "To see John Scott?"

"Please." It would be a first. A long-overdue first.

"Sure," she said, and she smiled as if it was nothing. And then she scooted to the john and started singing almost as soon as the door was shut.

MOISHE'S was overcrowded as usual. Steam rose from the shiny giant urns of coffee and loud talk boiled up from all of the tables. I was finished with my second bagel and my recap of the Laki case. I peered at Glenda over the rim of my coffee cup.

"Motives all over the place," she said. "But all emotional. I'd have preferred something harder-edged, like money."

"Everything goes to charity. It's in the will, according to Bench."

"Yeah," she said. She glanced at the counter in the front of the restaurant; she was debating whether or not to have a second bagel and cream cheese. "Insurance?" she said.

"I thought of that, being a former toiler in the insurance scam myself. Camelia gets a small amount under one policy—comparatively small, that is. And Guberian apparently didn't have Laki insured the way that most business partners insure each other. Maybe because he's only got a minority interest in Lakipix now. Or maybe he couldn't afford the premiums."

Glenda sighed. The bagel had lost the battle to the waistline. She gave her full attention to me. "Camelia could have done it, even though Guberian says she didn't have the time. She could have done it earlier, before he showed up. And anyway, how long does it take to poison somebody."

"And that's another thing."

"She could persuade him to take the poison?"

"Yeah."

"Another strike against Camelia." Glenda glanced at the food counter. "She had access to the stuff through her boyfriend—what was his name?"

"Dennis," I told her. I thought of the brawl in the Parkdale Tavern and I shuddered. "Michael Dennis."

"He could have done it because she asked him to. He was really hot for her, was he?" I nodded. Alan Laki was the only man I'd ever heard about who wasn't hot for her. "She could have had access to those bikers through him, too. Arranged to have you beaten up when she found you couldn't be controlled by Vanstone even though you were supposed to be working for her."

"Any of them could have got him to drink some stuff," I argued. "Randy, Guberian. Maybe they forced him to drink it. Remember what Chin said about the chipped tooth."

"Guberian?" said Glenda. "I thought you said he was a shrimp."

"He is," I conceded.

The waitress came by and Glenda raised a hand. "Cheesecake," she said, careful not to look at me. "Two pieces," she said. The waitress dashed off to fetch the calories.

"So?" I asked her. "Who did it?"

"Camelia," said Glenda.

"You're only saying that because I'm . . ."

"Gaga over her?"

"That's putting it rather strongly."

"She just feels right, Cage."

"Yeah," I said morosely.

"Or Randy," she added. I looked up. "The quiet one. Repressed. Still waters and all that crap." Glenda warmed to her notion. She wriggled a bit in her seat. "That's why Camelia is content to sit it out in the detention center. She's covering for her brother. She figures she'll be acquitted because of this Michael Dennis thing. But it's worth the risk. For her brother." I brightened. I liked that idea a whole lot better. "You did say his movie had killing in it." She spread her hands. "He got the chance to act out his fantasy."

The cheesecake came and we tucked into it with refills of coffee to wash it down. As we leaned back to rest, I said as matter-of-factly as possible, "Let's go to a hotel tonight."

Glenda gave me a puzzled look. "A dirty weekend?" she said with a half grin. "You've left it a bit late. It's Sunday already, Cage."

"You know me," I said. "Always a bit behind the times."

She frowned. "There's something else, isn't there?" Her frown cleared. "The break-in at your apartment. You're worried. About the killer coming after you. That's it, isn't it."

I started to shake my head. "There's no—"

"And you're worried about me. If we stay at my place . . ."

"I just want to be sure," I said.

"A hotel," she said. She shook her head. She looked at me and sighed. "Okay. But only for a couple of days. I'm not going to run and hide every time you stir up a hornet's nest. I won't live that way."

"Thanks," I said. "Just for a couple of days."

She got up from the table and paused for a moment in thought. "It could have been Guberian," she said consideringly. "Even though you don't like him, it could have been him."

"Thanks a whole lot for the advice," I said.

"Don't mention it." She was grinning. I put my arm around her. "I wonder why the will hasn't been filed yet," she said as we left Moishe's.

"JUST PUT THEM DOWN anywhere, lad." John Scott didn't even look at me, let alone at the stack of books I had brought. His attention was devoted to Glenda. He wheeled his chair forward without wincing at the pain. "I'm John Scott," he said. He offered a gnarled hand for her to take.

"Glenda Redway." They held each other's hands and smiled. I felt supernumerary.

"A walk?" I proposed.

"I've been looking forward to meeting you," said Glenda.

"And I you," said Scott.

"You were a friend of Cagey's father."

"Cagey? Is that what you call him? It's what his father used to call him, you know."

"I think all his friends call him that," said Glenda.

"It's a lovely day," I said.

"He has friends, then," said Scott.

Glenda laughed. "He's turning out fairly well," she said. "All things considered."

"I understand that you are a lawyer."

"Is that bad?"

"I certainly feel like a walk," I said.

"I shouldn't think that anything you do would be bad," said Scott. "Although, to be frank, I do have more than a few reservations about the law and its bureaucrats."

"Why don't we go for a walk," Glenda said. "You can tell me about them. Shall I push your chair?"

"Let John push," Scott said. "Walk next to me so I can see you."

And so it went. They nattered on as if I weren't there, and to tell the truth, I wasn't for much of the time. I was busy rotating three faces before my mind's eye: the beautiful face of Camelia Noone Laki, the unfinished one of her unhappy brother Randy, and Guberian's small, nasty countenance. I tried to look the conspirators in the eyes, to see through to the truth of Laki's death. But they only stared back at me in turn, mocking me, I thought, challenging me to untangle the mess they had made.

"Don't you agree?" Glenda asked me at one point. We were sitting on a bench under a big Norway maple, both of us facing Scott. I shrugged, lost.

"It's not a full life," said Scott. "Not a constructive one."

"It involves a search for the truth," Glenda said. They were obviously arguing.

"But about others," Scott objected. "It's not the self-examined life."

"No one comes at that directly," said Glenda. "We all look in by first looking out."

"And then what does he find?" asked Scott. They were talking about me, I realized. "Corruption, deception, violence."

"That sounds to me like the same kinds of things that you find when you consider society from your viewpoint."

"But I have a way of understanding it and a means for eradicating the evils. What does this offer him?"

"Individuals," said Glenda. "Not masses. Individuals with human faces." She was defending me with some heat.

"Bah!" said Scott. "False individualism, faked differences, phony uniqueness. Until the governing matrix is shattered, nothing truly individual can flourish."

"Who's winning?" I asked.

"Be quiet," said Scott.

"No one," said Glenda.

"How about an ice cream?" I offered.

"HE'S VERY FOND of you," said Glenda. She was going around the hotel room touching things, adjusting them slightly. I was lying on the bed admiring her.

"I'm fond of him, too," I said.

She opened the desk drawer and took out the Gideon Bible, the cardboard folder of stationery, and the white ballpoint pen with "Windsor Arms" written on it. Then she put them all back again. "He loves you, really."

"The son he never had," I said.

She turned toward me, wonderfully desirable in her delicate, skimpy underwear. "Don't be glib, Cagey. It's more than that. That, too. But..."

"Yes," I said. I found myself reluctant to say out loud that I loved John Scott. I cleared my throat. "My father," I said, and then I hesitated. Glenda pretended to interest herself in the arrangement of dried flowers on the coffee table. "Died," I said. "Died before I...we...got around to...to...talking about things like that."

"Things like that," she said. She got her bathrobe and slipped it on. It's a plain gingham thing. Unattractive. She sat in a chair and looked at me.

"Okay," I told her. "About love. We never did say that we loved each other. It was..."

"Taboo?"

"No." I could feel myself getting annoyed for no good reason. "No, it wasn't taboo; it's just that it was understood."

"Taken for granted."

"If you like. I knew he...he loved me. And he knew, too."

"That you..."

"That I...loved him. We just didn't have to say it."

"Odd, isn't it?"

"What's odd?" I was really uncomfortable. I had sat up on the bed, I realized, and had leaned back against the headboard with my knees drawn up and my arm crossed tight over my chest.

Glenda came and sat on the edge of the bed. She put a hand on my leg. "Odd how hard it is to say 'I love you.'"

"I love you," I said.

She shook her head a little. "Not for a man and a woman. Too easy, maybe." She smiled at me and traced a pattern on my skin. I thought maybe it was the word "love."

"For a man to say to a man?"

She frowned. "I don't know, Cage. I guess. Or for people to say to their parents." She looked me in the eyes. "Yes, maybe for men. Generally for men."

"I love you," I said.

She patted me. "Let's eat," she said.

We went down to dinner in the Grill Room, came back up, made love, and fell into sleep. I woke from a dream at two. I had been the victim of a crime and the cops had shown me a lineup. Through the one-way glass I saw a row of men wearing jackets and ties and pantyhose. The man on the far left was immensely fat, and the others decreased in size and corpulence until the suspect on the far right was short and skinny. It was my father next to me, urging me to be correct, to be precise. I began to feel dizzy and was led away by a nurse who looked like Elaine Younger. "There is danger," she said to me, "everywhere. Especially in running risks."

I looked at Glenda's form, indistinct in the dark. Danger everywhere, I thought. I tried to see out the window, but it only gave onto a courtyard and there was nothing to see.

TWENTY-THREE

WE HAD BREAKFAST in the hotel room, and then while Glenda hurriedly prepared to do battle with the forces of law, grumbling all the while about not having the right things to wear, I stalled over more coffee and the newspaper. The forces of lawlessness didn't keep to schedules, and any battling I might do could wait until I was good and ready. Besides, it helps to know who your enemy is, if you're thinking of combat, and I still couldn't choose among the three.

I nibbled on cold toast, sipped cold coffee, and listened to a lugubrious *Moldau* on the cheap radio built in to the hotel TV. The paper was full of the fact that we were bound to win the pennant, even though Fernandez had been limping almost as badly as I play patty-cake. I thought of Paulie Mac's tip. And that reminded me that I should press Broderick today for the information on Guberian Enterprises so that I could pay off Paulie for his help.

The bridge column described a perfect partial elimination play, which sounded exactly like something I could have used; but although I studied it for a good five minutes, the essence of the thing eluded me. Glenda kissed me on the forehead, en passant, and fled in a churning of perfume and purple linen. I sank lower in the hotel easy chair and regarded the detritus of breakfast as if it were the slough of despond.

Some time later—the radio was now playing a tinny version of a Beethoven trio—I forced myself upright and worked at retrieving my messages from the answering machine in my apartment. For once I did it right and found that my insurance company was more than happy to do its share in restoring my place to its former glory, that Vanstone was demanding my presence, that someone by the name of Unger wanted to hire me, and that the lab had finished working on the prints on the stuff from Elaine's.

I called the lab and the guy I deal with, Tom Polter, answered. "What do you have, Tom?"

"Hairbrush and phone gave us six good digits, and reckoning them as belonging to the occupant, we picked up four on the whisky bottle, ditto the drinking glass, and two on the pill bottle."

"Huh." Okay, so she'd handled the bottle. She'd poured for herself. The barbiturates would have been dissolved in the Scotch. She wouldn't have known that. And as for the pill bottle, because it was hers it was only natural that her prints would be on it. "Other prints?" This was the big question.

"Zero," Tom said. "Zilch."

"Too smeared?"

"Not present. Absent, as in not there at all."

"Shit," I said.

"Not entirely."

"How's that?"

"Think, Jantarro." Everybody was bent on my improvement.

"Wiped clean," I said. But that only reinforced my suspicion that Elaine had been murdered. What I needed was evidence that pointed in a particular direction.

"Possible," he said. "But if I was going to kill somebody this way, I'd try to make it look as natural as possible—make it look like suicide, right?"

"Right."

"So I wouldn't wipe. I'd handle the bottle with gloves. This is basic. Every kid knows this from the tube."

"What's your point, Tom?" He was sitting on something. I could hear the gloating in his voice.

Undeterred, he was going for mileage on this. "That way the ordinary prints from the liquor-store people would be on the bottle, right?"

"Right, Tom. What have you got?"

"Well, I wouldn't have noticed except that the bottle was so clean. Really clean. See, it wasn't bought at a liquor store, so it wasn't really handled at all. It's not part of the normal import stuff."

"What do you mean?"

"It's part of a batch specially imported directly from the distillery by... by... I've got it here in my notes... by Penner Brothers. Over on Adelaide Street."

"How can you tell?"

"I would never have noticed, except for the clean bottle. They get their little sticker put on the back at the factory—and feature this, Jantarro—each crate they import has a different set of numbers. I never knew that. Did you? Your unlucky bottle was part of crate number... oh-three-three-seven-four-one-eight-two."

"And Penner knows who they sold it to, am I right?"

"You're catching on. Hey, I hope you don't mind me playing detective like this. It's a real kick."

"Tom."

"Yeah?"

"Who, Tom?"

"A guy named Laki. Alan Laki."

"I'M NOT SAYING anything more." Randy was truculent, half-plastered, unshaven, and slumped in front of the big stereo Sony, the channel changer held tightly in his sweaty hand as though it were a magic sword.

"I just want a drink," I told him, smiling. "A Scotch."

He grinned sloppily. "Man after my own heart," he said. He made it to his feet on the second try. I tagged along with him all the way over to the liquor cabinet. "Scotch," he reminded himself. He reached inside the shiny mahogany and pulled out a bottle of Chivas.

"Johnnie Walker," I said. "If you have it."

"Johnnie Walker," he repeated and put the Chivas bottle back, banging it clumsily against the delicate door. He fumbled inside and withdrew the brand I wanted. I took it from him. "Help yourself," he said.

I turned the bottle around and there on the back was the little label Tom Polter had told me about. I got out my notepaper and compared numbers. It was dead clear: Elaine had drunk her last from a bottle of Laki's Scotch.

I considered Randy. "Elaine Younger," I said to him.

"Easter Bunny," he replied, hoisting his cut crystal tumbler in a parody of a toast.

"You know her, Randy?"

He frowned in a drunken attempt to understand what was going on around him. "Gossip," he said eventually. "Gossip column . . . column . . . writer." He beamed at me with wet lips. "Right?"

It wasn't Randy. This disorganized protoperson, this limp standard-bearer of ineffectualness could not have doctored her bottle and covered it up with such a convincing act of innocence. "Anybody borrow any Scotch from you recently, Randy?" I asked.

"Everybody drinks," he said, and in his incongruously booming bass it sounded like a judgment from above.

"Yeah, but not everybody buys."

He looked affronted. "You should talk," he said.

"Who borrowed a bottle?"

He waved the hand that held his drink and slopped half of it onto the broadloom. "Don't know," he said. "Everybody. Fucking Vanstone drinks like a fish. Thinks he owns the place. Fucking lawyer."

"Who else?"

"Go away," he said. He pronounced the words with exaggerated care. Then he weaved his way over to the couch and fell backward onto it.

Vanstone, I thought? Not one of the happy trio I had come to know and suspect? Stranger things have happened.

I PHONED Broderick from Laki's house before the cab came. He said he had some stuff for me, if I didn't mind it rough. I said things were rough enough right now that it would fit right in.

Then we were balancing coffee cups on our laps again. "You think you've got it bad," he said. He raised coffee to his lips. He was once again in a two-thousand-dollar suit, a glowing shirt of pure white Egyptian cotton, shoes that shone as if, inside, his feet were alight, and a tie so subtle it would never be remembered. If business was a confidence game, he had it won from the start.

"Guberian's in trouble?"

He smiled with his eyes, finished sipping his coffee, and then deliberately put the cup back on the saucer with a brittle-sounding china click. "Guberian Enterprises," he said quietly, "exists in name only. There is the bare minimum of assets surplus to liabilities, and I have sufficiently grave doubts about the true ownership of enough of the company's assets that I would bet they've been bankrupt for some time now."

I found this hard to believe. "I've seen his house," I protested. "He has four hundred acres and racehorses."

Broderick shook his head, presumably at my stupidity. "I would guess that when you come across a corpse in your line of work, it lies still; but in business things still twitch and stay upright for a surprisingly long time after death. Smoke and mirrors. Other people's hopes, credulity." He set his cup and saucer on the unblemished surface of his perfect desk. "You're dealing with a zombie, Jantarro. Stand clear when it falls."

"STAND CLEAR when it falls." I used Broderick's line with Paulie Mac. By giving him what I had learned from my financial expert, I had repaid him for the help he had given me.

He pursed his fat lips into an unlovely bow. The toy soldier in his hand jumped into the air twice, as he let his annoyance show. I shouldn't have believed him when he told me at the beginning that although Guberian was a heavy bettor, the man's downfall wouldn't bother him. He was bothered and showing it. "I see," he said.

"Hate to be the bearer of bad news," I said. I resisted the temptation to check my watch, even though I had a one o'clock appointment with Vanstone, made just after I'd seen Randy. There are certain formalities that have to be played out with people like Paulie Mac.

He inclined his head a fraction of an inch, acknowledging my unhappiness. "Used to chop their heads off," he said. "You read that? Used to kill the messenger."

I nodded. "I heard about that. Primitive custom."

"Yeah," he said. The toy soldier was bent, and he was trying to straighten him. He sighed a gust of wind from that giant chest of his. "It comes, it goes," he said. "Thanks, Jantarro."

I was on my feet. "No sweat," I said. "Anytime."

He smiled south of his eyes. "Your case," he said, "how's it going?"

"I'm getting there," I said not too convincingly.

"Don't bullshit me, Jantarro. You look like you're up a stump."

"Maybe," I said. "If I am, it's getting lower to the ground."

"Just don't fall off."

"Stand clear if I do," I said, and we both laughed.

"AND NOW, Mr. Jantarro, what have you to report?" Severe expectation best described the look on Vanstone's face: he was hungry but ready to upbraid the first person to tell him that.

"Later," I told him. "I'll report by the end of the day. I'm here with some questions."

His face darkened. "It's far too late," he blustered. "You promised, Mr. Jantarro. You gave an undertaking. By Sunday, you said."

I held up a hand to stem the flow. "A simple question. Do you know Elaine Younger?"

"Never heard of her in my life," he said. "Now, look, Jantarro, I've put up with all of the tomfoolery I'm going to take . . . wait," he said, interrupting himself. "Isn't she the newspaper woman, the gossip columnist? She just died, didn't she?" He narrowed his eyes. "That's it, Jantarro. You're fired. I will not have you wasting your time over some . . . some . . . *person* when our client—*my* client—wastes away in jail. It is a matter of complete and utter indifference to me that Elaine Younger suffered the fate that comes to us all. I will not have you charging off in this direction and that like some rogue elephant without a brain."

As Vanstone ran on, I realized that something had happened to switch on his lawyer mechanism to full blast. It wasn't simply the normal indignation you'd expect from a worried pompous twit. And then something Glenda had said came to me as clearly as if she'd been with me in the room. I smiled sweetly at the gabbling mouthpiece. "I wonder why the will hasn't been filed yet," I said.

That stopped him cold. I might have smacked him in the face. "I don't know what you're talking about," he said in a voice that betrayed him six ways to Sunday. "Will? What will would that be?"

"The will that Alan Laki made. With you as his lawyer, I think."

"The police have it."

"A copy," I said. "Maybe." Things were starting to fit together faster than I could make sense of them. "You could still have filed it. The cops wouldn't have cared."

"There is time," he objected. "I have six months. It's best to clear this"—he waved a trembling hand—"this mess out of the way first."

"And why is that? If the will leaves everything to charity. If it really does. The real will, that is."

"You have no reason—" he said, and then he stopped. He swallowed and tried again. "You have no reason to suspect . . . look, Jantarro—"

This time I cut him short. "Give it up, Vanstone. You make a lousy con. Do you tell me, or do I ruin your career? It's that simple."

He fell apart in front of my eyes, the way that witnesses are supposed to do under Perry Mason's questioning. His eyes went in different directions, his mouth tried to do too many things at once, and his hands couldn't decide whether to flee or to apply comfort to his sweating body. And all the while I kept at him with calm directions for him to tell me all about it. Eventually, like a frightened kid, he came around.

He told me about it. Then, with the enthusiasm that often follows relief, he pressed into my hands a copy of the last will and testament of Alan Laki, pointing out the terms and elaborating on them in great detail.

I had my answer. Even Bench would have had to agree. But because it would take only one more step to sew it up tight, to give me the pleasure of handing it to him trussed and trimmed, I declined to make the call I might have made. Instead, I phoned to arrange a meeting, and then I called for a cab.

When I left, Vanstone was shaking and patting himself to make sure he was still there. I was whistling through my grinning teeth. *I've got a lovely bunch of coconuts.*

TWENTY-FOUR

I NOTICED THINGS, on the drive over to Guberian's house. I noticed that the sky was so blue it should have drawn everything in the world up to it. I noticed that the trees were impossibly green and robust. That the cab was new and spotless. That my plastic hand didn't really look so bad. That the afternoon was warm, pleasantly warm.

I had won.

And it was a damn good thing, too. Because Guberian would have kept on trying to kill me.

Vanstone had confessed that at the time Laki had extorted control of Lakipix from Guberian part of the deal had been that Laki would remake his will and fix it by a contract so he couldn't change it afterward, at least so long as Guberian was alive. Vanstone explained all this in frustrating detail. Laki was to leave the lion's share of his assets to Guberian, and smaller sums to his wife and brother-in-law.

And there was the motive, as simple and as classic as any one could wish. Money.

Vanstone had agreed with Guberian to suppress the real will for the time being, to let the cops go on believing that the earlier will in which he cut out his family was the latest one. He had explained to me in nervous spurts that with Camelia as his client, and given that the true will provided for her, he had no obligation to give the cops evidence that could be used against her. That there was no conflict of interest between Guberian and Camelia—not really. After all, he had said, she was bound to be acquitted thanks to what I had uncovered about Michael Dennis; she might even be released after the preliminary inquiry, he had said. Didn't I think that was right, he had asked me pathetically? He wouldn't tell me how much Guberian had paid him.

It didn't seem plausible at first. One thing about Laki had become clear to me: he was nobody's fool. And if he's ha

Guberian by the short-and-curlies, as everyone seemed to think he'd had, then why would he have agreed to any demand from Guberian, let alone one that might benefit the little killer so greatly? And worse, wouldn't he have been smart enough to see this as the perfect invitation to murder that it turned out in fact to be?

Apparently, according to Vanstone, Guberian had been prepared to dig in his heels and fight the debt to Laki, promissory note or not. He would ultimately have lost, but he might have gained just enough time to raise the money elsewhere and prevent Laki's takeover of Lakipix; moreover, the fight might have resulted in the company's going into receivership, and that was something Laki wasn't prepared to risk. The business with the will, along with one or two other smaller concessions, was worked out by way of a compromise, and curiously enough it had been suggested by Laki himself. Vanstone seemed to think that it had been Laki's way of showing Guberian that, even faced with his militant determination, he could lead the little man around by the nose. Laki knew that Guberian had a soft spot and perhaps more for his wife, and that by offering to change his will so as to leave Camelia something, he could obtain Guberian's compliance.

It had been Laki's insult to announce that he would leave Guberian the lion's share, a way both of taunting him by putting great wealth in his name when it was clear that the chances of Laki's dying first were slim and of demonstrating his contempt for Guberian by saying clearly that Guberian wouldn't have the guts and the wit to collect on the possibility through murder. When Vanstone had mentioned the risk, Laki had laughed. "I know my enemies," he had said. He had held out his expressive hands to show how still they were. "See?" he had said. "I'm scared to death."

I gazed out of the window of the taxi at the brightly colored shapes of summer that sped by. My client had miscalculated, and now it was up to me to balance things out. To get Camelia out of jail. To take a killer.

"I KNOW ABOUT the will," I told Guberian. He was still in his suit, fresh from the office. I'd offered him the choice of meeting places and he'd chosen his home.

"Yes," he said with uncharacteristic meekness. He was ne[r]vous, and, unusual for him, sweating. A film of perspiratio[n] glazed his ugly little face and made it shine unpleasantl[y]. "Look, Jantarro," he began, his eyes averted from mine. An[d] then he stopped.

"I'm not interested in a deal," I told him. I dropped into on[e] of his gray leather couches and it gave out with a hundre[d] breathy sighs. The sunlight crept through the big window at th[e] end of the room and lay peacefully on the slate floor, resting f[or] the moment. Even the man's lizards were motionless behin[d] their glass. The case was over.

Somewhere across the room something expanded or co[n]tracted with a timid crack. "I don't believe you understand," Guberian said.

"I'D BET ON IT," said a wheezing voice.

I turned around as quickly as I could in the depths of th[e] couch. Paul MacMurtry stood beside a towering crystal cag[e] leaning on it with one plump hand in the effort of keeping h[is] flaccid bulk upright. He shot a quick smile at me and the[n] looked down to where, inside the cage, a great leathery bea[st] was snapping up at his pink fingers. He clicked his tongue [a] couple of times at the thing and said, "Sic 'em, boy. Sic 'em[.]"

"Paulie. What are you doing here?" My mind had seized u[p]. I needed answers to questions I hadn't even thought of.

"I've come for you," he said. He took a huge breath an[d] began the difficult trek to the center of the room.

"Guberian's going away," I said. "Going inside." I hea[rd] the hesitation in my tone.

Paulie Mac was intent on negotiating the two small steps tha[t] would bring him down to our level. "Dog," he said, st[ill] watching his feet, "take him, would you?"

"I LOVE IT, you know, Jantarro." Paulie Mac was slumped [in] the chair opposite me. "Gambling." He regarded me lazily ov[er] his heaving chest. Guberian perched on the edge of anoth[er] chair, holding on with both hands. Dog crouched on the sla[te] floor, grinning up at me. And I was lying on the couch, truss[ed] like a turkey. Dog had had the sense to take off my arm, and m[y] good hand was roped to the back of my belt. My feet were ti[ed] at the ankles. "You make a conjecture," Paulie Mac continued, "place a stake on it, and then enjoy the thrill."

"You and Guberian?" I said. The part of me that didn't hurt was still trying to figure things out. "You were in this together?"

"No," said Guberian, quietly but with force. "No. I didn't kill Laki. I didn't kill anyone."

"Now, you see"—Paulie Mac went on as though Guberian hadn't spoken—"you've just made a conjecture, but there can't be any thrill for you. Not anymore. You've got nothing left to put on it. No more stake." He explored the clear glass table beside him to see if there was anything to play with. My puny little Chiefs Special was there. My plastic arm lay just within his reach, and he drew his hand away to avoid touching it.

"It was Paulie Mac, then?" I asked Guberian.

"That's why you've got to protect your stake," said Paulie Mac, as though he were instructing a child. "And I've got to do that now, Jantarro. Or the thrill goes away. You understand."

Guberian looked at me, nodded, and looked away. "But you knew," I said to him. "You knew, didn't you?"

"I had to do that right from the beginning. I know you understand. This man here"—he pointed a pinkie at Guberian—"owed me far too much for me to let him be taken out of circulation." Paulie Mac had touched the surface of my prosthesis, and he was examining his fingertips to see if anything had rubbed off on them. I wondered if he would touch the rest of me when I was dead.

Now Guberian refused to look at me. "You can't let him do this," I said to him. "Guberian!"

He started from his seat. "No, Paulie," he said. "It's... it's..."

"Dog," said Paulie Mac, and a brief look of annoyance struggled to the surface of his fleshy face. Dog uncoiled himself and with a reach slapped Guberian's cheek. His glasses skittered along the slate floor; he sank to his knees and groped for them.

A BIG GLASS DOOR to one of the cages hung open. "What do you think?" Paulie Mac said to Guberian. A smell of decaying matter hesitated at the opening and then rushed into my nostrils. "Do you think they would?" He wanted to know if the things inside there would eat me.

Guberian was white and shrunken. He opened his mouth and nothing came out of it.

"Would they?" Paulie Mac asked again. And when Guberian said nothing, he roared the question: "Would they!"

"I...don't know," said Guberian timidly. "Please, Paulie...please."

Paulie Mac pushed his mouth into a petulant moue. "I tried to warn you off," he said to me. "Because I liked you, Jantarro." Damned if there weren't a pair of crocodile tears ballooning up in the corners of his eyes. He wiped at them and then moved his shoulders slightly. A shrug, I guess. "But the thrill comes before everything." He looked at the cage. "I wonder if they will," he said to himself. And then he looked at me. "That's it right there, Jantarro. The essence of the thing. The uncertainty of it. And you're the steak in this bet. Steak! Get it?" He laughed a wheezing laugh at his own witticism, snapped his fat fingers at Dog, and said, "Put him in. We can come back and finish the job if we have to." Then he nodded his head in the direction of the entrance to hell.

Dog took me by the belt and dragged me over to the opening. "Take his shoes off," said Paulie Mac. "Don't want him breaking any glass and cutting himself." Dog dropped me to the floor and did as he was told. "Then join us in the front room. We've got plans to make."

I was lifted up, swung back and forth, and then unceremoniously launched against a massive rock inside the cage. My stump flew up in an instinctive effort to ward off the blow, but it only got crushed beneath me, exploding with pain and all the buried memories of what it once had been. The door was shut behind me. I heard the key scrape against the glass before it entered the lock. Something touched the soles of my feet.

I WAS UPRIGHT and cowering in a corner of the cage, held at bay by a nine-foot dragon with a mouth big enough to admit my head and a jaw displaying the kind of teeth that could sever it. It would rise up on its squat legs, flick its tail, and exhale with a rough, hungry noise that sent my hairs upright. It's only a lizard, I told myself. A thousand times.

The glass behind me was thick. I had tried to break it by hurling myself into it, but the only thing that accomplished was a lot of pain and a loss of balance. Dancing around with tied feet wasn't easy; breaking out of the giant terrarium with tied feet and no hands was impossible.

The Komodo dragged its belly closer and lifted its big ugly head again. I could feel its hot breath on my legs, hotter still than the muggy, fetid air inside this box. I started to hop along the front wall of the cage, but that meant climbing a rocky hill, so my progress was slow and precarious. If I failed, there was a good chance I'd fall right on top of the beast.

I made it to a niche in the rock about a foot above the dragon's head, and there I had to stop and rest. A smaller animal, an iguana about a foot and a half from top to tail, scuttled across the rock top to greet me. In a quick series of dashes, it placed itself squarely on top of my stockinged feet. I could feel its cold weight, the animal motion inside its body, the twisting of its head and tail. I began to shudder. The thing began to force itself between my legs, wriggling, scratching with claws I hadn't noticed until now. Something sharp explored my calf. It was going to try to climb up my legs.

Panic began to uncoil in my chest. My legs felt as though they wanted to explode away from me. All I could think of was mutilation.

Abruptly, my body convulsed, and with a huge spastic jerk I tumbled to the rocky ground, striking the giant lizard on the muzzle. My head bounced off the other wall and bright tracers of pain flashed through my head. The great beast roared and backed off. I struggled frantically to a sitting position. Suddenly, its tail crashed into the glass above my head. I ducked to the side, hitting the wall again. The tail lashed out once more, connecting this time with a crushing violence.

My eyes came open reluctantly. Slowly, I discovered the nausea, the blurred vision, the pain of my predicament. An electric wire of fear shot through me as I thought about what the big Komodo dragon might have done to me while I was unconscious. But the only pain was the one banging away inside my head.

I managed to get to my knees. There was a stillness, a calm inside our cage. The other captives must have grown bored with my inert body, because none of them was in sight. Only the odd twitching of foliage betrayed their presence. In this moment of respite I managed to tell myself that the animals outside the cage were the ones I should really worry about. They wouldn't grow bored of me and wander off. They would return and do what human beings do to each other. They would kill me.

I needed to get my hand and feet free. I had no hope otherwise, and precious little even then. But my belt was a sturdy one, and there was no way I was going to be able to break it, not even if I'd had two good arms lashed to it. My stump flailed around with the uselessness of perfect impotence.

Then I thought that if I could get my pants off, my arm would come free with them. With that I began to pull down on the belt from the back, where my hand was tied. But no matter how I wriggled, I couldn't get more than an inch toward my hips. Now the narrow waist I was so proud of looked as though it was going to be a case of fatal vanity. But the pants weren't the problem, I thought. The belt was. And belts are made to come off.

If you have a free hand. And better, two.

Belly against the glass, I pressed and turned, pressed and turned, to see if I could tease the end of the belt out of its loops. One loop gave up and then another. Until the end stuck out from my waist. Now only the buckle remained as a problem.

Positioning my body as carefully as I could, I trapped the end against the glass and turned. I could imagine the buckle opening, the little tongue of brass popping free.

But after three tries I was as firmly caught as ever.

When you are one-armed, you learn to do a lot of things with your mouth, your teeth. I considered the possibilities. Quickly I sat down in the corner and bent over as far as I could. The tip of the belt danced before my face, a tantalizing inch away. I leaned back and rested my muscles. Then I bent forward, relaxed, and took the tip in my teeth. Clamping down hard, I twisted my head to the side, to free the leather from the buckle. As I turned I saw them.

Three big iguanas were climbing from the backside of the big central rock to join the dragon. With a wigwag motion that made their ugly wattles swing, they scrabbled higher until they stared down at me, perfect incarnations of Fear, Despair, and Death.

With a savage jerk of my head I tore the leather free of the catch. I felt my panic-bloated belly push against the button that held my pants. With my hand I tore down at the back. Somewhere in my frenzied wrestling, the button popped and my pants came loose. I hurried to get my hand down to where it could deal with the knot at my feet.

The biggest of the three lizards slid down the face of the rock and came to a stop a couple of feet from me. The other two began a lazier descent.

Numbed by terror, my hand fumbled with the knot. Dog had done a poor job of it, and I managed to free myself. I scrambled out of my pants and stood on two bare legs to face the lizards, waving the trousers still attached to my hand like a flag of distress. The beasts sighed in surprise and moved back, thrashing the ground with their meaty tails.

I needed a weapon. Something to break the glass. I scuttled along the face of the glass, eyes on the enemy, scraping along the ground with my hand like an ape. My fingers closed around a rock. Quickly I slid back to the lock on the glass panel and smashed the rock against the inside of it with as much force as I could muster. There was a loud, hollow, ringing sound and the rock disintegrated into powdery bits. Lava. That would have alerted Paulie Mac and Dog.

A lizard tail lashed at my leg, stinging me.

The obvious stone for the job stood in front of me, mocking me, because it would have needed two hands to lift it, two hands to throw it, two hands to get freedom.

Another lizard tail flashed my way. I jumped aside. And there, at my feet was the stone I needed. With a quick glance at the dragon, I bent down, picked it up, and spun with all my force at the lock in the glass.

TWENTY-FIVE

A FIST-SIZED SECTION of the glass went opaque and soft, like the glass in a windshield when it's hit. I felt rough lizard skin on my naked legs, and, terrorized, I smashed again and again. My fist went right through, and the glass panel swung open against my weight, toppling me headlong onto the floor.

"Hey!" Dog shouted behind me.

I shot across the slate, aiming for the table that had my gun on it. Dog tackled me and together we slid farther, hitting the luxurious softness of leather furniture. I could hear Paulie Mac barking commands, and farther away Guberian was shouting something.

Dog had his hand in my groin, groping for a hold. Blindly, I kicked back, missed, and kicked back again. This time I connected with a piece of him. He grunted and his arms disappeared from around my body. I clawed my way forward and slapped out my hand toward the gun.

I grasped it and just then felt my arm swing wildly away. Dog had grabbed my pants which were still attached to my wrist, and he was pulling at them to bring me where he could get at me.

The gun went off, and the pulling stopped. I rolled onto my back, saw Dog lunging for me, and fired point-blank at his chest. He fell on me with all the weight of the dead.

And then there was silence.

Slowly, I rolled Dog off me. Paulie Mac was trying to extricate something from his jacket and at the same time to descend the stairs into the main part of the living room. Both efforts were going slowly. I cocked the little revolver, aimed it at him from my bed on the floor, and said, "Don't."

"You wouldn't shoot me," he said. It was hard to read on that bloated face of his whether he believed his own words.

"I want to," I said. "I really do." Something in my tone conveyed itself to him, and his blimp of a hand floated empty out from under the linen jacket and drifted down to his side.

I stood up shakily. "Guberian," I called. "Guberian, get in here and get this goddamn thing off my hand." He appeared from behind Paulie Mac, blinked though his thick glasses at the scene of disaster in his oh-so-carefully arranged living room, and began hesitantly to pass the fat man. While Guberian went by, I held the cocked weapon aimed smack at Paulie Mac's face. Guberian shied away from the thing and circled toward me. I didn't blame him for being careful. All of the adrenaline that had been pumped into my system over the last hour or so was now seeking an outlet, and rage was a definite possibility.

Guberian fumbled at my wrist ineffectually for a minute. "Can't you hurry it up, for Christ's sake," I snapped at him.

He took his hands away. "I could do better," he said, "if you were to put the gun down." I looked at Paulie Mac, who hadn't moved a muscle since I'd frozen him on the steps. "Forget it," I said. I wasn't going to trust that fat, betraying son of a bitch one further inch. "Just go and phone the cops."

"And an ambulance, surely," Guberian said, as if seeking my permission.

"For Dog? Forget it. I killed him." Only twice before in my career have I had to say those words. Only twice before had I done the irretrievable act, for which there is no forgiveness, merely the waning of regret over time. I was starting to shake.

Guberian knelt down beside the biker. "He's breathing!" he said, announcing a triumph. Or a miracle of complicated design.

"Then go and phone," I said, weary all of a sudden. He practically ran to the phone at the other end of the room. I heard him dialing, talking, dialing again.

"I understand you, Jantarro." Paulie Mac was on the move. Slowly. Incrementally. Like a giant slug. "Congratulations," he said.

"Sit," I told him.

"What?"

"Sit down."

He looked around him as though there ought to have been a chair nearby. "Really, Jantarro—"

"Down!" I shouted. And his knees gave way, causing him to tumble like Humpty-Dumpty. I made my way over to where he had landed. He was striving for some dignity. "Talk to me, Paulie. Tell me about it."

He pursed his lips tight. And I wondered whether I would have to hit him. Whether I would have the strength.

SURPRISINGLY, the cops got there first. Guberian opened the door, and two uniforms came cautiously into the house, guns drawn, jumpy. They had a hard time getting a line on what had happened. Not that I blamed them. A man with his pants hanging from his hand—his one hand—holding a gun on a beached whale, while a biker pumped blood on the floor, all to be found in an outré salon. Quite a zoo. No wonder they wanted some persuading.

"He's armed, I think," I told the one who took my gun. I nodded at a deflated Paulie Mac.

"Jesus Christ!" The biggest iguana had ventured out and was rasping hoarsely in the other cop's direction. The Komodo dragon was nowhere to be seen.

"Don't shoot, don't shoot," Guberian cried. He dashed over, straddled the beast, and lifting, tugged it step-by-step back into the cage, as if it were nothing but a big puppy.

"Untie me," I asked the cop who'd got Paulie Mac's gun. I proffered my bound wrist. He ignored me and went to look at Dog.

The ambulance came. Another pair of uniforms arrived. Dog was taken out on a stretcher. Then the plainclothes got there. I leaned back on the couch, closed my eyes, and waited for my turn.

"UNTIE ME."

"Jesus Christ, Jantarro." Bench couldn't seem to close his mouth. It made him look almost human.

"I know, I know," I told him. "It was touch and go for a while. But you've got to stop being surprised when I solve a case. It's happened often enough."

He started laughing, something I don't think I've ever seen him do before. A rich, rolling laugh from deep in his belly. He was positively brimming over with human qualities. Then he

found the energy to point a finger at me as he hooted; and I realized I didn't like him any better human. "You..." he gasped,
"you...Jesus, you look funny."

"Think how you look with the wrong person in jail," I
snapped. It didn't seem to deter him one bit.

"You...you...look like...you got caught in a orgy...S and
M...Jesus, Jantarro." He was wiping his eyes and using a
handkerchief to do it, like the priss he is.

"Untie me, you asshole."

"Was it fun, Jantarro? Was it?" He started off again,
howling, bending over with the force of his schadenfreude.

I didn't want to, but I found myself starting to chuckle and
then to laugh outright. Maybe it was the release of all that
adrenaline. Hell, maybe I saw that I did look funny.

We guffawed and snorted and whooped, and then as the
mirth faded away, I wound up looking in his eyes, seeing there
something of a friendship I had lost, some hope that perhaps
I'd just mislaid it.

He tried to smile, but that was different from laughing and
he didn't quite make it. Neither did I. Then he untied the rope
from around my wrist, took it out from behind my belt, and
handed me my pants. I struggled into them, and he watched
intently as I did up my belt one-handed. "I've got shoes somewhere," I said.

"I think I saw them over there." He looked at my stump.
"And your arm," he said.

"Thanks."

"I don't need to tell you. You should have called."

"I tried that," I said. "About Elaine Younger, remember?" I debated about whether to go to all the trouble of
strapping on the prosthesis.

"Shit, Jantarro, I told you. I was busy. I have to work for a
living, you know. Besides, suicide isn't my bag." Bench handed
me the arm, holding it gingerly as if he might break it. I took it
from him, put it down on the couch, and began unbuttoning
my shirt.

I shook my head at him. "Not suicide. Murder, like I said."
He scowled at me. "Laki had told her about a movie that Camelia, her brother, and Guberian were making. He'd just discovered their little secret and he was trying to kill the project."

He handed me the arm again. He paid close attention to how I fitted it over the stump, how I worked the straps. A curious feeling of pride welled up in me. "She tried to put the bite on Guberian," I said. "Blackmail him, really. She figured that he wouldn't want the cops to know about it, what with Laki murdered. It wasn't just the money with her, although she could have used it. She drank up a lot of dough. I figure it was the power it gave her. Working around all the rich and famous, making them the center of her life, and then not having squat herself, not really. She saw this as a chance to climb on top, is my guess. Anyway, Guberian told Paulie Mac, the way he did with every problem that came up. And Paulie Mac fixed it. The way he did with every problem that Guberian told him about." I had tucked in my shirt. Bench handed me my jacket.

"Fixed it?"

"He asked around about Elaine. Found out she was an alkie. Told Guberian to get him a bottle from Laki's supply. I guess he figured that if anybody discovered where it came from it would only muddy the waters. Or point to Camelia somehow. He doctored it with barbiturates and had it delivered to her. Probably on behalf of Guberian—or that's what she thought. Bingo." I snapped my fingers. "That did it. One more threat to his golden goose removed."

"Guberian know this?"

I shrugged. "I don't know," I said. "Probably not consciously. My guess is he didn't want to know. A problem came up, he told Paulie, and the problem went away. He had to know somewhere inside himself." I shrugged again. Who could say what went on inside people?

"Can you prove this?"

I told him about the bottle at the lab. "And Dog will talk. If he lives. Paulie Mac said enough to me. I can testify."

"I think," said Bench looking around the room, "that perhaps you've done enough."

"Not quite. I've still got a client who's in jail." And a dead one who had told me to be concerned about his wife. "How soon can you get her out?"

Bench narrowed his eyes and ran a finger under his toothbrush mustache. "She's not . . . connected to any of this?" He waved his hands around.

I thought about the conspiracy to murder Alan Laki. "No," I said. "Certainly not so's you could prove it." I could testify, I thought. I shook my head. "No, she's not," I said emphatically. "Not at all."

TWENTY-SIX

GLENDA HAD arranged it all.

We sat in the back, while up at the front the second-best criminal lawyer in town waited her turn to let the state ask the judge to withdraw the charge against Camelia Laki. It was a formality. Ann, the aforementioned second-best criminal lawyer in town and also Glenda's partner, had tried to explain it to me. But I couldn't understand anything that required an innocent person to spend one more night in jail. All I knew was that when this rigmarole was done, my client would be free.

The courtroom was old, crowded, and noisy. Justice seemed to be flowing by at a great rate, surely too fast for the judge to be involved in it. Glenda patted my knee. "Go on," she said. I was explaining the case to her.

"Well, there isn't too much more to say." I was straining for a sight of Camelia, but I guessed they hadn't brought her up yet from the cells below.

"That poor man, Michael Dennis," she said, "he was just killed by accident?"

"I don't think so," I said. "I think that Paulie Mac's bikers were responsible."

"But why him? And how did they know he'd be there?"

"I think they were gunning for me," I said. "They were supposed to take us both out. Me for obvious reasons. And Dennis because Paulie Mac figured it would be a neat solution if a dead man got blamed for Laki's murder. That is, if Camelia didn't take the fall. And I guess Guberian was getting restive about that possibility. They were just following me, waiting for a good break. And they got it in the Parkdale Tavern. Until Groper's people dragged me out."

"So it was really all because of Guberian's gambling."

The cast of characters up front had changed for the umpteenth time, and I'd lost track of Ann. I still couldn't see Camelia. Glenda gave my leg a squeeze. "That was half of it," said. "I was a fool to have believed Paulie Mac when he told me he didn't care about whether Guberian got taken out of circulation."

"Would it have made any difference if he had cared?"

I turned to look at Glenda. I wanted her to quit asking the difficult questions. Her expression said that she was just curious, that the answer wasn't crucial in any way. "I don't know," I told her. I thought of how I'd told Paulie that I'd defer to his interests. "Probably not," I said. "I don't know."

She nodded. "Well, he certainly didn't think you'd lay off," she said.

"I guess Guberian was into him for too much for him to take any chances at all. It must have been too tempting when Guberian told him about the will. All the money Guberian owed him hanging out there on the thin thread of that man's life."

"The timing seems so...close. Almost as if Paulie Mac was Guberian's doppelgänger, his shadow. You know, doing everything Guberian really wanted without having to be asked. It's weird."

"Not when you realize that Guberian told Paulie Mac everything. Some men talk to shrinks, or to bartenders; Guberian talked to his bookie. What gamblers do, maybe. And besides, good timing is what you've got to have if you're going to be a big bookie. I reckon that Paulie started to make plans way back when Guberian told him he'd had to borrow from Laki to make the big bet. And when Laki took control of Lakipix away from Guberian, it must have become a serious plan. The will—and Laki's attempt to sink Camelia's film—just made it a cert. He had some of his people steal the elixir from Dennis, and then the strychnine. Then he used it."

"Well, you've got to say it was lucky for him that Camelia visited her husband just at the time that the murder was committed and got herself seen by the guard."

"Yeah," I said. "Gambler's luck." But I knew it wasn't. I knew that Paulie didn't take any risks he didn't have to. But I couldn't explain that to her because I hadn't told Glenda about the trio's conspiracy to murder Laki. And that, true to form, Guberian had told Paulie Mac all about it. Paulie couldn't risk losing his debtor to the cops by letting the amateurs go through with it the way they'd planned. He delayed Guberian at the

critical time, sent in his boys early to stuff the strychnine down
Laki's throat, and then stepped back to let Camelia find the
body and take the rap.

Camelia was standing in front of the judge. I leaned forward. Glenda took her hand off my leg. Ann approached the
bench with a man who looked untrustworthy, and they talked
to the judge for a bit. Then everybody got formal and said some
things that I couldn't hear too well because all the people
around me were talking as if nothing important was happening.

Ann and Camelia were walking down the aisle, smiles on
their faces. They were smiling at me. I stood up. Glenda stood
up. We all looked at each other. "Come outside," Ann said.

In the hall cops and robbers sat around on benches that
looked like church pews. Lawyers lounged and conferred.
Candy wrappers, half-filled Styrofoam coffee cups, and cigarette butts littered the floor. Camelia took my hand and held it.
Around us, desperate whispered conversations mingled with
bored, flat messages on the PA system, all bouncing between
the old marble floor and the high stone ceiling until they were
scrambled into the dull roar of criminal justice.

"Johnny," she said, still holding my hand. It was hot between hers.

"Camelia."

"I can't thank you."

"Don't worry about it."

"I can say thank you." She leaned forward and kissed my
cheek. "But that doesn't say the half of it."

"I have an idea," I said. She cocked an eyebrow and gave me
a crooked grin. I shook my head. "Finish your movie," I told
her.

"Yes," she said.

"And then live your own life."

"I will," she said so quietly that I had to read her lips to understand. She looked down at our hands. She stroked the back
of mine. And then she let it go. She squared her shoulders and
walked over to where her lawyer was waiting. Without anything more, the two of them set off down the hall.

Glenda was standing near me. "The other half of the case," I said to her, watching Camelia make her exist, "was Alan Laki. A miserable, rotten son of a bitch."

"Yes," she said.

"Arrogant, too," I said. "Did I tell you that?"

She put her arm through mine. "I have an idea," she said.

"I know my enemies. That's what he said. He was wrong. And too arrogant to realize that that's not good enough. You have to know your enemy's enemies as well."

"And your friends," said Glenda, drawing me gently in the direction of the day outside.

I looked down at her. "And your friends," I agreed.

Take 2 books & a surprise gift FREE

SPECIAL LIMITED-TIME OFFER

Mail to: The Mystery Library™
3010 Walden Ave.
P.O. Box 1867
Buffalo, N.Y. 14269-1867

YES! Please send me 2 free books from the Mystery Library™ and my free surprise gift. Then send me 2 mystery books, first time in paperback, every month. Bill me only $3.50 per book. There is *no* extra charge for shipping and handling! There is no minimum number of books I must purchase. I can always return a shipment at your cost simply by dropping it in the mail, or cancel at any time. Even if I never buy another book from The Mystery Library™, the 2 free books and the surprise gift are mine to keep forever.

414 BPY BP90

Name   (PLEASE PRINT)

Address   Apt. No.

City   State   Zip